MONSTERS IN THE MIST

C.G. MOSLEY

SEVERED PRESS
HOBART TASMANIA

MONSTERS IN THE MIST

ISBN: 978-1-925597-49-3

PROLOGUE

July 15, 1992, 3:19 p.m.
Acapulco, Mexico

Eric Gill took a sip of iced cola and then took a moment to loosen the collar of his dress shirt. It was a sweltering day, but the occasional strong gust of wind that came off the Pacific made the wait bearable. The man he was waiting for was a potential customer, and after speaking with him on the phone, Eric had a good feeling that his uncomfortable wait would be rewarded substantially.

After all, the view from the La Perla restaurant was not something he wanted to end abruptly. The restaurant was nestled high in the cliffs of La Quebrada, home of the famous cliff divers of Acapulco. Eric watched in awe as the men and boys of all various ages climbed the rock face, each taking a moment to pray to the Virgin of Guadalupe shrine before plunging head first into the blue waters 147 feet below. The dives had to be timed precisely with the wind and incoming waves so that the divers would have the adequate amount of depth needed to clear the rocky bottom.

The show was nearing its conclusion when Eric caught sight of an Arabian man in his mid-thirties approaching his table. The man wore a black business suit, and a turban to match. His beard was long and dark, although there was plenty of gray beginning to take over. The man was trailed by two other Arabian men, both of whom were dressed very similarly.

"Welcome," Eric said, rising from the table. "I'm afraid you've missed the show, but I hear they're going to be diving again in a few hours. This time it'll be dark, and they'll carry torches."

The Arabian man held up an apologetic hand and took a seat. "I'm sorry that I've kept you waiting, Mr. Gill. We were delayed by traffic," he said, then glanced toward the cliffs below. "I may return tonight to see these cliff divers; will you be here?"

Eric sat back down. "No, I'm afraid not. My flight leaves in a couple of hours and I have to get back to work," he said, then added, "hopefully when I return, it'll be you I'll be working for."

The Arabian man smiled slightly, but seemed to be going out of his way to keep the tone all business.

"All right," Eric said. "Let's get down to business. Firstly, I'd like to know how you found out about me and what I do."

The Arabian man grabbed the pitcher of water sitting in the center of the table and poured himself a glass. He drank it before speaking.

"Let's just say that we have mutual friends," he said finally. "I, like you, conduct a lot of my business in secret. I think that it would be best for both of us if we knew as little about each other as possible."

Eric crossed his arms and shifted in his chair. Something about this man made him terribly uncomfortable, but he dared not show it.

"Fair enough," he replied. "Well, how can I be of service to you?"

The man leaned forward to the point that his beard touched the table. "I'm interested in purchasing a tyrannosaur," he whispered.

Eric was in the middle of taking another swallow of cola when the man spoke, and the mere mention of the word 'tyrannosaur' made him choke. *A tyrannosaur? Was he crazy?*

After a brief moment of coughing and hacking, Eric finally regained his voice so that he could respond.

"Only one man has ever made a request like that," he replied. "And after I showed the man a picture of one, he changed his mind. A tyrannosaur would be extremely hard to contain."

The Arabian man was unnerved. "Can you fulfill the request, or not?"

"Yes, of course, I could do it," he replied. "It's you I'm worried about. I'm not sure you completely understand what you're asking for. A tyrannosaur, although admittedly not the nastiest animal we've got, is still one of the most terrifying. It would take a large area and a great deal of electric fencing to contain an animal that large. Just keeping it fed would take a lot of money. If carnivores are your thing, there are plenty of others to choose from that aren't nearly as large and easier to care for."

"How much for a juvenile tyrannosaur?" the man asked, seemingly ignoring his advice.

"An adult would cost you five," Eric replied.

"I'm not interested in an adult; I want a juvenile."

"Why a juvenile?" Eric asked. "Because if you think you can train the thing, you may as well forget it. Their brains are very small."

"How much for a juvenile?" the man repeated flatly.

"Two mil," Eric replied.

Without batting an eye, the Arabian man agreed. He extended his hand and Eric promptly shook it.

"Very well," Eric said, rising from the table. "Give me a week and I'll have the animal for you. Of course, you remember that I require ten percent up front."

"Of course," the Arabian man replied. He motioned toward one of his associates and a brown leather briefcase was suddenly placed on the table. Eric reached for it, but the man pulled it away.

"I'm not finished," he said. His steely eyes suddenly turned unfriendly.

Eric returned to his seat, and he wasn't sure if he should be happy about it or not.

"Are you saying you want to make another purchase?" he asked.

The Arabian man nodded slowly and then retrieved a piece of paper from his coat pocket.

"Do you have any of these on your island?" he asked, sliding the folded paper forward.

Eric reluctantly took the piece of paper and then carefully unfolded it. The species of dinosaur scrawled in black ink was not one that he expected to see. He suddenly broke out into a cold sweat.

"How do you know about this animal?" he asked.

"Do you have one?" the Arabian man asked again.

Eric closed his eyes and slumped down in his chair. He considered telling the man no. If he did, the man certainly wouldn't know any different. On the other hand, an animal such as this would bring in huge money. But why on earth would this man want an animal as nightmarish as this?

Eric couldn't think of any good reason for a man to ask for this particular species, but the real truth was that he didn't really care. If the man wanted to kill himself by stupidly purchasing an animal like this one, who was he to stop him?

"Considering their size and diet, I would estimate we have no more than five adult ones," Eric said finally. "We've only seen one, but evidence has been found to suggest that there are others."

"One will be just fine," the Arabian man replied. "How much will it cost?"

Eric breathed deeply through his nose and considered a price. He stared into the steely eyes of his client as he thought.

"Fifteen million," he said finally, never breaking eye contact.

"We have a deal," the man responded. "You'll find more than enough to cover the deposit for both animals in the briefcase," he said, rising from the table.

"I'll need at least one additional week to get the second animal," Eric said.

"Take three weeks if you need it; just make sure that the animals are delivered by the final week in June."

Eric reached out to shake the man's hand once more. He took it and rather forcefully tugged Eric toward him.

"Do not disappoint me, Mr. Gill," he whispered softly.

Eric jerked his hand back. "You won't be," he replied. "You just make sure you have the rest of my money and you'll get your dinosaurs."

With that, the Arabian man turned away and began to leave the restaurant.

"Why won't you tell me your name?" Eric called after him.

The man stopped abruptly and looked back at him over his left shoulder. "I told you my name," he replied.

Eric shook his head. "Somehow I don't think 'Mr. O' is your real name," he replied, somewhat irritated.

The Arabian man did not respond; he just turned away and left the restaurant, his associates following closely behind.

CHAPTER 1

Jackson, Mississippi

Jonathon Williams held his wife's hand and tried his best to put on a brave face. He and Lucy had been married for seven years now, and almost all of that time had been nothing short of wonderful. In fact, the only times that the two of them seemed unhappy was after Lucy regretfully informed her husband that another pregnancy test had come back negative. All of that finally changed four months ago.

When Lucy came running into the living room, the plastic test in her hand, he knew that the moment they'd dreamed about had finally arrived. As soon as he saw the two pink lines that indicated a positive test, Jonathon felt a mixture of pride and fear wash over him all at once. He knew Lucy was probably having the same emotions, although she'd never admit it.

After nine weeks went by, and he'd just started getting used to the idea of being a father, they went in for an ultrasound. The surreal sight of a tiny beating heart on the monitor brought both mother and father to tears. It was at that moment that it all began to fully sink in. They were going to be parents and their lives would never be the same again. Suddenly, it began to make total sense to Jonathon when he thought back to their ordeal on a tiny island in the center of the Bermuda Triangle seven years ago. There were many nights that he woke up in a cold sweat from the nightmares he experienced concerning hungry tyrannosaurs and terrifying pterosaurs. Worse yet, was the recurring dreams he had of the *Troodons* that inhabited the cave in which the fountain of youth was located. He would never be able to shake the mental image imprinted in his brain of Osvaldo being eaten alive by those vicious animals so that the rest of the survivors could escape. It was the eyes of the *Troodons* that troubled him the most. Those animals were far more intelligent than he or any other paleontologist had ever fully realized.

Despite all of those horrifying experiences, somehow he and Lucy escaped it all when there were others that did not. Now that there was a tiny person growing inside of Lucy, Jonathon truly felt that he knew the reason why. They were meant to be parents, and he dreamt of all of the things their child would accomplish. Those first four months of pregnancy were truly the greatest in their marriage, and it seemed as if their lives couldn't get any more perfect. And then—suddenly the door to the office they were sitting in swung open abruptly.

A man in a white lab coat stepped in, a stethoscope draped around his neck. Dr. George Hughes was balding, mid-fifties, with blue eyes and a face that seemed too boyish to belong to a doctor as experienced as he. He had a folder under his arm, and he took a moment to glance at it before taking a seat at his large, mahogany desk.

"Good morning," Dr. Hughes stated, almost shyly. "I'm sorry for keeping the two of you waiting."

"Good morning, and it's quite alright," Jonathon replied. *Just give me good news*, he thought to himself.

Lucy forced a smile, but there was no masking the true emotion of fear that was clearly at the forefront of her mind. She took a deep breath and then nervously repositioned herself in the cushy leather chair, the air softly hissing out of it as she did so. She squeezed Jonathon's hand tightly, preparing herself for the worst.

"I'll cut to the chase," Dr. Hughes said, his tone still reserved. Jonathon saw it as a bad sign.

"The lab results are back, and I'm sorry to say that cancer cells were found. Mrs. Williams, you're dealing with Grade 3 breast cancer."

Jonathon glanced over at his terrified wife; she opened her mouth to speak, but quickly closed it, unable to mutter a word. A single tear rolled down her cheek, and it was all Jonathon could do to keep it together himself. Someone had to ask the tough questions. Right now, it had to be him. He gave Lucy's hand a reassuring squeeze.

"What are the treatment options?" he asked, it was all he could get out at the moment.

***

Five Hours Later…

"No, I'm not doing it, and there isn't a single thing you can say to change my mind. I'm a mother now, and it's my job to do everything I can to protect this baby," she said, pointing to her large belly. Her face was red…her eyes redder. She'd been pleading her case to Jonathon ever since they'd left Dr. Hughes office, and the argument (if you could call it that) had completely drained her.

"Sweetheart, I—I can't lose you," Jonathon stammered, his eyes welling up. "We've been through so much together and we'll get through this. Refusing the treatment is absolutely the wrong answer."

"So you're okay with poisoning the baby? Is that what you're saying?" she asked.

"Oh for God's sake, Lucy…we wouldn't be poisoning the baby!"

"There are risks every time I expose this baby to radiation," she said. "I'm not taking the risks, no matter how minimal the exposure is."

Jonathon wanted to open his mouth and argue his side further. However, he thought better of it and stormed out of the house through the back door. He walked around the pool and plopped down on an outdoor chair near the edge of the modest, rectangular swimming pool. Once seated, he placed his face in the palms of his hands and let the tears flow. He was mad, he was hurt, and worst of all, he was terrified.

Why can't she see this my way? he thought. His head told him that this was her hormones taking over and that they were overpowering her judgment. However, his heart told him that her mind was made up on the matter. She wasn't going to take the radiation as Dr. Hughes recommended. He'd all but told her she had no chance of survival if the treatments did not start immediately. The cancer was aggressive, and she did not have another four months to spare. Were there risks for the baby? Of course, but Dr. Hughes made it clear that the radiation exposure would be minimal in the beginning and they would gradually increase it as the baby grew stronger. None of that mattered to Lucy. It seemed she'd focused on nothing but the risks for the baby.

Jonathon felt a warm body brush against his leg, and then a familiar cold, wet nose followed. It was Rex, his faithful golden retriever, and the dog could clearly sense his master needed him. Jonathon took the dog's large head in his hands and gently caressed his ears.

"I'll be alright, boy," he said.

Rex stared at him, his tail wagging slightly. It was obvious he didn't believe his master.

Jonathon continued to caress the dog's ears, and for the first time, he could see that the dog was showing its age. He'd gotten Rex when the dog was only a pup in December of 1982.

"You're pushing ten years old now," he said. "You're practically an old man."

The statement suddenly had him reliving the memories of the mysterious island and its dinosaur inhabitants. After all, it was Angus's dreams of conquering his own mortality that brought them there to begin with. The old man was tired of aging…he wanted to do something about it. He searched and searched until he found a way.

And then, an idea popped into Jonathon's head.

CHAPTER 2

Jackson-Evers Municipal Airport

"Oh come on, Henry," Julianne barked at her husband. "You survived the flight…congratulations! Now be a big boy and catch up."

Henry Williams rolled his eyes at his wife, but made no effort to increase his pace. Julianne always talked to him like he was a child; she'd done it all forty-four years he'd known her. As he thought about that, he tried very hard to think of a time when he'd raised his voice to the woman. He thought and thought, ultimately coming up with nothing.

"Do you see the boy?" he asked.

"Your eyesight is better than mine," she replied, squinting. "You tell me."

Henry stopped walking, took off his glasses, and rubbed them clean on his dress shirt. He then peered through the spectacles, scanning the crowd around them for any sign of his son. A couple of attempts later, he spotted him strolling their direction.

"Mom…Dad! It's good to see the both of you," Jonathon said, grabbing both of his parents at once.

"Easy, boy," Henry said. "Your mother and I are getting brittle."

"Speak for yourself," Julianne snapped, glaring at her husband. "There is nothing brittle about me because I stay active…I don't sit on the couch watching *Gunsmoke* reruns several hours a day."

Henry rolled his eyes again and did his best to ignore his wife's jest.

"Go easy on him, Mom," Jonathon said. "You know how much he hates flying. I'm sure he's a nervous wreck right now and you patronizing him isn't helping.

"Patronizing him? Oh, please," his mother responded. "I've had to baby this man his whole life."

"Show us to the car, will you, boy?" Henry said with a deep sigh. "These bags aren't getting any lighter."

Jonathon quickly grabbed one of the bags from his father.

"Sorry, Dad, sure…follow me," he said, trotting away.

Jonathon loaded the bags into the trunk and turned to get in the car. Before he could make his way to the driver's side door, Julianne grabbed his arm.

"Son, I'm terribly sorry," she said.

"Sorry?" he asked. "For what?"

"The last thing your father and I should be doing is quarreling," she said. "The entire reason we came down here is because of the terrible situation you and Lucy are experiencing. The last thing I want to do is add to your troubles."

"Are you kidding me?" Jonathon said. "I want you guys to be yourselves. I told you that the both of you didn't have to come."

"But, I insisted," Julianne said.

"That's right, and I'm glad to have you both stay with us...but please don't think you have to walk on egg shells while you're here. Lucy and I are dealing with things in our own way, and although my way and her way are far different, we're each doing what we have to do to get through it."

"You haven't stopped talking, have you?" Julianne asked.

Jonathon took a breath and said nothing. He got into the car.

"Leave the boy alone," Henry said as he made his way to the passenger side and got into the back seat. Julianne took the front.

"I'm assuming your refusal to answer the question is an indicator that the two of you have indeed stopped talking," she said once the car started moving.

"Mom, I really don't want to talk about it right now," Jonathon said.

"And you don't have to, son," Henry chimed in.

Julianne shot her husband a disapproving look.

"Sweetling, I didn't mean to pry. I just worry about the both of you," she said.

"I know, Mom. It's just complicated right now. Lucy refuses to take the treatment, and I want her to take the treatment. Every day that she doesn't is a day I can't get back. I just feel pretty helpless right now. The doctor says the best thing she can do right now is just stay off her feet and rest as much as possible. He's even tried to get her to go see a therapist, something else she refuses to do."

"See a therapist for what?" Julianne asked.

"Mom, you haven't seen her, you don't understand what this is doing to her. She certainly is staying off her feet as the doctor suggested. She lies in bed all day staring out the window, and when she isn't doing that, she is crying. She needs to see a therapist."

"My goodness," Julianne said. "Son, I'm so sorry. We had no idea things had gotten so bad."

"Well, I'm sorry that it's like this. Believe me, I am. I hate it."

"Well, how is her health?" Henry asked.

"She's alright, best I can tell, and so is the baby. The cancer isn't having any noticeable effect on her yet—well, besides the emotional part, I mean."

Julianne stared out the passenger side window and seemed to mull over everything Jonathon had said for a few moments. Henry said nothing too.

"Guys, don't do that," Jonathon said, attempting to break the awkward silence.

"Don't do what, dear?" Julianne asked.

"I don't want pity," he replied. "If you want to do something, try and get Lucy to talk. Try to get her to open up about how she's feeling because she certainly won't do it for me. I have a feeling if she just had the right person to talk to, she'd feel a lot better."

"Well, that's what her mother is for," Julianne said.

"Mom, you know that she hasn't spoken to her mother in years."

Julianne's mouth dropped open, a surprised look on her face. "Jonathon, are you telling me her own mother doesn't know what's going on?"

"Yes, that's what I'm telling you, and you better not say anything about it either," he said, wagging a finger at his mother.

"Alright, alright," she said defensively. "I'd just hate to know you would keep such a thing from me is all."

"The relationship you and I have is far different from the one Lucy has with her mother…you know that."

Jonathon pulled the black sedan into the garage and his parents followed him into the house. Julianne made a beeline for Lucy's bedroom. Suddenly, he and his father were all alone in the kitchen, neither man really knowing what to say.

After a few minutes, Henry drew near his son and placed a firm grip on his shoulder.

"Son, it's going to be alright," he said, seemingly reading Jonathon's worried thoughts.

Jonathon looked at his dad, his eyes welling up with tears. Henry, the smaller man of the two, pulled his son close to him and put his slender arms around him tightly.

"It's going to be alright, boy," he repeated. "You'll see."

"I can't tell you how much it helps to hear you say that, Dad," Jonathon replied.

"What do you say we go out and get a couple of drinks…you know, let your mother work her magic with Lucy," Henry suggested.

"Well, I don't want to just take off and leave mom here," Jonathon said. "You guys just got here."

"Son, you know your mother. She planned all this out before the plane ever touched down in Mississippi."

That made Jonathon smile, and then father and son left without discussing it any further.

They didn't go for drinks as Henry suggested. Instead, Jonathon drove them to a familiar spot he and his father spent a lot of time together at when he was a boy. He thought it would be the perfect place for them to talk about Jonathon's troubles, and it was probably the first time they'd been there together in over twenty years. He pulled the car over near a well-beaten trail that disappeared into a thicket of pine trees. Henry followed his son through the trail until it suddenly reached its end on a tall bank overlooking the Pearl River. It was now becoming late afternoon, and the sky was beginning to turn a brilliant hue of orange toward the west. It wasn't the river that brought them to this particular spot; instead, it was the large patch of fossilized clay containing hundreds, or perhaps thousands, of sand dollars and other fossils from the Cenozoic Era. It was where Jonathon received his introduction to paleontology and it was all thanks to Henry. They spent many summers in that fossil bed collecting all sorts of specimens.

"Dad, this is where the fondest memories of my childhood were made," Jonathon said.

"Yep, I have to admit I have a lot of fond memories of this place myself," Henry replied, taking a deep breath of the crisp evening air.

A long moment of silence passed. Henry pulled the gray fedora from his head and revealed his white, thinning hair as he was clearly trying to think of the right thing to say. Jonathon was growing tired of the awkward silences. He knew his father pitied him and he hated it. Even though he needed the strong embrace and reassurances from his father as fuel to keep going, he never could get comfortable burdening someone else with his troubles...even his own father. He'd brought his father to this spot for advice, not pity.

"Dad, I don't want to lose my wife," he said in a stern tone, looking toward the muddy, swirling waters of the river. He now removed his own hat, clutching it tightly in his fist.

"Well no one is saying you will, son," Henry said. "You have to keep thinking positive."

"I'm trying, but I don't think positive thoughts are going to save her life. The doctor made it pretty clear, at least to me, that the odds are heavily against her."

"Well, the doctor isn't the one who decides who stays and who goes," Henry said. "That's up to the big man upstairs, you know that."

Jonathon sighed.

"I know it's not what you want to hear, son," Henry said. "But some things are just beyond our control. Sometimes things are just left up to a higher power."

"Yeah…but what if it wasn't?"

"What?"

"What if it wasn't?" Jonathon repeated.

"Well, if it wasn't, obviously we'd do what was necessary to get her better," Henry answered, staring at his son.

Jonathon continued to stare into the muddy water of the Pearl River, a determined look on his face.

"Son, there is no use in dwelling on the things you can't do anything about," Henry said. "Don't do that to yourself."

"Dad, if you were in my shoes—I mean, if Mom were in Lucy's condition—and you figured out a way to save her, you'd do whatever was necessary to make it happen, right?"

Henry bit his lip as he tried to understand what Jonathon was getting at. "Well, of course I would, son. I'm her husband, and when I married her, I made a promise to take care of her no matter what."

Jonathon nodded. "That's right. So if I knew of a way to save Lucy, I should do what was necessary, no matter how dangerous the task was." He looked to his father for guidance.

"Son, what are you getting at?" Henry asked. "You're speaking about a bunch of theoretical scenarios that aren't possible. This isn't good for you."

"It's not a theory, Dad. It's a real possibility. I know a way to save—heal—her from the cancer."

Henry walked in front of Jonathon and placed both hands on his son's shoulders, looking him straight in the eye. "Son, pardon my bluntness, but what in the hell are you talking about?"

"Dad, Lucy and I have kept a secret from you and mom for seven long years. We swore we'd never talk about it with anyone except the other survivors, and we never have—until this very moment."

Henry shook his head. It was as if he was trying to shake loose the confused state he was feeling. "Survivors? What are you talking about, son?"

"Dad, I'm going to tell you something that you're going to have a hard time believing. So I'm going to ask you to do two things for me before I begin."

"Sure," Henry agreed. "Just tell me what."

"I'm going to first ask you to please try and have an open mind."

"Done," he replied. "I trust you, boy."

"Secondly," Jonathon continued. "Before I begin, I'm going to have to ask you to sit down."

CHAPTER 3

The Island in the Mist

Eric Gill stared out the windshield of the Learjet as he made his final approach to the freshly paved runway directly next to the base camp of his operation. He marveled at the shiny new facilities he'd seen built from the ground up over the past seven years. When he first set foot on the island, almost seven years ago now, his only goal was to find his missing boss. He'd come prepared with plenty of heavy firepower, but alas, it wasn't enough to prepare him for some of the dangerous animals that called the island home.

Eric had foolishly brought a few college kids with him as cheap labor, and looking back on it, he couldn't believe how stupid he'd been. Handing college kids assault rifles and telling them to shoot at any animal that attacked them was beyond stupid. It was downright idiotic. But that was exactly what he'd done, and they had been on the island exactly ten minutes before he suddenly realized how big of a mistake it truly was.

When the first tyrannosaur came lumbering onto the beach and opened its massive jaws, the roar it expelled was the most terrifying sound he'd ever heard in his life. He'd looked down at his gun at that moment, and it suddenly seemed no more useful than a squirt pistol. He and his young employees barely escaped with their lives, and Eric knew immediately that Angus Wedgeworth had to be dead. There was no way one man could survive on that island all alone.

On the voyage back to Florida, the wheels in Eric's head turned wildly, and it wasn't long before he came up with an idea to make a ton of money off the island. It was dangerous and it was crazy, but if he figured out how to pull it off, there would be no limit to the amount of money he could potentially make. The only other matter he had to address was the four college kids he'd foolishly hired to help him. They'd seen the tyrannosaur, and he knew they'd tell anyone who would listen about what they'd seen. Eric used a combination of fear and incentive to try and keep them quiet. He told them he was going to start a business on the island and that he'd soon be making millions. Eric offered them jobs on the spot in exchange for their silence.

He even made them sign a contract with very strict stipulations. One of the stipulations was that they had to drop out of college and go to work for him immediately. He'd saved up a good nest egg to keep them paid until he got the ball rolling. If they refused his offer…well, that was where the fear tactic came in. If they refused, he'd threaten to kill them. Fortunately, it never came to that. The young men, although somewhat rattled by the sight of the fearsome tyrannosaur, agreed to go to work for Eric immediately. All of the young men still worked for him to this very day, and he knew he owed a lot of the success his business had achieved to them.

The business that had literally made him millions was quite simple. He had a team of well-trained associates that helped him trap and sell all sorts of dinosaurs on the black market for incredibly high price tags. Eric had a history of smuggling all sorts of things in and out of the country on his airplanes, and that was actually how he'd become acquainted with Angus Wedgeworth so many years ago. He knew all sorts of rich, powerful men all over the world that would pay vast quantities of money just to own a real live dinosaur. His customers signed very strict contracts, and he made sure each of them knew how important it was to keep certain aspects of his business secret. No one knew the location of his island and he wanted to keep it that way. Trust was a major part of his trade, and if he didn't trust a potential customer, then he didn't make a deal.

So it was no surprise that he felt torn on his latest potential customer, Mr. O. The species of dinosaurs that Mr. O was interested in was far larger and more dangerous than any he'd ever sold before. But it would also be by far the most lucrative sales he would have ever made if he went through with it. Eric could not deny to himself that he definitely had some trust issues with Mr. O, but he also could not deny that he was very, very tempted by the seventeen-million-dollar sale within his grasp. Eric wasn't even sure why he was entertaining thoughts of turning Mr. O's offer down because he'd already accepted the deposit.

I could always return it, he thought.

The Learjet touched down so gently that the tires barely chirped. After Eric parked the plane in the hangar, he climbed down the stairs and was met by David Turner.

David Turner, or Dave as he liked to be called, was one of the college kids he'd hired to help find Angus. He kept his hair cut short as it became wild and shaggy if he let it get too long. He was a wiry young man, and his shirt and tie made him look like a young boy trying to play dress up in his father's clothes. What he lacked in appearance, he more than made up for with intellect. He'd become Eric's most trusted associate, and he always asked for Dave's input when it came time to make a new sale.

"So, how did it go?" Dave asked.

"Well," Eric said crossing his arms, "we could bring in seventeen million dollars if we accept the job."

Dave whistled. "Wow, that's WAY more than any other sale we've ever made before. I'm scared to ask what the guy wants."

"It's actually two different animals," Eric said, and he reached in his pocket and retrieved a pack of Jupiter brand cigarettes. He placed a stick in his mouth and followed that with the strike of a match to light it up.

Dave watched the end of the cig glow cherry red as his boss inhaled. "Well, let me guess, one of them is a tyrannosaur."

Eric nodded. "Bingo," he said, blowing smoke out his nose.

"It'd have to be for a price tag like that," said Dave. "So how are we gonna trap one of those? We've never gone after a dino that big before."

"Well, it shouldn't be too hard," Eric said, the cigarette twitching in his mouth as he spoke. "He's only asking for a juvenile."

Dave scratched his head. "Well, what did you charge him for the juvenile?"

"Two million dollars."

Dave gulped…he was suddenly worried. "Uh, so what is the other fifteen million for? Please don't say he wants the *Spinosaurus*…I thought you said you wouldn't sell that one."

Eric held up a hand and shook his head. To their knowledge, there was only one *Spinosaurus* on the entire island. The paleontologist that worked for Eric assured him this was actually a good thing since multiple spinosaurs would probably eventually wipe out the other carnivores on the island. The dinosaur was so fearsome there was little doubt that it would be able to kill a tyrannosaur in a one-on-one fight. Fortunately, however, the tyrannosaurs were much more social dinosaurs than what most experts believed. The *Spinosaurus* was unable to take on multiple tyrannosaurs at once, and for this reason, it seemed to stay on the opposite side of the valley.

"I'm not selling the *Spinosaurus*," he replied quickly. "That animal is unique since it's the only one we have."

Dave gave him a puzzled expression. "Well, if it's not the *Spinosaurus*, what else could it be for that kind of price tag?"

"*Sarcosuchus*," Eric replied. "He wants *Sarcosuchus*." He turned and began to walk away.

"Whoa, wait," Dave said, chasing after him. "Did you even think about this?"

"What is there to think about?" Eric asked. "He offered me fifteen million for one. One was seen recently on the southwest corner of the island, and there is reason to believe there are more. Anyway, it doesn't matter, all we need is one."

"Yeah, that's great, but the part you need to think about is the how."

"The how is not our department, we just make the deals. Let Dr. Cruz and Glenn figure out the how. That's their job."

"Glenn is going to go ape-shit about this—and what if they can't figure it out?" Dave asked, unable to contain his disbelief.

"Then we'll have to find someone who can," Eric replied as he entered the massive steel building.

***

"Are you out of your minds?" Dr. Casey Cruz snapped.

"No, I'm fully aware of what I'm asking for," Eric Gill replied.

Dr. Cruz slapped his hands down on the steel table and suddenly got up from his seat. He began pacing back and forth in the conference room.

"You're awfully quiet over there," Eric said to the thirty-something-year-old man that sat quietly at the opposite end of the table.

The man had a dark complexion, a clear indicator of the amount of time that he spent outdoors. He wore a weathered hat that looked something like the one Crocodile Dundee wore; however, the band was littered with raptor 'sickle' claws of all different sizes instead of crocodile teeth. He'd had to kill many of them that tried to take up residence outside the fences of the base camp. The raptors saw their human neighbors as an easy meal and often attacked the trucks coming to and from the facility. It was Glenn Hardcastle's job as the dinosaur-wrangler to keep them under control. His job was the most dangerous on the island. If it ever scared him, he hid it extremely well.

Hardcastle took his hat off his head and raked his fingers through sandy blond hair. He had a toothpick in his mouth, just as he always did. After replacing the hat, he stared at Eric a long moment with his gun-metal gray eyes before speaking.

"Mr. Gill, I don't think I need to say a damn thing about how extraordinarily dangerous what you're asking us to do is going to be. You just said yourself you already know what you're asking. If you want *Sarcosuchus*, then you need to be prepared for what comes along with that."

"Meaning what, exactly?" Eric asked.

"Meaning someone is probably going to die," Hardcastle replied.

"But it's your job to keep them under control," Eric shot back.

"I'm one man," Hardcastle said. "I'm one man and I'm damn good at what I do. I challenge you to find another man on the planet with the experience I have wrangling dinosaurs. I've wrestled a damn raptor to the ground and slit its throat just before it tried to rip my intestines out with its claws. I once drove my jeep in front of a charging *Triceratops* to keep it from impaling your boyfriend Dave there, and if I'm remembering right, I got a couple of cracked ribs in the process. Hell, I've even brought down an *Allosaurus* that tried to tear the northwest corner of the fence down with a perfectly placed bullet in the side of the animal's head."

Hardcastle paused a moment for dramatic effect and looked around the room. "I think I've done a damn good job of keeping them under control, Mr. Gill, and I dare say, I'm pretty qualified to give an honest opinion when it comes to catching dinosaurs. I'm telling you someone is probably going to die this time. I don't know who, and to be honest, I really don't care as long as it's not me. I didn't say I can't catch your damn dinosaur. I just want you to be prepared for what comes along with it.

"Now if you don't like what I have to say, and if you think you can find another dino-wrangler somewhere in the world with as many years' experience as I've got, then by all means, call the son of a gun up and give his ass my job. But if you want me to guarantee you I can catch this monster by myself, it ain't gonna happen. And if you want me to guarantee you I can catch this monster with help and keep everyone alive in the process, it ain't gonna happen. I'm one man, Mr. Gill."

"Very well," Eric said. "I value your opinion, Glenn. I'm aware of the risks, but just to be clear, you're saying you can catch the animal, right?"

Hardcastle clenched his jaw. "Where there's a will, there's a way," he replied.

"Great," Eric said, then turned his attention back to Dr. Cruz. "Okay, Casey, as our resident paleontologist, what can you tell us about *Sarcosuchus*?"

"I can tell you that it's the main reason the tyrannosaurs avoid the southwest corner of the island," he replied. "They're smart enough to avoid them and their brains are only the size of a walnut. What does that say about us?"

Dave couldn't help but chuckle at that.

"Okay, I think we've all established that these are some dangerous animals, but come on, give us some information we can use," Eric said.

"Well, they're basically a super-sized crocodile. Fully grown, they are forty-feet long. The head alone is six feet long, so it could basically swallow any of us whole in one gulp. The thing weighs at least eight tons, and it has a bite force of 18,000 psi. If a living thing gets caught in its jaws, there is absolutely no escape."

"Geez, it weighs eight tons?" Dave asked, his face turning slightly pale.

"That's right," Dr. Cruz replied. "Just moving the animal will be a big challenge."

"The best thing to do is have a massive ship ready on the southwest corner of the island," Hardcastle chimed in. "We'll need a barge near the beach to place the animal on. We'll drag the heavy bastard out to deeper water with tow cables and then we'll need a crane to get it on the ship."

"I like that plan," Eric said.

"Yeah, the only thing we have to do is figure out how to catch it," Dr. Cruz said.

"Well, that's what I want you two to figure out," Eric said, pointing to Cruz and Hardcastle. "Spend the rest of the day trying to figure it out if that's what it takes."

CHAPTER 4

Silas Treadwell kicked back in the large, yet rather comfortable, leather chair behind the desk of his personal office. He placed both feet on the finished oak surface before him and took a rather pleasant drag off the massive cigar locked between his lips. It was a sweet taste, and no matter how many cigars he smoked, it never ceased to be any less sweet. As he did this, he looked around the massive room before him. There were animals peering down at him from all different directions on the dark-stained wood panels. There was a massive head of a water buffalo to his left, along with a rhino, giraffe, and antelope.

On his right, a massive grizzly bear stood twelve feet off the ground on its hind legs, its massive paws stretched above its head with huge black claws extended. The animal's mouth gaped open, revealing fangs capable of ripping apart any living thing that dared get in its way—*or almost any living thing*, Silas thought. He knew full well that there were creatures he'd seen years ago that would probably cause even the mighty grizzly bear to flee in a panic.

There were lots of other trophies mounted on the walls surrounding him, but he always longed for one animal in particular—one animal that he swore he'd never pursue. His biggest fear was regret. He was pushing sixty-five now, and he'd done almost everything he wanted to do in his life. He'd shot and displayed every trophy he'd ever hoped to find—but that one animal in particular haunted him. It haunted him so much he truly wondered if he'd go mad when he finally stepped down from the job that made him famous.

Wild World had once been the most popular nature program on the planet. Silas Treadwell had taught so many families about the most dangerous creatures on the planet, and he'd captivated those same families by often putting his own life in danger just to get an up-close look at the animals. He did it for the people watching at home, but if he was really honest with himself, he probably did it mostly for himself. He did it for the thrill. Silas lived for the feeling he got when he was on the verge of being eaten alive, or trampled, or mauled—only to escape without a scratch on him (most of the time anyway). People saw him as a bit of a hero, and although he'd taken plenty of flak from the animal lovers of the world, he knew in his heart how much respect he had for the animal kingdom.

He looked around at his trophies again. Sure he'd killed plenty of animals for sport, but he'd compensated every one of those animals ten-fold in lots of other ways. He had a very successful foundation that paid millions every year toward animal conservation—and to be fair, he only killed a particular species of animal once. He just considered his trophies payment for all the good deeds he was doing.

However, the days of his admirers outnumbering his antagonists were now long gone. The folks in the '90s had gone soft, and it seemed no one wanted to see him tempting fate on a weekly basis anymore. The ratings for *Wild World* were now at an all-time low, and there were lots of fancy television executives that had had enough too. It seemed there was lots of new blood in the animal conservation industry that had television shows now, and they were younger, more attractive, and downright lovey-dovey with the animals on their shows. The grizzled hunter and conservationist Silas Treadwell had run his course.

Silas took another puff off his cigar and blew a smoke ring. He supposed it was all for the best because after all, although his life was far from over, the harsh reality was that he wasn't getting any younger. What else did he have to prove? And it was that line of thinking that got him right back to the one thing that haunted him. *A tyrannosaur would look mighty good right above the fireplace*, he thought.

The phone suddenly rang loudly, startling him. He gently laid the cigar down on the edge of an ashtray and snatched up the phone.

"Hello, Silas Treadwell speaking," he said gruffly.

"Well, listen to you; you sound all official."

Silas suddenly sat up straighter in his chair.

"Jonathon! Is that you?" he asked.

Jonathon chuckled. "It's me, old man…how are you, Silas?"

"Funny that you're picking this particular moment to call," he replied. "I was just sitting here thinking of our little adventure in the Bermuda Triangle."

"Really?" Jonathon said. "That's funny, because that's kind of why I'm calling."

Silas opened his mouth to speak, but suddenly stopped. *Why in the world is he calling about that?*

"Silas, are you there?" Jonathon said, noticing the awkward silence.

"Yes, of course I'm here," he said. "Just trying to think of any good reason why you'd be calling me about that place."

Jonathon sighed. "You have no idea how many times I picked up the phone to call you in the last few minutes, only to put it back down." He paused and laughed nervously.

"Calm down, boy," Silas said, picking up on his uneasiness. "What do you need?"

"I really need a favor," Jonathon said. "And before I ask, please understand I'll completely understand if you say no."

"What do you need?"

"Silas, I've got to make a trip back to the island," Jonathon said quickly. "I have no earthly idea how to get back to it. I was hoping that you might know the way since you piloted our ship back home. I'm not asking you to go on land with me; I'm just asking if you could get me there."

Silas was stunned. So much so, he found himself unable to respond.

"Silas?"

"Yes—sorry, I'm here," he replied finally. "I have to admit that's the last thing I expected you to say to me."

"I know," Jonathon replied. "I can imagine how crazy it must sound."

"I mean, after all," Silas continued, "you were the main one that was preaching to the rest of us about how critical it was for us to all keep quiet about that island—to never go back there again."

"I know—"

"You told us that it was up to all of us to keep that island and the animals on it safe because it was never meant to be interfered with by man," Silas said.

"Yes, well something's changed," Jonathon said.

"Well, that's obvious," Silas replied. "Because the guy speaking on the other end of this phone isn't the Jonathon I remember."

"Lucy has cancer," Jonathon blurted out. "She's pregnant and she is refusing treatment."

Silas slumped down in his chair; the words fell upon him like a ton of bricks. He reached over and grabbed his cigar to get another puff.

"My God," he said after a moment. "Jonathon, I'm so sorry to hear that."

"I'm desperate; I don't know what to do."

"I'm guessing you think that fountain can save her," Silas said.

"Yes, it's the only option I can think of," Jonathon replied. "I refuse to sit back and watch her die."

"Well, wait a minute, I'm confused. I thought that water only kept people young."

"Yes, it does. And it drops years off your age immediately. Osvaldo told us that once a person drank the water, they never get sick, and they never age. The only way they can die is if someone mortally wounds them. If Lucy drinks the water, it'll take years off her age—it'll cure the cancer and it'll be impossible for it to return."

Silas rubbed his eyes as he processed what Jonathon was telling him. "Alright, I follow you," he said. "So what does Lucy say about this?"

Jonathon said nothing.

"Oh, come now, man," Silas snapped. "Don't tell me you're going to trick her into drinking that water?"

"That's exactly what I'm going to do," Jonathon replied through clenched teeth.

"Wait, you need to slow down and think about this. If Lucy drinks that water, she'll never grow old. You will, but she will not. Do you want to grow old and die, only to leave her behind? Do you want your child to do the same thing? Jonathon, no disrespect intended because you know I love you like a brother, but do you have any idea how selfish this sounds? This isn't you."

"Actually, I've given a lot of thought to this," Jonathon replied. "To answer your first question, no, I don't want to leave her behind. That's why I'm considering drinking the water too."

There was another long moment of silence before Jonathon finally spoke again.

"So…are you going to get me to that island?"

Silas took a deep breath and exhaled slowly. "If I don't do it, will you give up?"

"Absolutely not. I'm not going to sit back and do nothing while she withers away," Jonathon answered.

"That's what I thought you'd say," Silas said. "Okay, we're going to do this, but since we're being selfish and returning to that godforsaken island, I've got something I need to do there as well."

Jonathon hesitated. "Silas, whatever it is, I'm obviously in no position to judge."

Silas eyed the empty space above the fireplace and smiled. "No, sir, you sure aren't."

CHAPTER 5

"How is she?" Jonathon asked his mother moments after concluding his phone call with Silas.

"She's sleeping now," Julianne replied. "I'm afraid she's fallen into full-blown depression."

Jonathon nodded. "Yes, it's getting worse."

He sat down on the couch and crouched over as if he were going to be sick. Julianne sat down beside him and placed a comforting hand on his back.

"Son, may I make a suggestion?"

"Yes, please do," he replied as he rested his face in his palms.

"You need to go talk to her some more," Julianne said.

"Mom, I've already tried that," he said, clearly discouraged.

"I know," she said. "But, even though she's not saying much back, believe me when I say she's listening. She told me she's very concerned about what this is doing to you and she feels guilty. I think you need to go in there and tell her to concentrate on her."

Jonathon sat straight up, wide-eyed. "She feels guilty? Why? This isn't her fault!"

"No, it's not. The both of us know that, your father knows that. But from her perspective, this illness—this cancer—it's tearing apart your whole little family unit. I think it would do wonders for her if you would just ease up on her about the treatment options. You need to go in there and be the rock she needs you to be right now."

Jonathon considered his mother's advice, and deep down, he knew she was right.

"I'll talk to her when she wakes up," he said.

"Very good," she said, getting up.

Jonathon grabbed his mother's hand to keep her from leaving. "Mom?"

"Yes, dear?"

"I've got a favor I need to ask of you."

"Of course," she said, sitting back down. "What do you need?"

"I need to get away for a few days—maybe a week," he said.

Julianne stared at him, bewildered. "Get away? Where?"

"Well, you pretty much just confirmed what I've already been thinking. My current state of mind isn't doing her any good right now. I need to get away for a few days to clear my head. I've already requested the time off at work, and under the circumstances, it was granted. It would help me out tremendously if you stay here with Lucy."

Julianne stared at her son in disbelief. She wanted to be angry with him, but the sadness in his eyes prevented her from doing so. Instead, she leaned over and embraced him.

"Of course, son," she said. "But I wish you'd reconsider. Lucy is not going to like this."

"She'll understand," he said. "I'm not going to go anywhere without explaining it to her myself first."

"Well, where are you going to go?"

"I'm not sure yet," he replied. "I'll figure that part out."

"We will worry about you," Julianne said.

"There's no reason to worry, Mom."

Julianne stood up, now visibly frustrated. "You're just going to leave and not even tell us where you're going? Why *shouldn't* I worry?"

"Because I'm going to be with him," Henry said from somewhere in the kitchen.

This response took Jonathon completely by surprise. He'd told his father about the dinosaurs and the fountain of youth. After the initial stage of shock and disbelief, his father eventually supported his decision. However, he'd made no suggestion about joining him on the trip.

"Dad, that's really not necessary," said Jonathon, doing his best to sound grateful, yet firm.

"Oh yes, I think it is, son," Henry said, now emerging from the kitchen. "I insist."

Julianne walked across the room to stand beside Henry. "Jonathon, I know this will come as a shock to you, but for once, I have to say that I agree with your father."

Henry smiled, knowing full well that Jonathon was between the proverbial rock and a hard place.

"No, I really will be alright, you can't come, Dad," he persisted. Jonathon stood from the couch and began to make his retreat from the room and the confrontation.

"Dear, I think it's been decided," Julianne called after him. "If you want a few days to clear your head, then that's fine, but your father is going with you. I'm going to take care of Lucy, but Henry is going to take care of you."

Jonathon stopped but did not turn to look back. "But, Mom, I—"

"It's settled, Jonathon," Julianne snapped. "Not another word about it."

***

Jonathon crept into the darkened master bedroom where he thought Lucy would be sleeping. She wasn't sleeping, but instead watching an episode of 60 Minutes. As Mike Wallace carried on about some middle-eastern terrorist named Bin Laden, Jonathon sat down on the bed beside her. She glanced over at him and offered her hand. He gently took it and brought it to the side of his face. The soft, warm skin against his face brought a great feeling of comfort over him and with it came a pang of sadness and guilt. He did not want to leave her, and this moment was making it even harder. Despite his best efforts to fight it off, a single tear rolled from the corner of his eye and onto Lucy's hand.

"Sweetheart, please don't cry," she said, her voice cracking.

"I'm sorry, I didn't expect that," he said, brushing the moisture from his eyes. He quickly straightened up. "Lucy, I've got something I need to tell you."

A look of concern flashed across her face, but Lucy patiently waited to hear exactly what that 'something' was.

"I've got to leave for a few days to take care of something," he said. "I should be gone no more than a week at most."

"And just where are you going?" she asked, obviously surprised by the news.

Jonathon thought to himself how nice it would be if people would just trust him and not ask questions. However, he knew that was wishful thinking.

"I don't know how to say this without it sounding incredibly selfish," he said. "I mean, you're the one that is sick and I'm perfectly healthy. I'm the one who should be strong...I should be the rock that you—"

"Jonathon," Lucy cut in. "Calm down and tell me what you need." She sat up on the bed and put a comforting arm around him.

"I've just got to get away for a few days," he said. "I just need to clear my head. I'm afraid I'm not doing you a lot of good right now, and I've just got a few things I need to work out."

She stared at him, and he noticed the look of surprise on her face fade to sadness.

"It's not you, Lucy," he said softly. "I've got things to work out with me. I'm just going to go somewhere quiet and think. Dad is coming with me and Mom is going to stay here with you."

Jonathon looked away from her. He didn't know how she could possibly take anything he'd just said in a positive way. There was just no good way to explain why he'd leave her at a time in which she needed him most, and he couldn't bear to see her break down and cry. If only he could tell her the real reason why he had to leave. If only she could know what he was about to go back to so that she could live.

"Okay," she said after a brief moment of silence.

Jonathon whipped his head back around to face her. There were no tears in her eyes.

"Okay?" he said, unable to hide the bewilderment laced on that single word.

"Okay," she said again, very nonchalantly. "I think you're right. It would do us both good to take a little mini break from each other."

Jonathon just stared at his wife in disbelief. Now he felt somewhat disappointed that his idea had not bothered her at least a little.

"Well, alright," he said finally. "If you're sure."

Lucy gave a slight chuckle. "Well, it was your idea, dear," she said. "Are *you* sure?"

"Yes," he replied. "I'm sure. Dad and I will leave in the morning."

"Alright," she said. She took his hand once more and squeezed it. "Just be careful," she said with piercing brown eyes that seemed to suggest she knew more than she let on.

CHAPTER 6

Glenn Hardcastle pulled the heavily armored jeep around to the main entrance of the base camp, or what their customers knew simply as the headquarters of Gill Enterprises. Once stopped, he beeped on the horn twice, and moments later, Dr. Casey Cruz trotted out and entered the vehicle.

"I don't like leaving the facility," Cruz said as he buckled in.

"Now that just don't make a lot of sense, Doc," Hardcastle replied. "You're a dino scientist and you don't want to be around the dinos?"

"No, I'm a paleontologist," Cruz corrected him. "That means I study fossilized prehistoric life, not living, breathing dinosaurs."

Hardcastle punched the accelerator and raced the heavy jeep through the main gate and onto the service road that circled the entire island. Their target was the southwest corner, and if they were lucky, they'd get an opportunity to study a *Sarcosuchus* up close. It was clearly not something Dr. Cruz was thrilled about doing, but Glenn was all about getting a thrill. *Sarcosuchus* would almost certainly provide that.

"Okay, I don't understand why you'd take a job that gets you up close with real live dinosaurs if you have no desire to be around them," Hardcastle said.

"Are you kidding?" Dr. Cruz answered. "How could one in my profession turn down such an opportunity as this when it was first presented? I was ecstatic when I first heard about this magical place. It was probably the most excited I'd been in my entire life."

"So what is the problem?"

"The problem is that what we all perceived dinosaurs to be in our minds, and what they actually are, are two entirely different things. Most of the animals on this island are monsters—they're killers! I admit I was a bit naïve when I took this job. I quickly discovered that I was much happier studying these animals when they were dead."

"So why don't you just quit then?" Hardcastle asked.

"The same reason you don't," Dr. Cruz said. "The money is too damn good."

The jeep sped along the road at a fast pace and Hardcastle noticed a sharp turn ahead. He knew the road like the back of his hand and he took the turn wide. This was in an effort to keep the jeep speeding along as quickly as possible at all times. Through the years, they'd all discovered this was the safest way to travel. If one could keep a vehicle going around fifty mph, there stood a good chance of staying out of reach of any of the nasty dinosaurs that may be lurking nearby.

Also, the jeeps were painted in camouflage consisting of many different shades of green. This allowed the vehicle to blend in beautifully with the surrounding jungle foliage and decrease the possibility of being spotted. To top all of that off, the jeep was covered in a heavy cage with a mounted machine gun turret on the top. It was enough to provide a great deal of protection from even the largest predators on the island. The only lettering on the vehicle was a large G.E. logo painted in black and centered on the doors, obviously standing for Gill Enterprises.

"The money is only the biggest reason I hang around here," Hardcastle said, continuing the conversation. "I also signed a contract that binds me for another six years, and to be totally honest, I love being on this side of the fence."

"Then you're nuts," Dr. Cruz replied. "You're going to get yourself killed, and do you think Eric will care?"

"Probably not," Hardcastle admitted. "But that doesn't bother me. This is a business, and I knew what I was signing up for when I agreed to come here. I also know how hard it would be to replace me," he added, smiling.

Hardcastle piloted the jeep for several more miles before they finally reached the southwest corner of the island. The terrain on that particular quadrant of land resembled something out of the bayous of Louisiana instead of a tropical paradise. Off the main road, it became quite swampy and completely impossible to drive through. Hardcastle hoped that they would not have to venture into the swamps to find the super-croc. The ideal situation would be luring and then catching the animal at the main road. There was little driving to do from that point to reach the coastline, and from there, they would be able to place the dinosaur on a barge and rendezvous with a ship in deeper water.

After bringing the jeep to an abrupt halt, Hardcastle immediately stood and took position on the machine gun turret mounted on top of the cage. He swiveled the gun in all directions, scanning the environment for any movement at all.

"Okay, it's clear," he announced.

Dr. Cruz pulled an expensive-looking pair of binoculars from the center console and began searching the surrounding swamp for any sign of *Sarcosuchus*.

"Anything?" Hardcastle whispered.

"Not yet," Cruz replied. "If there is one nearby, it is most likely submerged in water. We just need to wait for a little while."

"Patience is not one of my best traits," Hardcastle grumbled.

"If you want to see one of these things, it's going to have to be."

***

An hour had passed and there had been no sign of *Sarcosuchus*.

"This isn't happening," Hardcastle said. "I think we need to try and develop some sort of trap and come back."

Dr. Cruz glanced up at Glenn from his seated position and rolled his eyes. "Really? You think we can come up with a trap for an animal that big?"

"If we put our heads together, it's possible," Hardcastle replied. He angrily slapped at his neck in an attempt to flatten a bothersome mosquito.

Dr. Cruz shook his head and was just about to argue when a loud splashing sound erupted from somewhere off to his right. Hardcastle swung the heavy gun around in the direction from which the sound originated. The only evidence that remained was a massive rippling in the water thirty yards away.

"What the hell was that?" Hardcastle asked.

"I don't know," Dr. Cruz answered, "but I don't think it was our croc…it wasn't a big enough splash."

Hardcastle suddenly heard something pattering across the sandy road behind them. He spun around with the gun gripped firmly in his hands, ready to unleash a firestorm if need be. What he saw behind them was not what he expected. He didn't know whether to be disappointed or relieved.

"You're right, it wasn't *Sarcosuchus*," he said quietly. "It's just a hadrosaur."

Dr. Cruz slowly stood up beside Hardcastle for a better look. "Ah, that's an anatotitan," he said confidently. "Probably just munching on some of the cypress trees that grow here; I've noticed they're quite fond of it. It's probable that they're the main source of food for *Sarcosuchus*."

The anatotitan appeared to be roughly seven feet tall and its skin was an odd shade of orange. It fed on a cypress tree limb it had apparently snatched off a tree in the murky waters of the swamp. The animal chewed slowly with its duck-like bill and seemed completely indifferent to the pair of gawking humans watching from the nearby armored vehicle. It took its time, appearing to savor each bite as if it would be the hadrosaur's last meal.

Suddenly, with absolutely no warning at all, a pair of massive, hellish jaws burst from the water beside the road and clamped down onto the unsuspecting hadrosaur. The entire anatotitan, save half its tail, became enveloped inside the massive *Sarcosuchus's* jaws. As the dinosaur increased the bite pressure, the helpless hadrosaur ceased moving. *Sarcosuchus* began to open and close its large maw, and threw its head back so that its prey would slide further and further into the jaws and throat.

"Oh my God," Dr. Cruz said, his voice trembling. "That creature is massive."

"I've seen one bigger," Hardcastle whispered. "That's not the one I've seen."

"That one is big enough," Dr. Cruz said as he reached down for his notepad. He began furiously scribbling notes.

"So where do you think the money shot is gonna be?" Hardcastle asked.

"Oh, it's quite obvious there is only one really good spot," Dr. Cruz replied, pointing at the animal with his pen. "Just behind the head—around the neck area—seems to be the softest spot. The rest of that hide is entirely too tough. We'll have to double up the dosage; it's going to take far more than I anticipated."

The *Sarcosuchus* consumed the entire hadrosaur in mere minutes, and then it slowly dragged the rest of its submerged body from the murky roadside water. The animal looked like a nearly perfect copy of modern-day crocodiles, only frighteningly larger. When all forty feet of the *Sarcosuchus* was out of the water, the animal then turned into the direction of the jeep, only thirty yards away.

"What is that thing doing?" Hardcastle asked, his finger lightly resting on the trigger.

"I'm not sure," Dr. Cruz replied. "He just ate, surely he's not—"

It was at that moment that the massive crocodile scrambled frantically toward them, its jaws snapping as it charged. Hardcastle could see bloodstained teeth and rotting flesh within those terrifying jaws. He heard Dr. Cruz shout an obscenity, but he couldn't make out the exact choice of word.

"Get this jeep moving! NOW!" Hardcastle howled.

Dr. Cruz immediately scrambled into the driver seat, and it became nauseatingly clear that there was no way the jeep would get rolling before *Sarcosuchus* made it to them. Hardcastle did the only thing he could do: he squeezed the trigger on the powerful machine gun and the weapon erupted with a flurry of large-caliber bullets. The firepower made the jeep lurch and sent a wall of sand into the air as the bullets slammed into the earth just mere feet in front of the rampaging croc. The disruption gave them the mere seconds needed for Dr. Cruz to get the jeep rumbling down the service road and back to safety.

"Did you hit him?" Cruz shouted.

"No, I wasn't trying to," Hardcastle replied calmly.

"What? Why the hell not?"

"Because those things are in short supply as it is. We need one alive, and the last thing I want to do is make this task harder for us."

Dr. Cruz shook his head and did not offer a reply. He kept his eyes on the road and his foot firmly on the accelerator all the way back to base camp.

CHAPTER 7

On the way to Fort Lauderdale, Florida…

"You never told me you knew Silas Treadwell," Henry said, somewhat star struck.

"Well, as you've found out over the past couple of days, there's actually a lot I haven't told you, Dad," Jonathon replied. "Don't worry; he's a real down to earth guy. You'll like him."

"*Wild World* has been my favorite nature program for the past twenty years," Henry said. "Ole Silas has had many close calls with everything from lions to Komodo dragons, and somehow he always comes away unscathed. I can't wait to meet him."

"Well, I assure you that all of those animals don't hold a candle to a rampaging tyrannosaur, Dad," he replied.

Henry just shook his head and stared out the window without saying a word. Jonathon suspected something was on his mind.

"Dad, something seems to be bothering you," he said. "How about you tell me what it is?"

Henry glanced over at his son and smiled an uneasy smile. "Son, it's just that all this talk about dinosaurs is still hard for me to grasp. It's still sinking in."

Jonathon sighed and paused a moment before speaking. "Are you saying that you don't believe me?"

Henry turned in his seat to look at Jonathon. "No! Of course I'm not saying that, son. I believe you," he said, almost pleading. "But surely you understand how bizarre and unbelievable it sounds—even more so after I had time to think about it."

"Yes, I know how crazy it sounds, and I suppose I felt some of the same emotions you're feeling right now, but trust me," Jonathon's words became deadly serious, "when you see some of the horrors that live on that island, it will become VERY real."

Henry swallowed. "I'm sure it will," he said very quietly.

A few hours later, Jonathon wheeled the rental car into the nearest available parking spot at the marina and then immediately popped the trunk. He went to retrieve his gear and Henry did the same. Jonathon grabbed his wide-brimmed field hat and placed it on his head. He then unzipped his pack and retrieved the large hunting knife that saved his life more than once on his last visit to the island; he took a moment to fasten the knife's holster onto his belt. Henry retrieved a straw hat from the trunk, a cheap Panama Jack brand, and then grabbed his own bag of supplies. Jonathon was dressed in his usual field gear: durable brown cargo pants, work boots, and a gray button-up shirt. Henry wore his sport coat, oxford shirt, and khaki pants. He was hardly dressed in the proper attire for the trip, but Jonathon had been unable to convince him otherwise.

"Don't you think we need some sort of firearm?" Henry asked, glancing at Jonathon's knife. "I mean, I'm pretty good with a knife too, but can you even kill a dinosaur with that thing?"

Jonathon smiled, and patted the knife. "This one has killed two as a matter of fact, and as far as guns go, I assure you that Silas has that covered."

"You're darn right about that," a gruff voice said from behind them.

Jonathon turned to see Silas standing there. He was decked out in similar attire from their last visit to the island. A bush hat was on his head, and the tan shirt, shorts, and hiking boots completed the outfit nicely. One glaring difference was that almost all signs of blond in his hair and beard was all but gone and replaced completely with white.

"You look like Santa Claus," Jonathon said.

"What can I say?" Silas replied. "Time has never been good to me."

"I think you look pretty good myself," Henry said, holding out his hand.

Silas took it and shook it firmly. "Thank you, sir," he replied. "You must be Henry Williams, the sire of this crazy kid."

"That would be me," Henry replied, looking over at Jonathon, rather puzzled.

Silas caught on to Henry's bewilderment and said, "Jonathon, what all have you told your dad about our time in the Bermuda Triangle?"

"The bare minimum," he answered. "The dinosaurs, the thugs, the fountain—isn't that enough?"

Silas laughed; he couldn't help himself. "Oh, I don't know," he said. "What about the tyrannosaur that chased you off a cliff? Or how about those flying lizards that tried to eat you? Or the explosion on the ship that almost—?"

"Silas, okay," Jonathon snapped. "Fine, I didn't tell him everything—and they're not flying lizards, they're called pterosaurs."

Henry stared at his son, wide-eyed.

"Dad, don't look at me like that."

Henry rubbed the back of his neck and took a deep breath. "Son, when we're on that boat and headed for this godforsaken island, you're going to have plenty of time to fill me in."

"Okay, I will," Jonathon replied.

"I want to know everything," Henry said, forcefully grabbing his son's arm. "Do not hold a single thing back from me." He then turned to Silas. "And Mr. Treadwell—"

"Please, call me Silas," Silas replied.

"Silas, I'd very much appreciate it if you'd sit in on our conversation and fill in any gaps my son conveniently leaves out."

"Be glad to, Henry," Silas said with an irritating grin aimed directly at Jonathon. "Now follow me, gents; let's board the ship and get on with this."

***

Silas's ship, appropriately named *Wild Lady*, was a forty-foot-long fishing vessel that many fans of *Wild World* would be quite familiar with. Silas had filmed many adventures at sea chasing sharks, octopuses, whales, and a wide variety of dangerous fish. *Wild Lady* had become a character on those shows in her own right, and Henry grinned like a schoolboy as soon as he stepped on board.

"I can't believe I'm standing on this boat," he said in awe.

Silas was amused. "Henry, when we get done with this little adventure, you and I are going to go fishing wherever you'd like to go."

"Oh no, I'm not trying to imply that—"

"Henry," Silas interrupted. "The man that raised that tough son of a gun is more than worthy of going fishing with me on this girl whenever he wants," he said nodding toward Jonathon.

Jonathon did his best to not show the embarrassment Silas was making him feel. He wanted to say something but knew there would be a long discussion about the things he'd done on the island later. For now, something else had gotten his attention.

"What's that?" he asked, pointing toward a large, bulging object hidden under a heavy tarp on the deck.

"That's something I had some boys slap together for me the very afternoon you called me," Silas said, approaching the curious object. "It's an amphibious vehicle. It'll seat four people."

"You had them 'slap it together'?" Jonathon asked, confused.

"That's what I said," Silas replied as he jerked the tarp off the vehicle.

Once exposed, Jonathon could clearly see what Silas was referring to. And he instantly felt grateful. True enough, it was an amphibious all-terrain vehicle, and aside from the six wheels, it resembled a boat more than a car. But it was the steel cage mounted over the seating area of the vehicle that Silas was referring to. It was obviously added for protection from dinosaurs. The cage was painted the same color as the body of the vehicle…black.

"Very thoughtful of you," Jonathon said, clearly pleased.

"I thought you'd appreciate that," Silas said. "And don't worry, we tested it out. The weight is distributed evenly. Once that cage is locked, nothing is going to get inside there unless it reaches an arm inside and unlatches the door. And last I checked, those tyrannosaurs are severely lacking in the arm department."

Jonathon wrapped his hands around the cold steel tubing of the cage and tugged on it.

"It's going to add much-needed protection, no doubt," he said. "But, this won't save us from a tyrannosaur."

Silas seemed offended. "Oh come now, that's the same-sized tubing NASCAR uses for the roll cages in their race cars. If it's good enough for Richard Petty, it's good enough for us."

"Richard Petty isn't driving into the jaws of a tyrannosaur, Silas," Jonathon groaned.

Silas crossed his arms and shook his head; he seemed genuinely bothered by Jonathon's assessment.

"Look, I'm not trying to discourage you. I just don't want us taking any unnecessary risks because we're under some illusion that this thing will keep us completely safe. It will be a tremendous help, but we've still got to be extremely cautious."

"I know, I know," Silas conceded, "but, if it saves our lives, you're never going to hear the end of it."

"I have no doubts about that," Jonathon said with a chuckle.

CHAPTER 8

Eric leaned against the damp metal door of the hangar that sat at the far end of the tiny runway. After taking another drag off his cigarette, he peered up at the misty sky above him. This mist—or fog—whatever it was, kept everything damp all the time. No one knew why or how the mist just seemed to hover over the island, but it was due to that anomaly that the island had been kept secret and hidden for so many years.

He thought about Osvaldo, the Puerto Rican man that had literally stumbled upon the island over 500 years ago. It was Osvaldo, or Chief Macuya as he was known back then, that then discovered the fabled fountain of youth. He drank from the fountain and, after surviving for over 500 years unnoticed, later crossed paths with none other than furniture tycoon Angus Wedgeworth. The old man's obsession with cheating death eventually led them all to the island and now here he was.

Eric smiled as he thought about those series of events. *Was it a bunch of crazy coincidences? A bunch of chance encounters? Fate?*

Fate, ah yes, he thought. *What else could it be?*

Fate led Angus Wedgeworth to his eventual death, and it did the same to Osvaldo for that matter. Somehow, some way, Eric had managed to avoid that terrible outcome when two men before him had not. It seemed to him that very fact meant everything he found himself doing now was meant to be.

Fate.

He dropped the cigarette on the ground and crushed it with the heel of his boot. In the distance, he began to hear a sound. It was faint, but very distinct.

Whop-Whop-Whop-Whop…

His heart began to flutter. A smile formed on his face, and when he realized it, he then immediately rid himself of it. He felt like a goofy schoolboy. The sound grew louder.

Whop-Whop-Whop-Whop-Whop-Whop…

He looked to the skies and squinted, trying desperately to see anything.

"Damn mist," he whispered.

Before he knew it, the smile had returned to his face. This time, he didn't hide it. What was the point? He was downright giddy. He'd been trying for so many weeks and months to convince her to visit the island. And now—

Whop-Whop-Whop-Whop...

The chopper was *really* close now, and in mere minutes, she'd be standing on the same soil as he. She'd see what all he'd built. She'd see the fortress he'd built around the facility and finally she would realize that he was in control of this place. She would be safe here and now she would no longer have to rely on what he told her. She would see it for herself. If she was going to play any role in his business, she was going to have to start showing up at the office. He knew that day would arrive sooner or later. And now it was here.

The silhouette of the helicopter finally appeared over the trees. The vehicle was black with the familiar G.E. logo scrawled on the sides. The chopper touched down about forty yards away from him, and as soon as it did so, Eric rushed forward to greet a beautiful redhead that exited it.

Her red hair was straight, and very long. The helicopter did a masterful job of messing it up, but she was still gorgeous anyway. She wore a short, gray skirt with a white blouse to top it off. Her lips were a bright, candy apple red, by far the most striking feature after her hair.

"You made it!" Eric called out over the whirring sound the helicopter made as the engine shut down.

"I made it," the woman replied. "I can't believe you talked me into this!"

"Look around you," Eric said. "Nothing is getting through that fencing. And even if it did, I've got the men that can take care of it!"

The woman looked around in all directions, surveying the new environment. She noticed four guard towers, one on each corner, with men holding large rifles. Eric watched her and he could see the fear in her eyes. He noticed that soon her eyes drifted away from the buildings and fencing around her. It was the trees and dense vegetation surrounding the entire base that seemed to captivate her. He grabbed her by the shoulders and looked her in the eyes.

"Listen to me," he said. "What happened here seven years ago isn't going to happen again."

She nodded, but her eyes made it clear she was unconvinced.

"Annie," he said softly. "What happened to you last time isn't going to happen again. You're safe, I promise."

Annie smiled, and for the first time, she seemed to relax a bit. "I trust you," she replied. "If I didn't, there would be no way in hell you'd have talked me into coming back here. You just don't understand what it's like out there without all of these fences."

Eric laughed. Annie opened her mouth, appalled that he would laugh about such a terrifying memory. "Something funny?" she asked, annoyed.

"No, sweetheart," he answered, trying to sound apologetic. "It's just hard for me to accept the fact that you and old Angus share DNA. He was all gung-ho about coming here, dinosaurs be damned."

"Yeah, well after what he did to me back then, I'd be just fine if I somehow found out that we don't share any DNA at all."

"Don't say that, honey," Eric replied. "If it wasn't for your psychotic uncle, we'd have never even met."

"Can't argue with that," Annie said with a smile. She leaned forward and kissed him.

Eric pulled back from her and put his arms around her. "You're trembling."

"Yes, just cold, that's all," she said.

Eric quickly ushered her inside, and Annie was grateful that he bought her little lie. It was hardly cold enough to make her tremble.

CHAPTER 9

Atlantic Ocean

Henry Williams stared at his son in disbelief for several long seconds before looking back to Silas.

"My son did all of that?" he said just above a whisper.

"Darn right he did," Silas replied. "Saved our butts out there is what he did."

"Dad," Jonathon said. "Silas is exaggerating a lot of details. The tyrannosaur that chased me off the cliff never got close enough to really worry me."

Henry held up a dismissive hand. "Not another word, son. I don't care to hear any more about the death-defying stunts you performed all those years ago. All I care about is the fact that you made it through. And I have to insist that you don't take any unnecessary risks on this trip."

"Dad, nothing I did on my first visit was unnecessary. Everything I—*we*, went through…it was all about survival. I'll do whatever it takes to keep you guys and myself alive. If you have it in your mind that this is going to be easy, then you may as well stay on the boat. Actually, I'd prefer both of you to stay on the boat."

"Ain't gonna happen," Silas chimed in.

Jonathon shook his head and then turned to stare out the cabin window. "I know, Silas. I know why you're coming, and I want you to know I don't like it."

"And just what is it you think you know about me?" Silas growled.

Jonathon turned back to face him again. "You want another trophy. You want a tyrannosaur head to put on your wall. I'm not an idiot; I'm fully aware that was part of the deal you made with Angus before your last visit to the island."

Silas clenched his jaw and shook his head. "Whatever happened to that crap you said about not judging me? I mean, I'm not really crazy about your reasons for wanting to return either, by the way."

Jonathon sighed. "Yes, yes, I know." He closed his eyes and suddenly regretted what he'd said. "I'm sorry," he said softly. "I just think that the animals on that island have been disrupted enough by man. Going in there shooting them isn't the natural order in their world."

"True enough, and drinking some magic water to live eternally isn't the natural order in our world either," Silas countered.

Jonathon opened his mouth to argue his points further, but suddenly realized he had no argument. Silas was right, but that didn't mean he had to accept it.

Henry felt he'd let the bickering between the two men go on long enough. He stepped between them and accepted the role of peacemaker he felt was thrust upon him whether he liked it or not.

"Gentlemen, that's enough," he said calmly. "The fact of the matter here is that you are both right...and you are both wrong."

Jonathon and Silas stared at each other as they listened to Henry speak.

"And because of that fact, neither one of you has any right to try and persuade or counsel the other. You each have your own demons to battle here." He turned to face Jonathon and placed a firm hand on his shoulder. "Son, Silas is exactly right. What you're trying to do is not the natural order of things." He then glanced over at Silas. "And for the record, I think shooting animals that have managed to survive extinction for over 65 million years for sport isn't very sportsmanlike at all."

Silas huffed and turned away.

"But," Henry said, refocusing his attention on Jonathon, "you asked for Silas's help, son. You needed his help to find this place and he's provided this vessel we now stand upon and plenty of other weapons to use as protection. Not to mention that dino-proof all-terrain vehicle sitting on the deck. If he wants to kill one dinosaur as payment, then you have no right to deny him of that, whether you agree with it morally or not."

Jonathon pulled his wide-brimmed hat off his head and raked his fingers through his brown hair. He then placed the hat back on his head and rubbed his eyes. It was obvious his father's words had gotten through to him...and he hated it.

"Silas," Jonathon said. "I appreciate your help, really I do. I was out of line. I'm sorry."

Silas turned toward him and waved off the apology. "You don't owe me anything. I never expected you to like what I've been planning. Hell, I'd have been shocked if you hadn't put up some sort of fight. I don't expect you to understand it. Just know that this is something that I have to do. It's something that's been eating at me ever since I laid eyes on one of those vicious monsters. It's not that I want to bring down one of those beasts; it's that I have to do it. It's just who I am."

"I respect that," Jonathon said. "What I'm doing is something I feel I have to do as well." He held out his hand.

Silas shook it. "Well alright then," he said, turning to Henry. "Now where were we? Ah yes, did I tell you about the time a *Dromaeosaurus* pinned your son down on the ground and tried to rip his belly open with its claw?"

Henry suddenly turned white. "No," he muttered.

Jonathon wanted to intervene, but it was obvious to him that Silas was doing what he could to break the tension in the room. He decided to say nothing and just watch his poor father endure another terrifying story instead.

CHAPTER 10

Glenn Hardcastle took a liking to Annie Wedgeworth the first moment he laid eyes on her. He was, and never had been, the shy type. So it was no surprise to anyone when he rushed to greet her as soon as he caught sight of her in the foyer of the office building in which Eric Gill's business flourished. Hardcastle, without saying a word, removed his hat and took her hand. He then kissed it as he knelt on one knee.

"Will you marry me, honey?" he asked, theatrically.

Annie looked at the onlookers around her, one of which was Eric, and did her best to hide the embarrassment she knew was all over her face.

"Glenn, stop scaring my girlfriend," Eric said, and pulled Annie away with Dave Turner in tow.

Hardcastle scowled at him, but said nothing as he and Dr. Cruz followed them to the conference room.

"So what's the scoop on the super-croc?" Eric asked, no sooner after he'd shut the door.

"Well, *Sarcosuchus* certainly is super," Dr. Cruz replied with a somewhat nervous chuckle as he took a seat at the large, wooden conference table. "The beast nearly got to me and Glenn."

"Oh please," Hardcastle interrupted. "That thing never had a prayer once I trained the gun on her."

"Guys, all I want to know is what you learned and how it'll help us," Eric said.

"Well, we found out that they can eat an entire *Parasaurolophus* with relative ease," Dr. Cruz answered.

"Really?" Eric said, surprised. "Just the head on those things are around four feet long…isn't that right?"

"That's correct, and on average, they weigh about four tons."

"And our super-croc ate an entire one in front of you?"

"Yeah, he did," Hardcastle chimed in. "And he did it fast too."

Eric looked back to Dr. Cruz, clearly awaiting some sort of plan on how to catch the *Sarcosuchus*.

"The road that runs through the swamps on the southwest corner of the island," Dr. Cruz began. "Those swamps, as you know, are the only known place on the entire island where we've found *Sarcosuchus*. I'm thinking we capture a few *Parasaurolophus* and use them as bait along that road…maybe every mile or so."

"Okay, I'm with you so far," Eric said.

"Then we have scouts assigned to watch each animal from a safe distance. Of course, they'll all have to have a radio, and as soon as they spot one—"

"They alert a team that's armed and ready to capture the beast," Eric finished the statement.

"Exactly," Dr. Cruz said, happy that Eric seemingly liked his idea.

"Then what?" Dave Turner asked suddenly.

Dr. Cruz looked at the young man with an ever-so-brief expression of annoyance. He hadn't cared much for Dave and never understood why Eric treated the boy as his pet.

"Then," Dr. Cruz replied, "we tranquilize the animal and bind it with restraints."

"But how will you get it to sea?" Dave asked.

Glenn Hardcastle suddenly slapped the table with his hand, startling Dave and everyone else in the room. Annie shrieked.

"Then we drag the damn thing to the shoreline and onto a barge…it's not that far from the swampland. Then the barge can be pulled out to sea and deliver it to whoever this crazy S.O.B. is that wants it. Does that sound okay to you, Dave?" Hardcastle asked. He seemed to be just as annoyed with the young man as Dr. Cruz was.

Dave nodded, his face flushed red with embarrassment.

"I think that sounds like a helluva plan if I do say so myself," Eric said. "What do you think, Annie?" He asked the question in such a way that suggested he was merely trying to include her in some small way.

Annie smiled a pleasant smile and took a deep breath. She then looked around the room at the men surrounding her. "I think you're all going to die," she said, still smiling.

For a few moments, no one in the room said anything, but finally, Glenn Hardcastle spoke.

"That's funny," he said dryly. "I think I recall saying that very same thing the other day."

"Well, then you're officially the only sane man in this room," she replied to him.

Hardcastle bobbed his head toward Eric and flashed him a sly grin. Now it was Eric's turn to scowl.

***

Everyone else in the conference room had left, and only Eric and Dave remained. Dave had actually gotten up to leave with the others when Eric asked him to stay a moment.

"I need you to do something for me," Eric said. "And I'm afraid you're not going to like it."

Dave didn't like the way that sounded, but he shrugged it off. "Lay it on me. I'll do whatever you need me to do."

Eric smiled and took a deep breath. "Hardcastle and Cruz are going to make an attempt to capture the juvenile tyrannosaur tomorrow. I would like for you to accompany them."

Dave sighed and smiled nervously. "Are you sure about that? You know neither of those guys like me very much…Glenn especially."

Eric waved the suggestion off. "I know. They will obviously complain at first, but once those guys get down to business—well, just trust me when I say that the last thing they're going to be focusing on is you. Capturing a young tyrannosaur could potentially be more difficult that catching an adult one."

"And you want to send me with them?" Dave asked, dumbfounded.

Eric nodded. "This is the biggest sale we've ever made. I want to make darn sure everything goes through as smoothly and as quickly as possible. I don't think I'm going out on a limb by assuming our biggest challenge is going to be capturing the super-croc. We don't have a lot of time to waste chasing this juvenile rex. I want someone I can trust in the trenches with these guys on this one. Just your mere presence will be enough to keep them focused and determined to succeed on the first attempt. And if they don't—I mean, if they're sandbagging, I want to know about it."

Dave chewed his lip as he considered everything Eric had just said. He didn't like it, but he was beginning to understand that this was just one more instance where Eric was placing him in a position of authority.

"Can I count on you to see that Cruz and Hardcastle bag that *T-rex* tomorrow?" Eric asked.

Dave nodded. "Of course," he said. "You can count on me."

Eric smiled, clearly pleased. "Alright then, I'll let the guys know so they can get all of the complaining they're going to do over with." He turned to leave the room.

"No," Dave called out behind him.

Eric turned to face him, a puzzled look on his face.

"Let me be the one to tell them," Dave said. "Glenn isn't going to ever show me any respect until I show him that I'm not intimidated by him. I'm sure I'll bump into him at some point between now and tomorrow. Just let me break it to him, and maybe somehow I'll be able to reason with him."

"Reason with him?" Eric asked.

"Yeah, you know—make him understand," Dave said. "I want him to understand my role here."

Dave's words made Eric laugh. "Okay, hot shot," he said. "Break it to him yourself."

Eric then left the room and no sooner had the door closed did Dave suddenly begin to regret his decision.

CHAPTER 11

As soon as Jonathon caught sight of the familiar shroud of mist that surrounded the island, he felt a chill run up his spine. He glanced over at Silas and imagined the big man was having a similar reaction at the same moment.

"Never thought I'd see that sight again," Silas muttered softly.

"Me either," Jonathon replied. "A small part of me wondered if it would even still be here."

Silas looked at him, confused. "Why wouldn't it be here?"

Jonathon shook his head. "I don't know," he said. "I mean, this is the Bermuda Triangle, is it not?"

Silas chuckled and nodded. "I suppose so."

"Are you having second thoughts, son?" Henry asked as he quickly placed a hand on top of his hat to keep it from blowing away.

"Absolutely not," Jonathon replied sternly. "I didn't come all this way with the island in sight to stop now. I've got a job to do and I'm going to do it. But I stand by what I originally said: I really wish you'd stay on the boat, Dad."

"Not going to happen, son," Henry said, and now he too stared at the wall of mist that inched closer to them with every passing moment.

"I'm taking us to the beach on the opposite side of the island from where we landed seven years ago," Silas said. "From what I remember, the fountain was closer to that side, and it should keep us from having to cross that large valley in the center."

"Good idea," Jonathon agreed. "We'll skirt around the wood line— where it meets the valley. That way, we'll have a better view of what is around us and the chances are less likely for something to surprise us in the dense foliage."

"I remember the wood line surrounding the valley," Silas said. "It seems to be the safest way and the ATV should be able to navigate through the brush and cross whatever waterways we encounter. I seem to remember at least one stream."

"And what about your tyrannosaur?" Jonathon asked reluctantly.

Silas looked at him, and it was as if he was trying to read Jonathon's mind. It was hard to tell in that moment if Jonathon was being condescending or if he genuinely wanted to know.

"We'll get your water first," he finally responded. "Then I'll bag my tyrannosaur."

The ship began to drift into the shroud of mist, and all of the men felt a sudden cool dampness wash over their faces.

"I can't see anything at all," Henry said, excitement evident by the octave change in his voice.

"It will not last long," Jonathon assured him.

No sooner had he said the words than the fog began to thin out until finally it only remained high in the sky above them and behind them. Sunlight never made it to the island, and at first glance, it appeared that nothing at all had changed about the beach since the survivors escaped it seven years prior. The island remained a sad and gloomy sight, just as they remembered it. Silas and Jonathon even noticed the old shipping container that they'd gotten the ATVs out of all those years ago. It was still settled into the same position from which they'd found it, although the base of it seemed to be buried a little deeper in the sand.

After Silas dropped anchor and packed all their gear into the back of the amphibious vehicle, the three men spent a great deal of time wrestling with the crane to get it lowered safely into the calm waters below. Once they accomplished the unexpectedly difficult task, they each made their way down a ladder and into the vehicle.

"Alright, everyone strapped in?" Silas asked.

As soon as his passengers confirmed that they were, he reached toward the right side of the craft and pulled the heavy hinged cage over the top of them and latched it in place. He then throttled the vehicle forward and the trio slowly drifted toward the beach.

"Alright," Jonathon said, glancing toward Henry. "When we get to shore, it won't be long before you see some things that are going to knock your socks off."

"Oh, I'm quite sure," Henry said.

"No, Dad," Jonathon cut him off. "Whatever you're expecting, I promise you you're not expecting enough. Dad, the first time you see a tyrannosaur lumbering across the valley, for the first time in your life, you'll feel *real* fear."

"Alright," Henry said quietly, unsure how to respond.

"Don't panic. If you panic, you'll yell or shout, and all that will do is draw more carnivorous dinosaurs our direction. If you panic, you'll almost certainly make bad decisions that could not only jeopardize yourself, but Silas and me too."

Henry grabbed Jonathon's forearm tightly. "Son, I fear you've forgotten who you're talking to."

Silas glanced over at Jonathon and chuckled.

"I'm sorry, Dad," Jonathon said. "I'm just trying to prepare you."

"After living with your mother for nearly fifty years, the dinosaurs should be a piece of cake."

Silas laughed again, but Jonathon remained stone-faced.

Henry's face softened a little and he said, "Look, son, I know what you're trying to say, and I assure you I'm taking all of this deadly serious, but give your old man a little credit…and how about giving me a gun while you're at it."

"There are six rifles in the back," Silas said. "Didn't even bother bringing handguns; they won't do any good."

"Did you bring any knives, Dad?"

"Oh yeah," Silas muttered, remembering the stories Jonathon had told him. "Henry, I hear you used to throw knives professionally with the Misses."

"Well, I threw them at the Misses, yes," Henry replied. He pulled back his jacket, and Silas and Jonathon were both momentarily stunned at what they saw. "Does this answer your question?" Henry asked as he proudly displayed no fewer than twelve short throwing knives strapped to the liner inside his jacket.

Jonathon shook his head in disbelief. "That's my dad."

***

Once Silas piloted the amphibious vehicle onto the beach, he immediately sought out a path that the vehicle could maneuver through the dense tropical terrain so that they may find the valley nestled away at the heart of the island. Jonathon had taught him that such paths existed if you searched for them due to the frequent traffic inflicted by the islands large reptilian residents.

The only downside to using one of the dinosaur-made paths was the dinosaurs. The chances of encountering one on the very paths that they used was pretty high, and when Silas expressed his concern about that fact, Jonathon quickly reminded him that there were far more herbivores on the island than carnivores. "And besides," he added playfully. "You assured us the cage on this vehicle would keep a tyrannosaur out."

"And I stand by that!" Silas snapped. "But that doesn't mean I want to tempt fate either."

"Oh my God," Henry said suddenly, utter amazement in his voice.

Jonathon whipped his head around to see what had gotten his father's quick attention. He smiled when he saw it. "Stop the vehicle for a moment, Silas," he said.

The vehicle lurched to a sudden halt, but Henry's gaze never left the large majestic animal that moved slowly through the dense foliage roughly twenty yards away from them. The dinosaur was quite large and it walked on all fours. It had a long tail, and a head that was similar to that of the duck-billed hadrosaurs, but without the duck-bill. The hind legs were disproportionately larger than the much smaller front legs. The animal was a deep gray color, similar to that of an African elephant.

Jonathon leaned close to his father and whispered, "I believe it's an *Iguanodon.*"

"Ah," he replied. "Does it—er, will it eat us?"

"No," Jonathon answered. "It's an herbivore. It's not a threat to us as long as we leave it alone."

"Well, then by all means, let's leave it alone," Henry whispered.

"Alright, Silas," Jonathon said. "Let's move on...no sudden movements though. If we startle that thing, we could possibly attract unwanted attention by a carnivore."

Just before Silas began to pilot the vehicle away, he felt a very faint vibration originate from the steering wheel that was gripped tightly in his hands.

"Did you feel that?" he asked, looking over quickly at Jonathon.

"Feel what?" Jonathon asked softly. He instantly became attentive when he sensed a hint of concern in Silas's tone. He whipped his head around in all directions.

Silas didn't respond; he just stared forward, his hands still wrapped tightly around the steering wheel.

"What's wrong?" Jonathon whispered, still looking around in all directions. "Did you see—?"

He immediately quit speaking when he felt it too. There was a very subtle vibration originating from the ground and suddenly the *Iguanodon* noticed it too. The large dinosaur lifted its head and sniffed the air. Jonathon could see the large creature's eyes widen as it seemed to sense a sinister presence approaching.

"Something's coming," Henry said, unable to hide the fear in his voice.

Jonathon looked over at Silas. "We need to go...now!"

Silas nodded and immediately throttled the vehicle forward. As he did so, a massive dinosaur crashed through the dense jungle foliage and released a deafening roar. The dinosaur stood as tall as a tyrannosaur and had a mouth full of sharp teeth, but that was where the similarities ended. The carnivore had a large sail-like structure that blossomed from the vertebrae of its back. The "sail" was a reddish-orange color and had black stripes running vertically every several inches and resembled those of a zebra. The head was similar to that of a crocodile, and it had a long snout with teeth that seemed too long for its mouth.

"What is that thing?" Henry yelled as Silas frantically wheeled the ATV away from the danger.

"*Spinosaurus*," Jonathon replied, and he immediately began rummaging the back seat for a rifle.

"We're never going to outrun that thing!" Silas said as Jonathon returned to the front seat with the largest rifle he could find.

"No, but maybe we won't have to," Jonathon replied as he readied the weapon.

"And how is that?" Silas asked.

"It wasn't coming for us; it was coming for the *Iguanodon*," he explained.

At that moment, the large *Iguanodon* came charging alongside the ATV as it had clearly chosen to flee the *Spinosaurus* in the same direction as they had.

"You mean that *Iguanodon*?" Henry asked as the large herbivore galloped past them.

Jonathon gritted his teeth and turned to aim the rifle at the *Spinosaurus* that was in pursuit—he wasn't sure which prey the animal was focused on. What he was sure about was the fact that the animal was closing fast.

"What are you waiting on, shoot it!" Silas said, glancing over his shoulder.

Jonathon aimed the rifle toward the dinosaur's skull, but he was reluctant to fire it.

"What are you waiting on, son?" Henry asked.

Jonathon was staring at the dinosaur's eyes. He said nothing.

Silas again glanced over his shoulder to see where the animal was, and much to his dismay, he estimated the dinosaur was a mere thirty feet behind them. At the pace the animal was running, it would be on top of them in less than a minute. When he looked back ahead, the *Iguanodon* was still lumbering just in front of the ATV.

"Shoot it!" Silas screamed again at Jonathon.

Jonathon again remained silent. He kept the weapon trained on the animal's skull, but he stopped short of pulling the trigger. Henry looked over at his son and contemplated snatching the rifle from him.

"Son, if you don't take the shot, we're going to die," he said pleadingly.

The *Spinosaurus* was now bearing down on them, and it again released a roar that nearly made Henry pass out. Jonathon lowered the rifle and looked over his shoulder to Silas.

"Hit the brakes," he commanded.

Silas snapped his head around and looked at him as if he had gone completely mad. "Are you nuts?" he asked.

"Just do it…now!"

Silas took a deep breath and did as he Jonathon requested. He jammed his foot on the brake and the small amphibious vehicle came to a sliding stop. As it did so, the *Spinosaurus* continued stomping forward, and Silas feared that it was going to stop and give the roll cage on the ATV a good test. To his utter amazement, the animal stepped over the vehicle as if it wasn't even there and continued its pursuit of the terrified *Iguanodon*.

"I don't believe it," Henry said, grabbing at his chest.

The three men watched as the *Spinosaurus* quickly caught up to the *Iguanodon* and immediately sank its long teeth into the helpless animal's back. The *Iguanodon* wailed a pitiful cry and collapsed onto the sandy soil. The *Spinosaurus* then plunged its crocodilian snout into the animal's gut and the bloody mess that followed made Henry nauseous.

"How did you know?" Silas asked, amazed.

Jonathon shrugged. "I wasn't totally sure, but it looked like the *Spinosaurus* was focused totally on the *Iguanodon*. If I'd taken a shot at it, I'm sure that would've changed immediately and we'd probably be in deep trouble about right now."

Silas took a deep breath and wiped the sweat from his brow with the back of his hand. "I don't remember seeing one of those the last time we were here," he said as he continued to watch the animal eat.

"I didn't either," Jonathon said. "As if the tyrannosaurs weren't bad enough."

"Let's go find your water and get out of here," Silas muttered as he drove the ATV away from the carnage in front of them.

CHAPTER 12

Glenn Hardcastle jerked the refrigerator door open and snatched an ice-cold long neck from the top shelf. He used the bottle opener fastened to the side of the counter to remove the top. The small metal cap made a small tap as it hit the tile floor and Hardcastle made no effort to pick it up. Instead, he turned the bottle up and didn't stop until he'd chugged down half of its contents.

Suddenly, Dave Turner entered the employee break room and, as soon as he caught sight of Hardcastle, he became noticeably uneasy. Dave had always known Hardcastle, like most of the other employees at Gill Enterprises, didn't like him. He'd expressed his concerns about how the employees on the island viewed him to Eric, but his boss always seemed to downplay it and chalk it up to nothing more than grade-school jealousy. Eric made no bones about the fact that Dave was, despite his youth, his right-hand man. He put a great deal of trust in Dave, something he rarely did with anyone else. Dave knew more about his clients and business deals than anyone else on the island too. All of the other employee's roles at Gill Enterprises consisted mainly of getting the product out to the buyers. It was no big surprise to Dave that the other employees disliked him so much, but that still didn't change the fact that it bothered him. Nevertheless, he dealt with it.

And then there was Glenn Hardcastle.

Hardcastle took it to a completely different level. He talked down to Dave and made a point to embarrass him in front of other employees. The other employees in turn championed him for it, and Dave was often discouraged with the fact that Eric seemed to look the other way when it happened. Dave knew why, of course. Glenn Hardcastle was probably the most valuable employee with the company, and to make matters worse, he knew it.

Hardcastle had a great deal of experience with nearly every dinosaur on the island. Eric had his ways of dealing with him, and everyone on the island knew that Glenn had a way of getting under his skin at times (ironically something else he was championed for among his colleagues), but despite any issues he had with him, Eric always stopped short of any kind of disciplinary action against him. The unfortunate reality was that if the company lost Glenn Hardcastle, it would be a major setback. Major setbacks usually equated to a major loss of money.

As soon as Glenn noticed Dave's entrance, he smiled a sly grin at him and tipped his hat back a bit. The tension that filled the room was almost immediate and it seemed to smother Dave. He considered turning back and leaving, but he knew that would do nothing but reinforce Hardcastle's perception that he was intimidated by him. He was, of course, but there was no way in hell he'd ever admit it. And besides, there was a matter he needed to discuss with Hardcastle. This moment would be as good a time as any.

Dave strode toward the fridge, never even giving Glenn a passing glance. He opened the door and reached inside to retrieve a canned lemon iced tea. This made Hardcastle snicker, and he took another quick swig of his beer. Dave cracked open his can of tea and took a swig of his own. The two men stood in silence for a long, awkward moment.

"Glenn, I've got something I need to tell you," Dave said, finally deciding the blunter he was about this matter, the better.

Hardcastle squinted at Dave and gave a sideways smirk. "Oh, you do?" he said. "Well hang on just a second…let me take a seat."

Hardcastle pulled a chair out from the nearby table and plopped down. He took another pull from his beer and then rather forcefully slammed the bottle down on the table.

Dave felt it was best if he remained standing. "I've heard the news about tomorrow. I know that you and Dr. Cruz are going out to try and catch the baby tyrannosaur. I just wanted you to know that I'll be accompanying you."

Hardcastle drummed the fingers of his right hand on the table and gave Dave an icy stare. "Like hell you are," he growled.

Dave swallowed. "Now, Glenn, I'm afraid this isn't up for debate. Eric wants me out there and I'm going to go. That's just the way it is, and the sooner you accept it, the better it's going to be for all of us."

Dave felt all of the blood rush to his face. He hated confrontation, especially with Glenn. Despite his best attempts to hide his embarrassment, the expression on Hardcastle's face revealed how badly he had failed.

Hardcastle remained seated and continued to dole out that same uncomfortable stare at Dave.

"Oh, is that right?" he said, in a surprisingly calm tone.

"That's right," Dave answered, surprised at how calm he sounded as well. "We both have a job to do. I think it's clear that you don't like me, and that's okay."

Hardcastle rolled his eyes and grinned. Something about the way Hardcastle reacted to his last statement triggered something inside of Dave that he'd always hoped was there, but was never quite sure. He suddenly began to feel an abundance of confidence wash over his entire body. The embarrassment and awkward feelings he'd been experiencing mere minutes earlier were suddenly vanishing. He returned a glare of his own to Glenn and then continued speaking.

"And now that we've gotten that out, I think I should clear the air about something else," he said. "I have authority over you."

Hardcastle suddenly sat straight up. His grin disappeared and was replaced with a scowl. "What did you just say?" he spat.

"Let me rephrase," Dave said, "I'm not your equal in this company—I never have been. I'm actually superior to you, and I think that from this moment forward, I'm going to start acting like it."

Glenn Hardcastle popped out of his chair and got his face within an inch of Dave's. He was slightly shorter than Dave, so he had no choice but to look up slightly. This small detail only added to the wave of confidence Dave was riding. It was all he could do not to smile

"You're saying you're better than me?" Hardcastle growled.

"No," Dave replied. "I'm saying that in the eyes of Eric and Gill Enterprises, I am your superior."

Now it was Hardcastle's turn to turn a shade of red—although, his change in color was due to another emotion. The rage he now felt was clearly evident due to the fact the man was beginning to tremble. Hardcastle kept his face inches away from Dave's, and if anything, he got slightly closer.

Dave saw the gesture for what it was: a pathetic attempt to intimidate him. Well, the schoolboy antics weren't going to work any longer. He'd had enough of Glenn Hardcastle.

"Are you going to hit me?" Dave asked.

Hardcastle continued to stare him down, but he made no reply.

"Because if you're going to hit me, make it a good one," Dave said. "And when you're done, you'll be on the first ship off this island."

Hardcastle breathed in deeply through his nose, and Dave feared that in another few moments, smoke would begin to wisp out of the man's ears. He was literally shaking now and seemed to be on the verge of an aneurysm.

Another minute passed, and when neither man said another word, Hardcastle suddenly turned away and headed for the door, the beer bottle in his right hand.

"Oh, Glenn," Dave called out to him.

Hardcastle stopped in his tracks. He said nothing, and he didn't turn to look back at him.

"I think you need to pick up that bottle cap you left on the floor," Dave said.

Once again, Hardcastle said nothing and made no attempt to pick up the bottle cap. This didn't surprise Dave, and he never expected him to actually pick it up. He was, however, making a point. The days of Glenn Hardcastle bullying him were now over and in the past.

Glenn stomped toward the door, but before he left the room, he took a final moment to throw his empty bottle in the trash can. He threw the bottle with enough force to make the glass shatter loudly. His anger and fury couldn't have made Dave any happier.

CHAPTER 13

"Are you absolutely sure?" Silas asked, unable to believe what he was hearing.

"Yes," Jonathon answered. He was kneeling on the ground several yards ahead of the vehicle where Silas and Henry remained within the relative safety of the cage. Moments before, while Silas was driving and Henry was still trying to slow his heart rate after the encounter with the *Spinosaurus*, Jonathon had noticed something rather odd ahead of him. As soon as he'd noticed it, he immediately asked Silas to bring the vehicle to a stop so that he could investigate on foot. Now he was looking at something that not only puzzled him, but somehow left him with a sick feeling in the pit of his stomach.

"It's definitely a dirt road," he said. His tone suggested he was having trouble believing it himself.

"Well, are you sure it wasn't there before?" Silas asked.

"Positive," Jonathon said, his eyes trained on what he knew were relatively fresh tire tracks.

"Well, why the hell would a road be here now?" Silas asked.

"A very good question," Jonathon answered. "Something is wrong here…very wrong."

"Could there be someone else on this island?" Henry asked.

"There are tire tracks here," Jonathon said. "I'd say the chances are really good we're not alone on this island."

A loud, thunderous roar suddenly echoed somewhere deep within the jungle foliage to the left of them.

"Wh—what was that?" Henry stammered. "It sounded…big."

"*T-rex*," Silas whispered, his eyes wide.

"Are you sure?" Henry said.

Silas nodded, his blue eyes unblinking. "I could never forget that sound," he answered.

"He's right," Jonathon said, as he stood and returned to the vehicle. He lifted the cage and returned to the seat next to Silas. "That's a tyrannosaur. They seem to be plentiful on this part of the island."

"And this is the side of the island you two decide we should land on?" Henry asked, noticeably worried. When Silas and Jonathon made no reply, he said, "So what do we do?"

Jonathon looked up at the sky and then down at his watch. Nightfall was going to hit soon. "We go deeper into this island, and we find a place to camp for the night. In the morning, we find the cave as quickly as possible so that I can get what I came for—and then we head back."

"And then we go after what *I* came for," Silas added, jerking a thumb toward his chest. He cranked up the all-terrain vehicle and eased it forward.

Jonathon nodded, but said nothing.

"Well, what about the tyrannosaurs?" Henry asked, his voice trembling slightly. "What are the chances of one of them attacking us?"

Jonathon peered in both directions as Silas eased their vehicle across the dirt road. The road stretched at least a mile in both directions before disappearing beyond a curve in the distance. "It's not really the dinosaurs I'm afraid of right now," he said, taking one final glance at the tire tracks imprinted on the loose soil.

***

Finding a home away from home for the night proved to be a lot more difficult than Jonathon thought it would be. It seemed his first trip to the island provided a lot more options for shelter and protection from dinosaurs. He thought of the large metal shipping container on the beach that he, Silas, and Annie Wedgeworth had slept in all those years ago and found himself longing for it immensely.

As the light continued to fade, he found himself on the verge of giving up. They would just have to find enough wood to build a large enough fire to keep the animals away for the night. Although they'd have to take shifts sleeping, it could work. He even remembered Lucy telling him that Angus and his thugs had done just that the night after they'd kidnapped her.

But then Jonathon looked at his father. He'd never be the same if anything happened to him, especially in such a land as foreign as where they now found themselves. It was his fault that his father was here on an island inhabited by dangerous dinosaurs. He was the dinosaur expert and, although Silas didn't like to admit it, even he relied heavily on Jonathon's expertise. The fact was that the overall safety of both men fell squarely on his shoulders.

Would a fire really be good enough?

He knew the answer was a definitive no. He had to keep looking. And besides, although a fire would probably be a great deterrent for dinosaurs, it could have the opposite effect for any humans that may be on the island. Orange flames flickering within the blackness of the jungle wouldn't be hard to spot and would surely be investigated.

"Over here!" Silas called out just a little louder than Jonathon would've liked.

He trudged over to where the shout had originated and found Silas and Henry peering into a hole near the base of an enormous tree.

"Get away from there!" Jonathon snapped. "You don't know wha—"

Suddenly, a loud shrill cut off Jonathon's sentence and made all three men startle. Henry stumbled to the ground as he backed away from the hole and Silas quickly jerked him back to his feet.

A beaked mouth, resembling that of a large parrot, protruded from the dark void and opened. The same shrill rang out again. As Silas and Henry backed away even further, the animal boldly revealed the rest of its oddly shaped head. The dinosaur was dark brown in color, very similar to the color of the soil from which its subterranean home was constructed. A large neck frill (but no horns), and the mere size of the creature, was a dead giveaway that Silas and Henry had stumbled upon the nest of a *Protoceratops*.

Jonathon thought it odd that the second dinosaur he encountered on his first visit to the island was in fact the second dinosaur he'd encountered on his second visit there. The underground home the animal had built underneath the enormous tree would've probably been large enough for all three men to enjoy for the night. Talking the *Protoceratops* into leaving, however, would be a difficult task.

Silas suddenly pulled out his revolver and pulled back the hammer.

"No!" Jonathon shouted.

Silas quickly pointed the gun downward and away from the animal. "What?" he asked, genuinely puzzled.

"It's not going to hurt you," Jonathon replied. "It may have young down in that nest. It's not an aggressive animal. You don't have to kill it!"

"But it's got exactly what we need," Silas argued, pointing at the burrow with the barrel of his gun. "How else are we going to get it to leave?"

"My, you're eager to shoot something," Jonathon quipped. "We're not shooting it to take its home," he added.

Silas begrudgingly returned his weapon to the holster on his belt. He shook his head and grumbled something that Jonathon was unable to make out. The *Protoceratops* continued to protest very loudly.

"Son," Henry said.

Jonathon whipped around to face his father. "Yeah, Dad?"

"Forgive me, because I know you're the dino expert here, but is all the racket this thing is doing going to attract the more dangerous dinosaurs?" he asked with a worried expression.

"Yes," Jonathon answered flatly. He then gazed up at the enormous leafy tree above them and marveled at how large and sturdy its branches were. As he examined the bottom branches, an idea suddenly occurred to him. "Silas, did I see you pack a large tarp in the storage compartment of the ATV?"

"Yes" he replied. "It's camouflaged. I brought it in case we came across an area we had to travel on foot. I thought we could cover it up the vehicle and hide it from the dinos."

Jonathon smiled to himself at the silly notion. He doubted that the dinosaurs would have anything to do with the ATV, camouflage tarp or no. Nevertheless, he was now grateful that Silas had brought the item as he had another use for it.

"I know what we can do," he said. "Get that tarp."

CHAPTER 14

The next morning was bright, or at least as bright as it could be considering sunlight was in short supply on the island. Usually when the sky was as bright as it currently was, it meant that the day was going to become uncomfortably hot and sticky. However, when Dave took a morning jog around the perimeter fencing, as was his usual morning ritual, he noticed a slight chill in the air. Part of him wondered if that was some sort of omen; a sign trying to tell him that accompanying Glenn Hardcastle on the day's hunt was a doomed endeavor. Dave shook the unpleasant thought out of his head and continued his jog.

An hour later, he showered and dressed in attire fitting for the day's activities. He rarely wore blue jeans, and he only had a single pair to his name on the island. He'd joked to Eric that there would be no way he'd be caught dead wearing any of his nice clothing outside of the fencing in the past. It seemed today he had an opportunity to put that statement to the test, and thus he'd found himself putting on the blue jeans without even really thinking about it. He put on the plain white T-shirt he'd decided on the night before, but he didn't count on it being as chilly as it was. He grabbed a gray, hooded sweatshirt that zipped up in the front for added warmth.

Before heading out to meet Hardcastle and the others, Dave had one more stop to make. Eric had ordered him to check in with him before venturing off the island. There was something he needed to give him. When Dave arrived, Eric was already seated behind his large desk, reading a National Geographic. He was kicked back in the chair, his feet on the marble top.

"You wanted me to stop by?" Dave asked.

Eric took his feet off the desk and leaned forward in his chair. He threw the yellow magazine off to the side. "Dave! Yes, come in," he said. "I've got something for you."

Eric reached over and pulled open his top right desk drawer. He retrieved a silver revolver.

Dave shook his head. "There's no need for—"

"Yes, there is a need for it," Eric argued. "Now, I know you're not crazy about guns, but you're going to take this one. Take care of yourself out there," he said, carefully sliding the weapon across the desk in his direction.

Dave reluctantly took it and shoved it into his rear waistband.

"You nervous?" Eric asked.

Dave chuckled uneasily. "Would it matter to you if I am?" he said.

Eric frowned. "Look, I know you're kind of stepping out of your comfort zone here, but that's exactly why I'm making you do it. Everything will be just fine, and besides, all you have to do is supervise the operation. Let Glenn and Dr. Cruz do their thing. They run the show, and you run them…got it?"

Dave scratched his head and smiled. "Yeah, I got it." He thought about his confrontation with Hardcastle the night before. "Have you seen Glenn this morning?"

"No," Eric replied. "But that's not unusual. He usually sleeps late." Eric paused and looked at his watch. "But, by now he's probably at the hangar getting the trucks ready as we speak—why do you ask?"

"No reason," Dave replied. "Just wondering," he added wistfully. "Well, I suppose I'll head on over and get ready to head out with them. You got anything else for me?"

Eric shook his head. "Nah, you be careful and bring me back a juvenile tyrannosaur."

Dave nodded and turned to walk away.

"Oh Dave," Eric called out after him. Dave stopped and glanced back as Eric tossed something at him. He caught the item—it was a candy bar.

"In case you get hungry," Eric said. "Good luck."

Dave put the candy bar to his brow and saluted it to Eric as he turned away.

***

The eight thousand square foot hangar only had one airplane and two helicopters in it. The rest of the space was occupied with four jeeps and two large trucks. All of the vehicles were army surplus and were perfect for the terrain on the island. Aside from the black paint jobs, Gill Enterprises logos, and the outfitting of the protective metal cages on the jeeps, the vehicles were otherwise in the exact same condition they were upon purchase. They'd been reliable and durable. Dave knew that Glenn Hardcastle knew that better than anyone. He'd had to depend on the jeeps a time or two to escape rampaging dinosaurs.

Upon his arrival at the hangar, Dave spotted Hardcastle backing one of the jeeps up to a caged single-axle trailer. The trailer appeared to be five feet by eight feet and was painted completely black to match the jeep. There was another man standing at the tongue of the trailer and immediately began lowering the jack once the jeep was in position. With the trailer attached, Hardcastle jumped out of the vehicle and headed for a second jeep parked behind the trailer. Dave briskly trailed him.

"So what's the plan today, Glenn?"

At first, Hardcastle seemed to ignore the question. He reached into the glove box of the jeep and retrieved a first aid kit. After examining its contents, he turned his attention to Dave.

"I think we'll head to the wood line on the southern portion of the island. It's only about four miles from here. Most of the tyrannosaurs nest along that interior edge of the jungle. It'll be the best place to find a juvenile," Hardcastle said, though he never actually looked at Dave.

Dave was surprised and caught off guard with the fact that Hardcastle had made no attempt to insult him or initiate any kind of confrontation. It was a welcomed change.

"Well, why do you think the tyrannosaurs nest on the interior edge of the jungle?" Dave asked, trying to make conversation.

"Because they feed off the herbivores that inhabit most of the valley in the center of the island," Glenn replied. He climbed into the back of the jeep and studied the large mounted machine gun. "There are also a lot of smaller dinosaurs that live in the jungle between the valley and the southern beach. There are lots of opportunities for the tyrannosaurs to find a meal in all directions around where they nest."

Dave nodded, and he was genuinely impressed with how well Glenn knew what he was talking about. "So...on a scale of one to ten, how difficult do you think this is going to be?"

For the first time, Glenn stopped what he was doing and looked at Dave. "I'd say ten, but I'm saving that for the dino-croc. So I suppose I'll have to settle for nine."

Dave swallowed hard. That wasn't what he wanted to hear. "Really?" he said, doing his best to sound unrattled. "That high?"

"Well yeah," Hardcastle answered. "The terrain is going to be difficult. There are lots of gulleys and sandy soil in that area. It's really easy to turn over one of these jeeps if you don't know what you're doing. On top of that, we're going after a kid belonging to one of the nastiest dinosaurs on this island. God help us if Mama gets wind of what we've done."

"I see," Dave said, still trying to sound confident.

Glenn Hardcastle could see right through it. "Oh, don't worry, Dave," he said, climbing down out of the jeep. "You've got me to look after you," he said, slapping him on the back as he strode past. "It's a good thing we're such great friends." He grinned as he said the words.

Something about that grin troubled Dave considerably.

CHAPTER 15

Jonathon awoke with a nagging backache. He supposed it could've been worse considering his sleeping arrangement. Silas and Henry had been the lucky ones in his opinion. The three of them had fashioned a pretty nifty hammock the night before using the camouflage tarpaulin and rope stored away in the ATV's storage compartment.

The hammock was hidden in some of the thick lower branches of the large tree his father had discovered, and soon after, the *Protoceratops* living underneath. Jonathon had volunteered to sleep on the ground within, what he still considered to be, the minimal safety of the armored amphibious ATV. He'd slept with one of Silas's large rifles in his arms, and he clung to it with the ferocious grip of a toddler with a favorite teddy bear. Truthfully, he didn't get much sleep at all, and what he did get didn't seem to do him a whole lot of good. Now he was aching, and still tired.

"You alright down there?" Silas grumbled to him from somewhere above.

"Yeah, relatively speaking," he answered softly. He unlocked the cage and swung it open, allowing himself the first opportunity to stand. He stood right there in the ATV and stretched. The jointed appendages on his body popped and cracked so loudly he feared the nearby *Protoceratops* would hear the sounds and protrude it's wailing head out of the burrow again, drawing unwanted attention. The stretching did do wonders for his aching body, however, and for the first time, he felt ready to take on the day. The task at hand was simply finding the fountain of youth as quickly as possible and then getting the hell off the island.

Jonathon had to admit to himself that he was immensely curious about the road that they'd encountered the afternoon before. That curiosity was in fact partly responsible for his lack of sleep. He'd tried to imagine the whos and the whys all night and had been unable to come up with a good explanation for any of it. Finally, he told himself that he really didn't care. He had to stay focused on his reason for being there in the first place. Lucy's life depended on it.

"So, what's for breakfast?" Henry asked rather loudly, shortly after arriving on the ground again.

Jonathon held a finger to his mouth in an attempt to shush his father. Henry's brow tightened, but then softened when he realized his son was pointing to the burrow where the *Protoceratops* lived.

"There's food in the ATV," he whispered. "We'll talk when we find a safer spot."

Henry nodded. He and Silas then climbed back into their respective seats in the vehicle.

***

Dave clasped the handle mounted on the dashboard and held on for dear life. Glenn Hardcastle was driving like a madman, and he was sure it was all in an effort to scare him. It was becoming more and more apparent that Glenn had decided he'd attack him all day with subtle jabs. Dave was determined not to give in. The important thing was that Glenn had still not made a single insult, nor had even tried to start the slightest hint of a confrontation. That was progress; the proverbial train seemed to be on track, and Dave wasn't going to do anything to cause it to derail.

Occasionally, Glenn would glance over at him, but Dave would only look back and smile as if to suggest, will this thing go any faster? Dr. Cruz, and a middle-aged African-American man named George Powell, trailed behind them in the jeep hauling the trailer. George was a likeable fellow, and Dave was certain he had no enemies to be found on the island. He'd gone on many hunts with Hardcastle in the past and seemed to be almost as fearless as he.

"How much further do we have to go?" Dave asked loudly, trying to be heard over the whining of the jeep engine.

"About another mile," Hardcastle shouted back.

"So what's the plan when we get there?"

"Patience," Hardcastle replied. "We're almost there. You'll find out soon enough."

Less than five minutes later, Hardcastle slammed hard on the brakes and the jeep skidded to a stop in an area where the edge of the jungle met the valley in the center of the island. Dave peered out at the flat land and noticed a herd of *Triceratops* moving toward the large lake that all of the animals frequented for water. There were other, smaller dinosaurs scurrying about. Some of them were in herds, while some of them seemed to be all alone. Moments later, George and Dr. Cruz arrived with the trailer. Hardcastle stood up in the jeep and directed his attention to them.

"Alright, gentlemen…are we ready?" he asked.

"We're ready," Dr. Cruz replied. He glanced disapprovingly over at Dave. "Are you sure you don't want George to accompany you?"

Hardcastle laughed off his suggestion. "Of course not! We've got this…right, Dave?"

Dave said, "I'm just here to make sure we come back with the prize. You guys do what you do best."

Hardcastle laughed again. "That's the spirit, Dave," he said. "You guys be ready to snag that baby *T-rex* when the window is opened," he said, pointing at them.

George nodded and said, "Good luck, Glenn, you crazy fool."

With that, Hardcastle slumped back into the driver's seat and stood on the gas. The jeep took off, leaving a plume of sand in its wake. Dave held onto the edge of his seat and suddenly felt very confused. *What is he doing?*

Hardcastle piloted the jeep along the wood line until he found a spot where there was no grass, only a narrow road roughly ten feet wide. The road originated from somewhere within the dense foliage of the jungle. The canopy of trees and flowering vegetation seemed to create a natural-made tunnel where the road eventually disappeared into the shadows. Hardcastle stopped the jeep a moment at the entrance and tried to look within those shadows.

Dave caught a whiff of a pungent odor. It was an odor he'd never smelled before and it favored death and decay. He started to comment on it, but when he glanced over at Hardcastle, it was apparent he was concentrating. He thought it best not to interrupt. This was Glenn's domain, and he was going to let the man do his job.

Suddenly, Glenn whipped the jeep around and put the vehicle in reverse. He was now slowly backing down the shadowy narrow road.

Dave's curiosity was getting the better of him. He had tried to be quiet, but now he felt his clueless state could potentially cause problems. What was Glenn doing? He had to ask.

"Glenn," he whispered. "Where does this road go?"

"This ain't no road," he snapped back. "Now keep quiet and listen!"

"Listen for what?" Dave asked nervously.

It was then that he noticed it. There on the ground, just outside of the jeep, was the largest three-toed footprint he'd ever seen. It had to belong to a tyrannosaur, and suddenly it became quite obvious what Hardcastle was doing. After he noticed the large footprint, then he noticed the bones. There were perhaps hundreds of them littering both sides of what Dave had thought (until Glenn corrected him) was a road. The bones were all different sizes and many still had chunks of rotting flesh clinging to them. Flies were buzzing everywhere. Hardcastle was exactly right when he said what they were on wasn't a road. It was a game trail—an extremely large game trail. Dave trembled when he considered what the trail probably led to. Hardcastle was backing the jeep into a tyrannosaur nest!

"Are you nuts?" Dave whispered through clenched teeth. "Get me the hell out of here!"

"Shut up!" Hardcastle growled. "You wanted to accompany me on a hunt, well you're here. So shut up before you get us killed!"

"No," Dave argued. "This is not what I meant. Get me out of here right now!"

Suddenly, there was a rustle in the foliage behind them. Dave watched in terror as entire trees seemed to sway back and forth. A monstrous creature was headed for them from somewhere further down the road. The ground vibrated slightly underneath them.

"Showtime," Hardcastle said with a low grumble. "These things hunt a lot and often they'll carelessly leave the young ones behind."

"So how are we going to get by the big ones?" Dave asked.

"We're not," Hardcastle replied. "We want Mama and Daddy to chase us so that George and the doc can go after junior."

Dave felt as if he were going to faint. He broke out in a cold sweat. "We—we're…the bait?" he asked, unable to believe it.

"That's right," Hardcastle said, a sly grin on his face.

"Damn you," Dave snapped. "Damn you!" He pulled the gun Eric had given him and pointed it at Hardcastle. "Take me out of here…NOW!"

Hardcastle glanced over at the revolver and then back at the large tyrannosaur lumbering out of the shadows. "I'd put that away if you're interested in living," he said. "You shoot me and we're going nowhere at all."

As soon as he finished his sentence, Hardcastle jammed the jeep in drive and stomped on the gas. He didn't waste any time to see if Dave had heeded his warning. Instead, he focused on the terrain ahead and piloted the vehicle straight into the widespread valley. His goal was to drive into a herd of smaller dinosaurs in hopes that the tyrannosaur would lose interest in chasing after them and instead go after its normal prey. Then, what he feared might possibly happen, actually did.

"There are two of them!" Dave screamed.

For an ever so brief moment, Hardcastle wondered if Dave was going to begin weeping. He'd always thought the man was a coward, but seeing how quickly fear had taken him over—it was somewhat disappointing. *This one's got no backbone at all*, he thought. It was quite obvious the big chicken believed he was going to die.

That's not to say that Hardcastle himself wasn't feeling any fear at the moment. That couldn't be further from the truth. The tyrannosaurs were every bit as terrifying as he'd imagined they would be as a child. The jagged teeth jutting from the animal's jaws were by far the most striking and frightening feature. He'd seen them before today, of course, and had even had a few close calls. But no matter how often he'd seen them, or how many times he'd managed to evade them, one never got used to the sheer majesty and overwhelming presence of such a nightmarish beast. In Hardcastle's mind, the main difference between him and Dave was the fact that he was managing to keep his composure. Keeping one's composure in a situation such as the one they were now in was crucial to survival.

It seemed with every beat of Hardcastle's heart, those snapping jaws drew ever so closer to the rear of the jeep, and his view of the animal in the mirror became more and more detailed. The skin was a shade of brownish-green color. The tyrannosaur's back was darkest and the coloring became lightest on the stomach and chest. The eyes were an unsettling shade of orange, lifeless and seemingly non-blinking.

"I was hoping we'd get lucky and only have to contend with one," Hardcastle yelled as he wheeled the jeep around a large tree stump. Dave's body slammed against the door during the sudden motion. He shoved the handgun back into his waistband for fear that it would be jostled out of his grip. "But I knew going in that we might have to deal with two. All we've got to do is keep them busy long enough for Cruz and George to snatch the baby up. Of course, that's assuming that these two have a kid!"

"What?!" Dave wailed. "You don't even know if there is a juvenile in the nest?"

"No, I don't," Hardcastle replied matter-of-factly. "Did you see one?"

Dave dropped his head in his hands and did not offer a reply. Glenn continued to maneuver the jeep around any obstacles he could spot in an effort to slow their rampaging pursuer.

"It's been several months since mating season," he added thoughtfully. "I'd say that the chances are good there's a kid in that nest. Have a little faith, Dave."

Hardcastle peered into his side view mirror and saw the larger of the two tyrannosaurs charging in closer to them. The smaller, the female, fell further behind and drifted to the right as if anticipating that they might turn in that direction. He caught sight of a large group of styracosaurs marching toward the lake. *Styracosaurus* was a bluish-gray, large frilled dinosaur that was similar to the triceratops in stature. The frill was quite large and adorned no less than six spikes that jutted upward. The nose of the animal was armed with a two-foot horn, also similar to a triceratops.

This particular species of herbivore was not what Hardcastle had in mind to use as a means of getting the tyrannosaur off their tail, but it was the closest herd in their vicinity. He had to give it a try.

He held the throttle wide open and pointed the vehicle straight toward the seemingly oblivious group of herbivores. As he did so, he spent more time looking in the rearview mirror than he did out of the windshield. Unfortunately, this kept him from seeing a large terrace straight ahead of them. When the jeep hit the abrupt incline, the vehicle launched into the air. The jeep flew high enough for all four wheels to leave the ground. When they returned to earth, the jolt sent Dave hurtling upward and his head struck the protective cage. He landed awkwardly between the two seats, inadvertently knocking the vehicle out of gear and into neutral. The engine revved loudly, and by the time Hardcastle realized what had happened, it was too late.

The pursuing tyrannosaur pulled even with the jeep and then violently slammed its entire right flank into the side of the vehicle. The jeep went on two wheels and, despite Hardcastle's best efforts to keep it upright, went into a barrel roll. When it finally stopped rolling, fortunately, the jeep settled on its wheels. The tyrannosaur stomped toward the vehicle as if it were peering down at a wounded animal and released a deafening roar.

Hardcastle felt as if he was on the verge of falling unconscious, but the sound erupting from the tyrannosaur quickly snatched him back. He could feel that his hat was gone, and he then felt a trickle of warm blood flowing down from the top of his head and across the front of his face. The vehicle's roll cage was severely damaged, and the hinged part that fastened over the passenger side was ripped away. It was then that Hardcastle realized Dave was gone. If he wasn't in so much fear of losing his own life, he may have smiled at that, but there was no time for it right then.

To his surprise, the jeep was still running. As the tyrannosaur lumbered closer, Hardcastle stomped on the accelerator and sped away. The jeep shook so badly he thought his teeth would shatter, and smoke began to wisp out from under the hood. None of that mattered to him now, as long as the jeep held together long enough to get him to safety. Hardcastle thought the tyrannosaur had turned to chase after him, but a glance in the cracked and dangling side view mirror showed that the fearsome animal had instead decided to give chase after one of the *Styracosaurus* younglings that had fallen behind the rest of the herd.

Glenn briefly scanned the environment for any sign of Dave. He saw no sign of him among the tall grasses of the plain. He wondered to himself if he'd have even stopped if he did. Probably not, he decided finally. Little smart-ass got what was coming to him.

CHAPTER 16

The trio had been traveling at a safe speed just within the shadows of the wood line where the jungle met the plain. Jonathon had passed out breakfast, which consisted of only a package of Pop-Tarts for each man. Each of them had been quiet for the most part as they ate, all of them very much aware of the fact that silence in a part of the jungle where tyrannosaurs had been known to roam was currently a necessity. It was only when Silas noticed an odd occurrence that the silence was broken.

"Look," he said excitedly, pointing toward the wide-open valley. "Do you see that?"

Jonathon sat upright in the rear seat and leaned over to the left side of the vehicle for a better look. He heard it before he saw it. "Is that a jeep?" he asked, surprised.

Although they'd all recently discovered the road, it was still rather odd seeing another sign of the outside world on the island.

"Yes, it is," Silas replied, "and do you see what's behind it?"

Jonathon scanned his view further behind the vehicle and then noticed the large two-legged carnivore chasing after it. "My God," he whispered. "That's a tyrannosaur."

Henry pulled the brim of his hat down over his eyes to shield the brightness of the sky and then gasped when he spotted the most well-known dinosaur of all time. He felt his pulse quicken, and although they were a healthy distance away, he began to feel an overwhelming feeling of dread.

"Well, what are we going to do?" he asked, suddenly feeling sorry for the strangers in the jeep.

"Stop the vehicle," Jonathon said flatly, and Silas brought them to a halt. "We're not going to do anything...yet," he replied to his father. He reached over and grabbed a pair of nearby binoculars. He got a good look at the fleeing jeep and could easily see there were two men inside of it. "That jeep has a lot of armor, similar to the cage you put on this thing, Silas," he said, still peering through the binoculars. "They're traveling at a high rate of speed, if they keep that up they should be able to outrun— oh no!"

It was at that moment that the jeep hit something and became airborne. After landing, it appeared that either the vehicle was damaged, or its driver was rattled, because the jeep slowed down enough to allow the pursuing tyrannosaur to catch up. Jonathon looked on in amazement as the animal thrust its entire body into the side of the automobile, sending it rolling violently across the earth.

"Whoa!" Silas shouted. "They're in BIG trouble now!"

"I think I saw one of them fly out of the vehicle," Henry said somberly. "He looked like a rag doll, pitched into the air."

"I saw it too," Jonathon replied, bringing the binoculars down. "He came down near those boulders," he said, pointing to a cluster of large rocks near some fallen trees.

"We should do something," Henry said, obviously deeply concerned.

Jonathon watched in amazement as the man in the jeep somehow got the vehicle rumbling away again. For a moment, it seemed that the tyrannosaur would chase after its wounded prey, but then it seemed as if the animal realized the retreating object wasn't prey after all. It decided instead to go after a young *Styracosaurus*, thus allowing the jeep to flee back to wherever it had come from.

"If we go out there, we're taking a huge risk," Jonathon muttered.

"I think that's an understatement," Silas added. "It would be suicide."

Henry looked at the both of them, surprise on his face. "We have a moral obligation to try and help that man," he said.

"He could already be dead," Silas argued. "And then we could join him!"

"You don't know that," Henry countered. "He could be seriously injured though…he could be suffering."

"And just what are we supposed to do for him if he is?" Silas asked. "We've got a first aid kit, but nothing to treat a broken back or internal injuries."

"Well, we're not going to know if we can treat him or not unless we go look," Henry replied, sounding more irritated. "We'd all want someone to come check on us if we—"

"We'll wait," Jonathon interrupted his father. "If we go out there right this minute, we won't stand a chance. Let's wait for the tyrannosaur to leave the area and then we'll go check."

"Are you nuts?" Silas said, obviously agitated. "We've got a plan and we need to stick to it."

"Silas, did you notice the direction from where the tyrannosaur was running? It's straight ahead of where we're going. There's a good possibility we may run into more tyrannosaurs if we keep this same course."

"But we've come this way before," Silas argued. "We need to go the way we know!"

"We came this way seven years ago! A lot can change in seven years, Silas. I say we scope this area out until we feel it's safe to cross. We cut straight across the valley and make a stop by those boulders to check on the stranger."

"Sounds like a good plan to me," Henry said.

Silas huffed and shook his head. "Well, it seems I'm outvoted," he grumbled. "Fine, we'll do it your way."

***

Hardcastle limped the jeep back to the tyrannosaur nest where he'd last seen George and Dr. Cruz. As he approached, he heard screaming and then a frightening realization suddenly occurred to him. He'd completely lost track of the second tyrannosaur!

The first thing he spotted was the swishing tail of the female, and she was rather forcefully snapping her jaws low at something behind the other jeep. Hardcastle could see that the trailer was still attached, and soon after he noticed George inside it, he then spotted the juvenile tyrannosaur lying motionless behind him. The female was trying frantically to fit her large maw into the open door at the end of the trailer. She was successful, until her head widened to the point where she could go no further. Her large jaws snapped furiously at George, and he was unable to back away any further. With every failed attempt to sink her large teeth into him, the trailer rocked violently back and forth, and it did the same thing to the jeep attached to it.

Hardcastle was pleased to see that George had gotten the juvenile into the trailer and sedated it, but, with the angry tyrannosaur jostling it about, he wondered how long the trailer would remain attached to the jeep. He then noticed that Dr. Cruz was not inside the jeep, as he'd first assumed.

Normal procedure required one man on the turret at all times when on a hunt. Hardcastle had purposely broken that procedure with Dave already. He knew that Dave had no experience with a weapon that powerful, and he had been confident that he could outrun the pursuing tyrannosaur without the help of the gun. He couldn't have been more wrong, and he had already known he was going to have to come up with one hell of a story once he returned to base camp.

Now, for whatever reason, it seemed George and Dr. Cruz had veered away from procedure as well. And now George found himself in a difficult predicament because of it. The tyrannosaur continued to snap furiously at her prey, just out of reach in the trailer. She was oblivious to

Hardcastle, now only thirty yards away. He stopped the vehicle and reluctantly made his way to the overhead turret.

He found what he feared. The turret was heavily damaged during the rollover, but on the positive side, the gun was not. The gun was turned awkwardly away from where Hardcastle needed to aim it. He jerked hard and repeatedly tried to get the turret turned in the right direction, but no matter how hard he pulled, it refused to break free. He knew time was running out, sooner or later, the angry female was going to get to George.

Think, he told himself. Hardcastle considered getting back into the jeep and turning the vehicle around so that the gun would be pointed the right direction, but he knew he'd only have one shot at it. If the gun was not pointed just right, he'd have to scramble back down into the driver's seat and move the vehicle again. This would not only waste precious time, but it would also make him way more vulnerable than he wanted to be. As he considered his options once more, he heard a shout that changed everything.

Hardcastle discovered where Dr. Cruz had been; it was his shouting that had gotten his attention. Apparently, he'd been hiding underneath the trailer. He'd probably been assisting George on getting the juvenile into the trailer when the two of them were suddenly attacked. George managed to scramble into the trailer, while Dr. Cruz had to slide underneath it.

Now, when he'd finally spotted Hardcastle's jeep nearby, he decided to make a run for it. Hardcastle cringed when he heard his colleague shouting and running his way. Of all the people on the island, Dr. Casey Cruz should've known better than anyone how not to act around the animals. He was the resident paleontologist, and it was he that often advised everyone else on what not to do around the animals. One of the things he'd made abundantly clear was to never panic and do something stupid to draw attention to one's self. He'd preached that to everyone on more than one occasion. So it was shocking for Hardcastle to now see the same man shouting and running frantically in his direction. Dr. Cruz was in a total panic, and it was a long thirty-yard run to the jeep. Hardcastle wanted to shout at him to stop…he wanted to ask him what he was doing. But now it was too late for any of that.

Just as the female tyrannosaur noticed the fleeing man and began to turn her attention to him, Hardcastle clumsily made his way from the gun and back to the driver's seat of the jeep. He mashed the accelerator, but the wounded machine responded slowly. The engine seemed to wail in protest, as if it were a living, breathing thing. It had already been pushed to its limits; there was just not much left for the vehicle to give.

Hardcastle hoped the machine would hold together just a little bit longer. He set his sights on the approaching Dr. Cruz, fully aware that the tyrannosaur had done the same. She began trotting—slowly at first, and then the trot evolved into a swift run. The animal seemed to bring its head forward, and down; the tail stood straight out behind it as it ran.

Dr. Cruz ran with all of the speed a man his age and build could muster. Reluctantly, he forced himself to glance over his shoulder as he ran. When he did so, he was horrified to see the towering monster charging swiftly after him. He turned his head back forward and managed to look Hardcastle in the eyes as the jeep rumbled ever so closer to him. When the two men's eyes met, each of them knew it was hopeless.

Glenn Hardcastle opened his mouth to scream, but no sound came out. The female tyrannosaur ducked her head forward and suddenly plucked Dr. Cruz off the ground, just out of Hardcastle's reach. He looked on in horror as the animal's jaws tightened around the screaming man's torso. A shower of red rained from her jaws as she did so, and any sound originating from Dr. Cruz immediately ceased.

Hardcastle only had a moment to react to prevent the jeep from colliding with the tyrannosaur. He jerked the wheel to the left, and as he did so, the right rear tire ever so slightly caught the right foot of the dinosaur. The vehicle was spun by the abrupt collision, and for the second time in only a matter of minutes, the jeep rolled over. The roll was slow and clumsy, and when it was over, the vehicle rested on the already battered roll cage.

Amazingly, Hardcastle had managed to avoid injuring himself any worse than he already was. He frantically began to clamber out of the overturned vehicle, but his foot became caught in some coiled rope that had fallen out of a storage compartment during one of the rollovers. Hardcastle tugged at his leg furiously, but it seemed the harder he pulled his leg, the tighter the rope cut into his ankle. He reached into his pocket and tried to pull his pocketknife out. As he did so, he felt a vibration that he knew could only be the tyrannosaur stomping toward him. After a brief struggle, he finally retrieved the knife. He opened it quickly, and just as he was about to begin cutting on the rope, a large shadow drifted over him. Hardcastle took a deep breath and bit his lip. He rolled over on his back and stared up at the intimidating silhouette standing above him. The tyrannosaur cocked its head to the side, much like a dog, and slightly opened its mouth to reveal all of the bloody teeth within. Warm saliva dripped off the monster's tongue and fell onto Hardcastle's forehead. This did nothing but enrage him.

"Come on!" he shouted. "Get on with it!" He threw the open pocketknife toward the dinosaur's eye in a pathetic attempt to inflict some sort of pain on the creature before it killed him. The knife flew past the head without so much as grazing it on the way by. The tyrannosaur began to dip her head forward, and Hardcastle closed his eyes as he awaited the same fate that had just taken Dr. Cruz from the world.

Suddenly, he heard gunfire erupt from somewhere behind the dinosaur. He opened his eyes again just in time to see the damage large-caliber bullets could inflict on a mighty tyrannosaur. The animal immediately lost interest in Hardcastle and turned its attention toward whatever strange creature it perceived to be attacking it. During all of the chaos, George had escaped the trailer, taken control of the gun turret on the other jeep, and narrowly saved Hardcastle from certain death. The tyrannosaur roared with a sound obviously full of rage. It began to trot toward George (who was not about to relinquish firing the gun), but the trot never evolved into anything faster this time. Instead, the massive creature stopped about ten yards away, and crashed hard onto the ground.

With the tyrannosaur dead, Hardcastle had more time to work his ankle out of the rope. As soon as he was free, he jogged toward the jeep. He glanced at the tranquilized juvenile tyrannosaur sleeping soundly in the trailer as he climbed behind the steering wheel. George kept his place on the gun, and he remained there until they returned to base camp.

CHAPTER 17

When Dave Turner regained consciousness, the first thing he heard was the pathetic wailing cries of a nearby dinosaur. The animal seemed to scream in terror and then the sound abruptly stopped. Dave slowly rose from his lying position and to his right, about seventy yards away, he spotted the hindquarters of the male tyrannosaur that had caused the jeep to roll. The large animal was kneeling over a fresh kill and feasting as if it had not eaten in days. He eyed the dead animal the tyrannosaur was eating and noticed how small it was. It would be consumed quickly and Dave feared he would be next. He surveyed his surroundings for a place to hide. To his left, there was a cluster of five or six large boulders and at the base of the one nearest to him were the remains of a massive fallen tree. All that was really left was a hollowed-out trunk, and Dave wondered if the *T-rex* would be able to break through it to get to him if he climbed inside. As there appeared to be no other suitable hiding place, Dave began to Army-crawl his way toward the log.

As he made his way into the log, he briefly considered the possibility that some other deadly animal may already be inside, using the log as a home. He forced himself to dismiss the notion, as he clearly had no other option. It was tight inside, and to his dismay, there were indeed other creatures using the log as home, but they were the tiny six-legged kind. He hoped they were not ants and kept wiggling his way further inside.

It soon became apparent that the tyrannosaur had either finished its meal, or noticed him enter the log, because no sooner had he immersed himself deep inside it, did he begin to feel the earth beneath him shake and vibrate with each powerful step of the approaching dinosaur. To Dave's horror, it seemed that the tyrannosaur knew exactly where he was. He felt each step draw closer and closer until finally they stopped. Dave held his breath and hoped with all his being that the monster would lose interest in him and leave. He'd never been a religious man, but he suddenly caught himself praying silently to himself, begging for some sort of divine intervention.

The tyrannosaur leaned over the log and deeply, and rather powerfully, sniffed the cylindrical hollow object from one end to the other. Dave felt something scratching the outside of the log and guessed the animal was using one of its scrawny arms in a futile attempt to make a hole into it. After what seemed like an eternity of scratching, the animal seemingly became frustrated and released a deafening roar that literally rattled Dave's skeleton. He squeezed his eyes so tight that he began to feel tears stream down his face past whatever insect was crawling over him at the same time.

After the male tyrannosaur released its furious roar, there was a long moment of silence. Dave began to allow himself to entertain the thought that the *T-rex* might have grown bored with him after all. The moment, however, was short-lived. The angry tyrannosaur suddenly stomped a large foot onto the end of the log and the smashed portion disintegrated into an explosion of splinters, mere feet away from Dave's head. Remaining silent was impossible now, and Dave screamed frantically as he began to wriggle away from the smashed end of the log.

As he shuffled away, the tyrannosaur again slammed its large foot onto the log, again barely missing Dave's head. He dug his nails into the side of the log, desperately searching for some sort of grip so that he may pull himself forward and away from the stomping tyrannosaur at a quicker pace. Once again, the dinosaur crushed another section of log, and just as Dave's feet popped out of the opposite end, a loud, repetitive popping sound erupted from somewhere in the direction of the tyrannosaur nest.

The male tyrannosaur raised and cocked its head sideways as it peered into the direction of the sound. Dave peeked out of the broken end of the log and watched as the dinosaur began to trot off to investigate the strange noises originating near its home. The animal had lost interest in him just as quickly as it had found it. Dave, for what seemed like the first time in an eternity, relaxed and breathed a sigh of relief. As he did so, for the first time, he felt a tremendous amount of pain radiating from his right leg. He glanced in the direction of the pain and found the source of his discomfort: a jagged stick pierced straight through the back of his calf and protruded diagonally through the front of his pants leg. He wanted to howl in pain, but the fear of the nearby tyrannosaurs hearing him kept him quiet.

***

"What is that thing doing?" Henry asked as he and the other men watched the tyrannosaur's strange behavior.

The large animal seemed to be stomping at something on the ground. The dinosaur resembled a kid doing his damnedest to try and smash a bug with his sneaker. The act was almost comical, and probably would have been, if they had not been aware that an injured man was near the ruckus.

"I'm not really sure what he's doing," Jonathon whispered. "These animals have been gone for 65 million years and there is so much we don't have a clue about." He held the binoculars up to his face and observed the tyrannosaur's muscular legs rise and fall to the earth repeatedly. It seemed to be smashing a log to bits. "I don't see the man anywhere. I don't know if the rex is trying to get him…or if he's after something else."

Suddenly, the clacking of repetitive gunfire began from somewhere near the wood line. Jonathon spun toward it and focused the binoculars. He watched in awe as another tyrannosaur towered over a man lying on the ground. Jonathon recognized the man as the driver of the jeep they'd already witnessed roll over once mere minutes earlier. He then scanned the environment further to the west and found another jeep parked nearby with a trailer attached. There was a large machine gun turret on the back, and a man seemed to be putting every bullet he had at his disposal into the tyrannosaur's back.

Jonathon looked on and could not help but feel a small amount of pity for the animal as the injuries began to take their toll. The dinosaur slowly tried to turn to face its attacker, but in doing so lost its footing and crashed to the earth. The man on the ground appeared to be very bewildered, but he swiftly seized the opportunity and made a dash toward the other jeep.

"I'll be damned," Silas said. "He's leaving!"

Jonathon lowered the binoculars and returned his attention to the other tyrannosaur. Upon hearing the commotion from the wood line, the dinosaur turned and trotted away to investigate.

"Now's as good a time as any to check on that other fellow," Henry said.

Jonathon peered through the binoculars once more toward the large log the tyrannosaur seemed so interested in. He spotted two feet protruding from one end of it and realized his father was right. If they were going to save the man, now was the time to do so. He glanced over at Silas.

"Drive straight for that log," he said, pointing. "It'll only take a moment to figure out if that guy is dead or alive."

Silas shook his head, and the expression on his face suggested that he wanted to protest. However, he also knew he was outvoted by the father-and-son duo. Without saying a word, he mashed the accelerator on the tiny vehicle and sped in the direction of the log.

As they approached, Jonathon scanned their environment for dinosaurs. It seemed the frightening tyrannosaur had done a marvelous job of clearing the area. He saw a herd of triceratops several hundred yards away moving in the opposite direction, but aside from that, he spotted no dinosaurs in their vicinity at all. Silas brought the vehicle to a stop next to the log, and the men immediately noticed movement from the protruding feet. Jonathon quickly opened the caged door above his head and clambered out onto the ground. He then pulled the large hunting knife from the sheath on his belt and approached the man.

"Are you hurt?" he said rather forcefully.

There was a pause and the man's feet suddenly became still.

"Look, we don't have a lot of time," Jonathon said. He looked around to survey the area for danger again. "Are you hurt or not?"

"My leg," the man said. The words sounded as if they were spoken through clenched teeth.

"What about it? Is it broken?"

"No," the man replied. "Can you pull me out?"

Jonathon glanced back at the ATV, and Silas stood up and aimed his rifle toward the log.

Without saying another word, Jonathon reached down and began to pull the man out by his ankles. It startled him when the man howled in pain, but he continued to pull until the man was completely exposed. It was then that Jonathon, Henry, and Silas noticed why he screamed.

"Ouch," Jonathon said, staring at the gruesome wound. The stick protruded from the front of the leg by about seven inches and probably a couple of inches less in the back.

After briefly surveying the injury, Jonathon looked over the strange man. He was young and slim, with a mop of brown hair. He was a good-looking kid and so out of place for an island such as the one they were on.

Jonathon held out a hand and the young man reluctantly took it. He then pulled him to his feet. The young man again yelped in pain.

"You got a name?" Jonathon asked.

"Dave," he muttered.

"Dave, grab the side of the ATV with both hands, will you?"

Dave really wanted to ask why, but he was in too much pain to care. Besides, his leg hurt so badly now that he was standing, all he wanted to do was lean against something to get his weight off of it. He limped over to the vehicle and did as he was told. He grabbed one of the roll bars across the top and for the first time noticed Silas pointing a gun at him.

"Wait," he said, startled. "Why are you pointing that thin— OWWW!"

Jonathon jerked the stick from Dave's leg before he'd even known what was happening. Dave released several curse words and tears streamed from his eyes. He fell to his hands and knees, and Jonathon thought he was going to throw up.

"Come on, Dave," Jonathon said, grabbing him by the back of his shirt collar.

Dave was nearly choked as he was dragged upward, but he was in no condition to fight back. Jonathon motioned for him to get into the vehicle, and with Henry's assistance, he got in. Jonathon climbed in behind him and pulled the cage shut over his head.

"Where to now?" Silas asked as he put the vehicle in gear.

"Let's get across the valley first," Jonathon answered. "Then I've got some questions for our new friend here."

CHAPTER 18

The juvenile tyrannosaur produced the best roar it could muster, but it was more comical than intimidating. The young dinosaur made a noise that more closely resembled the trumpeting sound of an elephant than that of one of the most fearsome predators to ever walk the face of the earth. It was still inside of the battered trailer, parked safely inside the dark hangar.

Eric Gill grabbed the bars of the animal's cage and stared at its frightened, confused eyes. *Were Dr. Cruz's and Dave's lives worth this*? he thought. He turned to face Glenn Hardcastle and George Powell, doing his best to contain the bitter mixture of anger and sorrow he now felt.

"You're certain that nothing could've been done to prevent this disaster?" he asked rather quietly.

Hardcastle sighed before speaking. "I've already told you—"

"Then tell me again," Eric interrupted. This time his words were anything but quiet.

"I tried to lure the parents away from the nest, just as I've done many times before," Hardcastle said. "But this time, for whatever reason, the female gave up on chasing us and headed back to the nest. The male still pursued, and I had to deal with him before I could go after the female. The male attacked my jeep, and Dr. Cruz was killed. While this was going on, George and Dave were being attacked by the female. I got there as soon as I could…"

Glenn paused and jerked his hat off his head. He rubbed his eyes and wrenched at the hat before giving another hard look to Eric. "There was nothing I could do," he muttered. "You have to believe that."

Eric glanced over at a wide-eyed George Powell. "Is that what happened, George?"

George set his gaze upon Hardcastle; he'd noticed the slight variation in Glenn's story. It was Glenn that had taken Dave, and it was Dr. Cruz that had remained with him. He knew that Hardcastle had made the change because Eric would've been furious if he'd known Dave had been carelessly put in harm's way.

Glenn Hardcastle's eyes seemed to beg him to concur with his story. George considered telling the truth, but what difference would it have made? If Dr. Cruz and Dave had swapped places, the end result would've almost certainly been the same. He took a long moment to give Glenn a hard gaze, as if to say, you now owe me big time.

"That's what happened," George said finally, turning back to Eric. "There was nothing we could've done. We didn't even have time to bring back their remains."

Eric trusted George, and with his reassurance, he considered the matter closed. They now had the juvenile tyrannosaur, and there was only one animal left to capture to fulfill the order. There would be plenty of time to mourn the losses of his men later. Right now, he had to focus. He would need another paleontologist. Fortunately for him, he had several applicants begging for him to call them. He walked over in front of George and Glenn. Both men stared at the ground, and regardless of what he felt about Hardcastle, Eric could tell the man was visibly shaken by what had occurred. He grabbed both men by the shoulders.

"You did well, gentlemen," he said, forcing a smile. "Let's not let their deaths be in vain. It's time to finish the job." Eric turned to walk away, but stopped abruptly as a thought occurred to him. "Oh, one more thing," he said as he turned to face them. "News of what has happened is going to eventually get out," he said. "However, I don't want any of you volunteering any information to Annie until I say so. It's probably best just to keep it as quiet as possible until she leaves at the end of the week."

The two men stared at him, bewildered.

"It's taken me months to convince her to visit and make her feel that this is a safe place. I don't want to undo all of that work. Can I count on the two of you to keep this quiet?"

"Well, yeah," Hardcastle replied. "But why is she so afraid of this place? She's never even gone outside of the fence since she's been here."

As Eric opened the door to leave, he turned back to face Glenn. "She's been here before," he answered. "Before any of us, and she's seen things like what you have seen today." Eric turned away and closed the door behind him.

"Then she's got to be one of the looniest people on this island to even fathom coming back here," Hardcastle muttered under his breath.

***

"Okay, I prefer to do this the easiest way possible," Jonathon said as he dragged Dave out onto the ground.

They'd driven for a very lengthy time until they found a wide clearing inside the jungle and just north of the great valley where Dave had been attacked. The surrounding terrain was lush and vibrant with tropical flowers and many colorful birds. Jonathon surveyed the area for any dinosaur remains, and when he found none, he felt the area would be safe enough for an interrogation.

Dave winced when he fell upon the ground, the throb of his aching leg forcing him to do so. "I prefer easy," he said. "Please...you have nothing to fear from me."

"Oh, we know that, boy," Silas growled at him, a handgun gripped firmly in his right hand. "The only one with something to fear right now is you."

Jonathon raised a hand to stifle Silas's threats. "Tell us what you're doing on this island and why you were being chased by those tyrannosaurs," Jonathon said.

Dave sighed deeply and slapped at a mosquito biting him on the neck. The jungle was full of mosquitos. "We were trying to lure the parent tyrannosaurs away so that we could catch one of the juveniles at their nest."

Jonathon stared at him, surprised at his answer. "You were trying to catch a juvenile tyrannosaur?"

Dave nodded and looked away.

"For what purpose?" Silas growled. "Do you have a death wish, son?"

Dave continued to look away from his captors and said nothing. Jonathon looked at Silas and Henry; all three men were bewildered.

"He asked you a question," Jonathon said. "Messing with tyrannosaurs? That's just nuts, kid. Why on earth would you do such a thing?"

"I can't tell you," Dave said, suddenly realizing he was on the verge of giving away the secrets of Eric's enterprise.

Jonathon was taken aback. "What do you mean you can't tell me?" he asked. "You've got a lot to tell us so you better get started."

Dave shook his head and remained tight-lipped.

"Who was the other man with you?" Jonathon asked. "Are there others like him on this island?"

Dave remained silent.

Silas barged forward and grabbed Dave off the ground by his shirt collar. "We don't have time for this!" he spat. "Answer his questions!"

"I'm sorry," Dave stammered. "I can't tell you any more."

Jonathon could sense the young man was afraid and they didn't *really* want to hurt him. But, he also realized their lives could be in danger. They had to find out what this kid knew before roaming the island any further. Suddenly, he felt a warm hand grip his upper arm.

"Let me have a try," Henry said softly.

Jonathon chuckled and adjusted his hat. "No offense, dad, but you're not exactly the intimidating type." He began to walk away when his father jerked him back.

"I have my ways," Henry said.

Suddenly, Jonathon caught on to his dad's suggestion. He smiled. "Alright, Dad, get him to talk."

Henry took a moment to survey the land around him for a large tree. He finally found one he felt would suit his needs and began to approach it.

"Silas," he called out. "Grab the rope from the ATV and the both of you tie our young friend to this tree. Make certain that he is unable to move."

Silas grabbed the rope and then began to shuffle Dave toward the tree. Dave tried to resist at first, but quickly discovered doing so caused greater discomfort in his injured leg. He had no choice but to go along with their demands. With Jonathon's help, Silas tied Dave tightly against the large trunk of the tree.

"Come on, guys," Dave said nervously. "Is this really necessary?"

His captors made no reply, and it soon occurred to Dave that he was actually trying to seem more intimidated than he was. These men did not strike him as the type that would harm another human being, but at the same time, it seemed that it would be in his best interest to make them think that he believed they would. They seemed to be buying it—for the moment at least.

Satisfied with Dave's fixed position, Henry carefully removed his coat and placed it on a nearby boulder. He left it opened so that the inside pockets were exposed. Dave caught a glimmer of shiny metal reflecting light off the afternoon sun and squinted to try and make out what it was. Henry reached over and removed one of the shiny metal objects and held it up for all to see. It was a small knife, and Dave felt his pulse quicken.

"What are you going to do with that?" Dave asked, his voice raising an octave.

Henry tossed the knife into the air, end over end. He caught it effortlessly by the blunt end. "Son, there's no reason for anyone to get hurt," he said, turning away. "Just tell us what we want to know." Henry had walked about twenty-five feet away from Dave's tree.

Jonathon and Silas stood a safe distance to the right of where Henry stared Dave down. Jonathon stood with his arms crossed and Silas towered next to him, the rifle slung over his shoulder. Both men's eyes were as attentive as a kid on Christmas morning. Silas leaned over and whispered just loud enough for Jonathon to hear.

"You sure about this?"

Jonathon nodded, then whispered back, "Just watch the old man work."

"I told you," Dave stammered again. "I can't tell you the things you want to know. Now, don't get me wrong, I'm grateful that you guys saved me. But that still doesn't mean—"

A knife hurtled out of Henry's hand end over end at lightning speed. The blade pierced deeply into the meat of the tree trunk all the way to the hilt, just mere inches from Dave's right thigh.

"Whoa!" Dave shouted. He instinctively tried to escape, thrashing and jerking his body from side to side. The rope cruelly refused to budge the slightest bit. "What are you doing? Are you nuts?"

Henry retrieved another knife from his jacket. "My wife seems to think I am," he quipped. "Now quit all that squirming around; it's been a while since I've done this. The blades may not look rusty, but believe me, kid, when I tell you that I am!" He hurtled another knife at the tree and again the blade sank deep into the tree's flesh, this time just inches off Dave's left thigh.

Jonathon smiled broadly and Silas held his hand over his mouth in amazement.

"Are you ready to talk yet?" Jonathon asked flatly.

Dave, though paler in complexion than he had been, remained stubborn and shook his head in defiance. Before Jonathon had an opportunity to speak again, two more knives whistled through the air and landed into the tree, one on either side of Dave's torso. This time, the knives were even closer, and one of them had managed to cut the fabric on the left side of Dave's shirt. The sight of the torn cloth worried Jonathon.

"Dad, you alright?" he asked.

Henry held up a hand to silence his son. "Now, Dave," he said. "I need you to start talking, son." He looked around the jungle. "I know you already know what kinds of monsters are lurking around us. We don't like to stay in any one place for very long. I'm ready for you to start talking so that we can all get moving. If you don't talk, you're going to agitate me, and I assure you my aim is off when I'm agitated."

Dave stared at Henry, his eyes unblinking.

"So what'll it be, son?"

Dave licked his lips. "We catch dinosaurs," he said just above a whisper.

Jonathon took a step closer. "Why?" he demanded.

Dave looked at him, then allowed his head to slump forward as if he'd been defeated. "It's a business. We catch the dinosaurs and we sell them," he replied, his mop of disheveled brown hair dangling in front of his face.

Jonathon shook his head in disbelief. "You—sell them?"

Dave nodded, but refused to look up.

"Sell them to who?"

"Whoever will buy them—and people will," Dave said. "People pay a lot of money for a dinosaur."

Jonathon looked over at his father, and then to Silas. He was wondering if they were finding Dave's revelation as unnerving as he was. Each of them seemed to shrug as if unsure what to say or how to digest it all.

"Who do you work for?" Jonathon asked.

Dave sighed and shook his head, another display of stubborn refusal to answer the question. Henry wasted no time whistling another knife through the air and into the tree trunk, just inches away from Dave right ear.

"Eric Gill!" he shouted, for fear of getting another knife thrown at him.

Jonathon marched forward. "Did you say Eric Gill?"

"Yes!" Dave spat. "Just stop throwing knives at me! You know everything now."

"That little bastard," Silas growled. "Ole Angus dies and I guess he figured he'd pick up where the old man left off."

"No, we came and looked for him," Dave said. "We looked for a day, but the dinosaurs—they were just too dangerous. We couldn't continue and Eric just knew that Mr. Wedgeworth had to be dead."

"Angus Wedgeworth *is* dead," Jonathon said. "But he had a different reason for coming to this godforsaken island." He paused to let the statement hang in the air a moment. Dave had not mentioned the fountain of youth and he wondered if Eric had found it.

After a long minute, Dave said, "So why did he come here then?"

"Oh, like you really don't know," Silas said, drawing closer to the conversation. "Don't pretend like Eric doesn't know—"

"Silas!" Jonathon interrupted. Silas whipped around to face him. Jonathon shook his head and Silas took his meaning.

"So you know Eric?" Dave asked.

Jonathon and Silas looked at each other again, and then back to Dave. "Yeah, we've met," Silas answered.

"When? How did you meet him?" Dave questioned.

"The whens, whys, and hows don't matter," Jonathon replied. "What does matter right now is how willing you're going to be to cooperate with us right now."

Dave chewed on the inside of his lip and squinted. "What do you want me to do?"

"You're going to take me to Eric Gill. I need to have a chat with him," Jonathon said.

Silas said, "But what about the—?"

"It can wait," Jonathon barked, cutting him off. He wished Silas would quit taking the conversation back to the fountain. If Eric didn't know about it, he intended to keep it that way.

"I'll be glad to take you back to Eric," Dave said. "I'll do anything to get out of this jungle and back to safety."

Jonathon laughed. "Safety? Please tell me where safety exists on this island!"

Dave huffed, somewhat perturbed by Jonathon's smug change in attitude.

"Eric's built a facility on the other end of the island with high electric fencing and stationed men with guns at every corner. We've had a few dinos try, but none have succeeded getting past the fences," he replied proudly.

Jonathon's curiosity had now peaked. He was interested in seeing just what sort of compound Eric had put together over the past several years. They'd already encountered roads, and they'd seen the heavily armored vehicles that Dave and other men had been piloting. He contemplated making an attempt to reach the compound before nightfall. He looked up at the gray veil of mist above his head. It was getting darker, a clear indicator that they were nearing the end of the day.

"What are the chances of us making it there before nightfall?"

Dave shook his head. "Traveling at night is strictly forbidden. It's extremely dangerous, and that little vehicle of yours isn't going to go fast enough to get there before the sun completely sets. The *Velociraptors* are particularly more active at night, and there is no hope for us if we come across a pack of them."

Silas shook his head, seemingly amused. "And how do you think we got through the night, boy?"

Dave stared at him for a long moment; he seemed to be confused. "What? If you spent a night out here, then you've got to be either the stupidest or luckiest fools I've ever met," he replied.

"Watch it," Silas growled taking a step forward.

Dave flattened his body against the tree—a futile attempt at escaping the large man's reach. "I'm by no means suggesting spending the night out here," Dave stammered. "There is another option."

"What other option?" Jonathon asked.

"We've got a safety net, so to speak, a little less than a mile from here."

"What do you mean a safety net?" Henry asked.

"It's an underground bunker. It was put in place just in case someone got stranded out here just before nightfall. It's a safe place to spend the night until someone can come and get them first thing in the morning," Dave explained.

Jonathon glanced over at Silas and then to Henry. Without saying a word, the three men all seemed to telepathically come to an agreement.

"Alright, cut him loose, Silas," Jonathon said. "Take us to this hidden bunker, Dave."

Silas cut him loose and Dave took a moment to rub the soreness out of the places on his body where the rope had cut into him. Without saying a word, he began to limp toward the ATV. Jonathon grabbed him tightly by the arm as made his way past him.

"I'm warning you, kid," he said. "You try anything funny, the dinosaurs will no longer be what you fear most on this island. Are we clear?"

Dave nodded, wretched his arm loose, and continued his awkward stroll toward the ATV.

CHAPTER 19

"What's wrong with you?" Annie asked. Her delicate voice had an immediate calming effect.

"Why do you think something is wrong?" Eric asked with a smile, doing his best to sound cheerful.

"Because of that," Annie replied, pointing to the Jupiter cigarette with the smoldering cherry hanging out of his mouth. "You're on your second pack. It's hard enough for me to get past you smoking the six or seven sticks you already smoke a day. You never, ever, smoke this much unless something particularly bad is bothering you."

They were seated at the dining room table of Eric's lavish apartment space (his was the nicest and largest of all the others on the island). His apartment was in what had been dubbed the 'Triangle Building' by everyone at the facility. The Triangle Building got its name because it looked very much like a triangle, wide at the base and decreasing in width until it reached the peak. The building consisted of 25 apartments, and it was where everyone called home while they were working on the island (which was almost all year). Eric's apartment was perched on the very top, overlooking the entire compound. It even had a rather pleasant view of the coastline. The surf rolled onto the white sand rather gently, and he spotted a group of gulls swarming over what appeared to be the carcass of a smaller dead dinosaur. Probably a *Parksosaurus*; they roamed all over the beach and were very territorial. It wasn't unusual to find a dead one from time to time. If a member of a pack got lost, or went rogue, it was quickly disposed of by a rival group. The busy scene on the coastline was what he'd been gazing upon when Annie began badgering him.

He looked at her, smiled another fake smile, and then looked away.

"Call me a liar, Eric Gill," she added stubbornly.

Eric took the cigarette he'd been pulling from, rather forcefully extinguished it in the ashtray in front of him, and then rubbed his tired eyes.

"I'm just exhausted," he grumbled.

Annie got up from where she was sitting and stood up behind him. She began to massage his shoulders. "I'm sorry, sweetie," she whispered. Then she leaned over and began kissing his neck. "I'll make you feel better, just you—"

Eric pulled away from her and abruptly stood from the table. He crossed his arms and strolled over to the large picture window overlooking the coastline. After a moment of silence from Annie, he slowly glanced back to see where she was. Annie just stood right where he'd left her. Her arms were crossed; a look of confusion and sadness was on her face.

"I'm sorry," he whispered, turning away again.

"So am I," she said. She then stormed out of the apartment, slamming the door behind her.

***

"Here we are," Dave said, sounding more relieved than anything else.

"What are you talking about? I don't see anything," Silas said, seemingly peering at nothing but dense foliage.

"It's the bamboo," Dave answered. "We surrounded the bunkers with the stalks so we'd be able to find them easily, but at the same time the tall plants provide an excellent hiding place."

"Smart," Henry said. "But you said bunkers...with an 'S.' There is more than one on the island?"

"There are three," Dave said. "This one is the furthest from the base camp."

Jonathon had to wrestle with the protective cage on the amphibious vehicle to get it open. It was becoming an increasingly more difficult task each time.

"Silas, this thing needs some WD-40," he grumbled. "It's getting harder to get it open." He punched a shoulder into the door and it finally gave way. The four men clambered out into the dangerous environment and carefully made their way to the bunker door.

Jonathon reached for the silver handle and turned it downward...nothing happened. He once again called upon the aid of his broad shoulder and tried to shove the door open while he once again twisted and turned at the handle. The door refused to budge.

"Get out of the way, please," Dave said as he hobbled forward. "It has an electronic combination lock."

He reached for a small panel to the left of the door. The panel had a protective lid that flipped up and revealed a keypad of numbers. He began to enter the first number to the combination when he suddenly realized Jonathon was still leaning against the door with his shoulder...watching him.

"Do you mind?" Dave asked. He tried to make the request sound polite, but it was obviously forced.

"Are you kidding?" Jonathon asked without blinking.

"This entire facility is top secret. I can't let you see the code to this bunker."

Jonathon rolled his eyes and stepped away.

Dave quickly punched in the combination. The men could all hear some sort of mechanism moving within the wall, and within a second later, the door opened gently toward the interior. Dave smiled and gestured for the men to step inside. Henry and Silas stepped in first, but Jonathon stood still.

"You first," he said. "You're not locking us in there."

Dave looked genuinely surprised. "The thought never crossed my—"

"Yeah, yeah, get in there," Jonathon snapped, pushing him into the bunker.

Once the four of them were all inside, he pushed the door shut.

***

Annie walked gingerly toward the main office building within the compound. It was the building where Eric spent most of his time strategizing and coming up with elaborate plans on how to catch dinosaurs, and who to sell the beasts to. She'd sat in on some of those meetings, and some of them had actually been quite interesting. But now she only had one thing on here mind.

Eric had done a fantastic job of blowing her off and, more importantly, pissing her off, so there was only one thing on this forsaken island that could cheer her up now. The one thing that the office building had, that none of the other buildings had, was a vending machine. The machine was full of various candy bars and she suddenly had a craving for one. She always ate junk food when she got mad, so naturally, she immediately targeted the one place on the island where she could get it.

Once she arrived at her destination, she inserted two quarters into the large machine and punched in E4. She then waited for the spiral doo-hickey to release the chocolaty goodness so she could eat and contemplate how in the world she was going to expedite her exit from the wretched island. The wire spiraled away, and just as the candy bar was about to drop, it stopped.

"Shit," she cursed under her breath. She lightly tapped at the glass. The candy bar didn't move. "Come on now," she whined. She slapped the glass a little harder, but nothing happened. "Give me that damn candy bar!" she screamed. Annie began slapping the glass with both hands. She continued to scream and curse at the machine. Tears began to stream down her face, and after she'd pounded on the glass so hard that her hands hurt, she fell to her knees and sobbed. It wasn't just the candy bar that angered her. It was Eric, it was this stupid island, and most of all, she was angry at herself for going against her better judgment and even coming here.

"Wow," a calm, male voice muttered from the doorway. "I'd always heard redheads were hot heads, but honey you take the cake."

Annie glared over at Glenn Hardcastle. After she gave him an icy stare, she looked away, suddenly embarrassed. She shook her head and said, "Please, just go away."

Hardcastle ignored her and strutted over to the vending machine. He retrieved an odd-looking key from his pocket and used it to open up the front of the machine. He grabbed the candy bar and handed it to her.

Annie looked up at him, and after a long moment, she reluctantly took the candy bar. Glenn then took a moment to swipe a candy bar of his own before he locked the machine back up.

"Your boyfriend doesn't know I have this key," he said, holding the silver object up to the light. "I'd like to keep it that way."

Annie took a bite of her therapeutic chocolate bar, and despite her best efforts not to, she smiled.

Hardcastle reached a hand downward. "Come," he said. "We'll eat up in my office."

Annie stared at his hand, and then back up to his face. "And why would I want to do that?" she asked, wiping away tears.

Hardcastle pulled his hand away and used it to rub the back of his neck. "Look, I don't know what's got you so upset and truthfully, I don't care. But I've heard a rumor that this island has you a little jumpy."

"Of course you have," Annie said, pursing her lips into a pout. "I suppose Eric told you that."

"Sort of," Hardcastle replied. "He also told me something else. He told me you've been here before—before all of this," he said, referring to all that Eric had built.

"Yeah...so what?" she said, taking another bite of candy bar.

"Well, if you come to my office, I'll show you something that I think will ease your mind a little."

Annie thought on his offer, and she quickly remembered where she was and the situation she found herself in. "What the heck," she said. "Where else am I going to go?" She raised a hand and Hardcastle pulled her up.

He led her out of the doorway and down a long hallway to an office with a piece of copy paper stuck to the door courtesy of a large knife piercing into the wood. The piece of paper had his name scrawled on it in font and artwork that looked like something off of an AC/DC album cover. There were lightning bolts, and shooting stars, and nightmarish-looking demons doodled all over it. Hardcastle punched a code into a nearby keypad and the door opened instantly. He threw his arm outward to invite her in.

"Welcome to my office," he said.

Annie stepped inside the dimly lit room. The source of light came from the seven monitors that lined the wall and desk. The office was tiny, and as her eyes adjusted, she noticed some vicious-looking dinosaur skulls staring menacingly at her from a rickety-looking shelf on the wall. There was something that resembled a mini fridge under the desk, but it was hard to tell since it was partially hidden behind a small mountain of trash collected in the corner of the room. Glenn Hardcastle could tell she was looking the place over and judging him already.

"Alright, you can nag about my housekeeping later," he quipped. "Have a seat."

He pulled over a rolling chair from another darkened corner of the room and parked it next to the large one behind the desk. He took that chair for himself and Annie, rather reluctantly, took a seat in the one he rolled out for her.

"Take a look at these monitors," Hardcastle said, pointing. "What do you see?"

Annie squinted and peered at each monitor, giving each equal attention before she answered. She could tell that each one was showing a different view somewhere outdoors, but the screens were nearly completely black (it was night after all).

"It looks like cameras surrounding the facility," she finally answered.

Hardcastle shook his head. "No. Although we do have multiple cameras on each fence around this facility, none of these are them. Those cameras are watched by members of our security team."

Annie looked at the monitors again. She thought she noticed a shadow move past on one of them. "Then where exactly are all of these?"

"We've got eyes all over this island," he answered. "And just because there are only seven monitors does not mean I only have seven cameras. I've got a total of fourteen cameras hooked up to these monitors. Each one shares feed for two cameras. All I have to do is toggle between the feeds," he explained, and then he showed her by punching some buttons on his keyboard.

Annie noticed that the feeds did indeed change, but due to the darkness, she could still see very little.

"I know you can't see much right now, but trust me, there is a lot going on," Hardcastle said. "I've been on your boyfriend about getting some night vision hooked up, but he's being a cheapskate." Hardcastle paused a moment, and it was clear a thought suddenly occurred to him. "Hey, maybe you can talk him into it?"

"Oh, I see," Annie replied dryly. "You called me in here to show me all of this with some sort of false hope that I can get Eric to get you some fancy night vision cameras…well, you can forget it because he's so stubborn; I can't even get through to him."

Hardcastle rolled his chair back from the desk and held up an apologetic hand. "No, no, no," he said quickly. "That's not why I called you in here."

"Well, why then?"

"Two reasons: One, I know this place makes you uneasy, and I wanted to show you just how much we're able to keep tabs on all the dinosaurs out there—especially the really nasty ones."

"And the second?" she asked.

Hardcastle gave a sideways smirk. "Well, I'd like to know more about your last visit here."

Annie's demeanor suddenly changed. A frown appeared, and she sighed deeply. "I guess that jackass told you I've been here before," she said after a long pause.

"Yeah, he let it slip," Hardcastle replied. "What happened? How did you get here, and why were you here?"

Annie considered getting up and leaving right then and there, but she remembered again that she had nowhere else to go at the time. Now more than ever, she did not want to go back and face Eric.

"Well, you've heard of Angus Wedgeworth?" she asked.

Hardcastle nodded.

"He's my uncle—was my uncle—and he dragged me out here with promises of getting me a Pulitzer Prize winning shot," Annie explained. "So I grabbed my camera and followed him here with a few other ignorant souls and once we got here…well, it got bad."

"How bad?" Hardcastle asked.

"Bad enough that people died," she replied somberly. "Bad enough that I still can't make it a whole week without having at least one night where I wake up screaming and soaking wet with sweat."

"What happened?"

Annie shook her head. "I don't want to talk about it anymore," she replied.

"Oh come on," Hardcastle pressed. "What happened?"

Annie shot him a hard glare. "I said I don't want to talk about it anymore."

Hardcastle huffed and shook his head, clearly wanting to argue, but knew better. "Fine," he said finally. "But if it was that bad, why would you ever want to come back?"

"That was seven years ago," Annie replied. "Eric has done a lot of begging and put forth a lot of effort showing me pictures of what he's built here to convince me to come back."

"You love him that much?"

"I thought I did," she said. "Now I'm not so sure. But I think it was more than just that. You know…all that facing your fears to overcome them nonsense probably played into it."

Hardcastle was about to try and pry a little more information out of her, when suddenly something on the computer screen got his attention.

"What is that?" Annie asked, noticing it too.

"I'll be darned," Hardcastle replied. He peered at the little window that had popped up on the screen a few seconds more to make sure his eyes weren't deceiving him.

"What is it?" Annie asked again. She could clearly tell that whatever was on the screen was important.

"Someone just entered the safety bunker on the other end of the island," Hardcastle muttered.

CHAPTER 20

Once they were all locked inside, fluorescent lighting lit up the ceiling and revealed a narrow staircase that descended deeper into the bunker. Jonathon, Henry, and Silas all waited for Dave to lead the way. None of them said anything, but even Dave could sense their skepticism.

"Guys, relax," Dave said as he began to hobble down the stairs. "You guys have me outnumbered three to one, and my leg is probably going to end up so infected that I'll have to have it amputated."

"Well, I don't know about getting your leg amputated, but if you try anything funny in here, that possibility will become the least of your worries," Jonathon grumbled.

Dave offered no response, but soon led them to a room that measured approximately twenty feet across in all directions, and roughly seven feet in height. The three walls opposite of where the staircase came down were covered with shelves and cabinets. There was plenty of canned food and water available. There were two cots in the center of the room and a couple of wooden chairs.

Silas grabbed a can of peaches and began rummaging for something to open it with.

"You guys think of everything except a darn can opener," he snapped.

"Here," Jonathon said, reaching for the large knife sheathed on his belt.

"Much obliged," Silas said, and mere seconds later, he began plucking peach slices from the opened can.

"I found pineapple," Henry said, and he took the knife and began working on his own can.

"Alright, well since you've fed us, why don't you go ahead and entertain us with a little dinner conversation," Jonathon suggested.

Dave looked confused. "What else do you want to know?" he asked. "I've told you everything."

"I want to know more about what you morons are doing on this island," Jonathon replied.

Dave sighed an exasperated breath. "I've told you more than I should've already."

"Well, tell us more," Silas said as he threw the last peach slice into his mouth.

Dave bit his lip and crossed his arms. He sat down in one of the chairs, and Jonathon pulled the other one closer to him and sat as well.

"Come on, Dave," he said. "Don't make my dad get the knives out again."

"What do you want to know?" Dave spat, clearly agitated.

"How many animals have you shipped off of this island?" Jonathon asked.

Dave thought a moment. "Somewhere in the neighborhood of thirty, I think."

Jonathon's eye's widened. "Thirty? That's just wonderful," he said, slumping down into the chair.

"We are careful. The animals that are sold are all neutered or spayed. They are unable to reproduce, and even if they were, we've never sold two animals of different genders," Dave explained. "If we sell a male *Triceratops*, that's all we will ever sell in the future."

"And the animals that you're selling…how many of them are dangerous?" Jonathon asked.

"We've sold a couple of raptors, but for the most part, it's been small herbivores. We've sold quite a few *Protoceratops*. They're plentiful on the island, they're small, and they're not dangerous at all."

"And now you're selling juvenile tyrannosaurs," Henry said, as he settled onto one of the cots.

Dave suddenly got quiet.

"Do you have any idea how extraordinarily stupid bringing a tyrannosaur to civilization is?" Jonathon asked.

"The buyer is paying an extraordinarily large amount of money for it," Dave countered.

"We can't let it happen," Jonathon said sternly. "I won't let it happen."

Dave considered what he said a long moment, and suddenly his mood softened. "Okay, look," he said. "The truth is, I wasn't crazy about the tyrannosaur either. But once Eric sees the dollar signs, he won't back down."

"Yeah, he's obviously blinded by greed so much that he was willing to sacrifice you," Jonathon said. "Did that thought ever occur to you?"

"No," Dave said, shaking his head. "It wasn't Eric. It was the guy that was driving the jeep I was in. He's what you'd call our resident dinosaur wrangler. His name is Glenn Hardcastle, and unfortunately for me, he hates me. He probably wanted the dinosaur to kill me, and when I see Eric, I'm going to tell him all about it."

"And how do you think you're going to see Eric?" Silas asked. "We've got you, son."

Dave laughed. "Do you really think they're not going to come looking for me?"

"Not if they think you're dead," Jonathon said.

"Even if they did think I was dead," Dave argued, "this end of the island will be crawling with Eric, Glenn, and many others as they try to fulfill the other half of the order. Sooner or later, you'll be found out."

Jonathon perked up. "What do you mean, the other half of the order?"

Dave clenched his teeth and shut his eyes. He couldn't believe he'd been so careless.

Jonathon stood from the chair. "What else are they after?" he said, noticing how disturbed Dave had become because of his error.

Dave remained silent. Jonathon grew angrier. He grabbed Dave by his shirt collar and jerked him out of the chair. "What are they after?"

"I can't even pronounce the name of it!" Dave shouted fearfully. "Sarco—something…it's some kind of prehistoric crocodile. I don't know exactly what it's called!"

"*Sarcosuchus*," Jonathon said, abruptly dropping Dave back into the chair.

Henry sat up from the bed. "Son, you sound worried…and if you're worried, I'm worried."

"I've been around plenty of crocs while shooting *Wild World*," Silas said. "A prehistoric one can't be good."

Jonathon swallowed hard. He took his wide-brimmed hat off his head and ran his fingers through his hair. "It's not good at all," he said somberly. "It's basically a forty-foot crocodile with a mouth large enough to gulp down your entire body in one catastrophic chomp. The hide on it has to be almost impenetrable."

"It is," Dave said. "According to our paleontologist, it's the most dangerous animal on the entire island. They're planning on capturing an adult one."

Jonathon clenched his teeth and wrung his hat in his hands. "I won't let them capture it," he said angrily. "It will not happen on my watch!"

"What sort of customer would want something like that?" Henry asked.

"Someone with a lot of money," Dave replied flatly.

"Someone up to no good," Silas countered. "Do you guys check out who you're selling to?"

Dave looked away and said nothing.

***

Glenn Hardcastle had endured a rough night. Sleeping was next to impossible after what he'd discovered on the computer monitor the night before. Someone had entered an emergency bunker during the night, and he was certain that it had to mean that Dave was alive. Initially, he wasn't sure if the discovery was good news or not. On one hand, Eric would be thrilled when he found out that Dave was indeed alive, and he would undoubtedly be pleased with Glenn for figuring it out. But on the other hand, Dave being alive also meant that he would probably waste no time at all expressing his displeasure with how Glenn had treated him, and he would certainly make it known how reckless he had been.

Ever since he'd quickly ushered Annie out of the room, and encouraged her to return to Eric, Glenn had been unable to concentrate on anything else. Truthfully, he could care less if she never spoke to Eric again, but given his latest discovery, he needed time to think. And so it was, thinking was all he did the entire night. After giving it so much thought, he finally decided that the benefits of going forward to Eric with the information outweighed anything negative that could result from it by a good margin.

He'd call him as soon as the sun came up and let him know what he'd found. Then he'd spearhead the mission to go after him, and maybe, just maybe, Dave might be so relieved to see him, he'd conveniently let bygones be bygones. And after all, if he didn't say anything about the bunker, someone else would almost certainly figure it out and notify Eric if he didn't hurry up and do it first.

Morning finally did arrive a short time later, and after making his decision, Glenn somehow managed to get at least an hour of sleep. As soon as he was up, he marched straight to Eric's apartment. He raised a fist to knock on the door, but then suddenly an awkward thought occurred to him. He'd sent Annie back several hours ago. *Lord knows what happened after that*, he thought.

He'd just about decided to spend some time packing the jeep first when suddenly the door opened. It was Annie. Her hair was disheveled, her makeup looked terrible, her clothes were in disarray, but somehow she still looked stunningly beautiful. She was understandably surprised to see him standing there.

"What are you doing here?" she asked, in a voice just above a whisper. She looked over her shoulder as she spoke.

Glenn got straight to the point. "I'm here to see Eric. I'd have waited, but it's pretty important." He could now clearly hear water running.

"Well he's uh...he's taking a shower," she said in a tone that suggested she was embarrassed.

Glenn read between the lines, but he certainly didn't see any reason for her to feel embarrassed. If anyone should've felt embarrassed now, he felt it was certainly him.

"Well, tell him I'll be in the hangar. Tell him to come find me as soon as he gets out. It's about Dave," he said, turning away to leave.

"What about Dave?" she asked.

Hardcastle stopped, but didn't turn back to face her. He suddenly remembered that Annie knew nothing about Dave's disappearance. "I'd rather speak to Eric directly about it," he said very matter-of-factly.

"I see," she replied. "I suppose that means it's something bad," she said in a worried tone.

Glenn kept his back to her and rolled his eyes. "No, it's actually something good," he said. "In fact, tell Eric that the news I have about Dave is good; you can tell him that."

Dave was just about to walk away again when he heard a muffled voice call out from somewhere further toward the interior of the apartment. Glenn had never ventured inside Eric's apartment before.

Eric's jabbering had gotten Annie's attention. She leaned back to listen, seemed to understand, and replied, "It's Glenn...he says he's got good news about Dave!"

The water immediately turned off and Glenn could hear what sounded like a shower curtain shuffling about.

"Glenn! Wait!"

Moments later, Eric jogged into the doorway with a towel wrapped around his waist. He was soaking wet, and it suddenly occurred to Glenn he'd never seen Eric shirtless before. The man obviously was working out and his athletic appearance only made Glenn despise him more.

"What's up with Dave?" Eric asked.

Hardcastle kept his mouth shut and glanced over at Annie. Eric suddenly remembered she didn't know what all had occurred the day before.

"Sweetie...err, excuse us a moment," Eric said, and he stepped outside and shut the door behind him.

Hardcastle looked around. He wondered what would be thought or said by any of his coworkers if they caught a glimpse of him standing with a naked Eric—and outside his apartment to boot.

"I think he's alive," Glenn said. "I got a ping off the bunker at the other end of the island. Someone went inside it last night."

Eric smiled, but it disappeared almost immediately. "I thought you said you saw Dave die."

Glenn shook his head. He was ready for this. "No," he said, holding up a hand. "I never said I saw him die. I said I saw the tyrannosaur attack him, but he was in the truck. Everything happened too fast, and to tell you the truth, I was in survival mode at that point. When things were obviously hopeless for Dr. Cruz and Dave, I had to do what I could to protect George and myself. Dave must've somehow slipped out and escaped. I never got a clear, unobstructed view."

Eric let out a breath and closed his eyes. He was letting it all process.

"I'm telling you," Glenn continued. "If there was anything I could've done, I would've."

"You've never liked Dave," Eric said, a little too coldly for Glenn's taste.

"Look, I'm a jerk, and I can be—difficult, I know all that," Glenn replied. "And yeah, I've never been fond of Dave because he's always come across as a kiss-ass. But you know how serious I am about my job, and part of my job is protecting you and everyone else in this corporation from these monsters. I wouldn't purposely do anything to get someone killed."

Eric stared at him a long minute. He took another deep breath and exhaled slowly.

"Well, Dave's out there all alone with those monsters all around him right now," Eric said. "So what are you going to do about it?"

"I'm going to go get the little pain in the ass," Glenn said with a grin.

Eric smirked. "Yes, you are," he replied. "And I'm going with you—after I get dressed."

He opened the door to the apartment, and as he was about to go inside, he stopped and turned back to Hardcastle.

"Oh, I almost forgot," he said. "Our new paleontologist arrived during the night."

Glenn was taken aback. "New paleontologist...already?"

"Finding a paleontologist to come to this island will never be a problem," Eric said. "And coming during the night is the best way to get them here discreetly."

"But Dr. Cruz has been dead less than twenty-four hours," Glenn said somberly. He was surprised at how much it bothered him that the man was so quickly replaced.

"I know," Eric said. "But you know Casey would want us to push onward. We've got a big croc out there to get. We need all the help we can get and we don't have any time to waste. The bunker is close to where the super crocs are. This little adventure to go and get Dave will be her first taste of what this island has to offer." And with that, Eric disappeared into the apartment and abruptly shut the door.

Her? Glenn thought to himself.

CHAPTER 21

Charlotte Nelson, or "Charlie" as her friends knew her, was a go-getter. She'd always been labeled that by anyone that truly knew her. She was a gal that was willing to get her hands dirty and do whatever it took to get where she wanted to go. She became fascinated with dinosaurs at an early age. She was very much aware of the fact that most other children were fascinated with dinosaurs also, but for her, the fascination never faded. It became a passion, and ultimately, a lifestyle. She'd learned from the best in the Badlands of Montana, and eventually, she became a professor at a major university. Dinosaurs—more specifically, paleontology—was all that she ever thought about. So when a strange, good-looking fellow named Eric Gill had visited her six months ago, the cryptic things he'd said and hinted about had left her with a lot of unanswered questions. He kept referring to 'animals' that were related to her field. He'd made it clear that he was not offering her a job, but simply recruiting for a possible opening in the future. He, in a polite way, threatened her with legal action if she did not keep quiet about their meeting, and made it abundantly clear that if she did speak to anyone, she would most definitely be taken off his list of potential candidates. He'd said just enough to make her insanely curious and interested. He'd said just enough to make her want to keep quiet. And she did…almost.

***

Eric Gill's operation depended on many things for success. The dependable, armored protection that his small fleet of four jeeps provided was certainly among the most important of all. The jeeps were used for everything from scouting missions all the way up to capturing and towing dinosaurs back to base camp for their eventual sale. Unfortunately, after the mishap with Dave, the operation was now down to three fully functional jeeps. This didn't seem like a major setback to one without inside knowledge, but Hardcastle, of course, had inside knowledge. Multiple jeeps were often used in a choreographed way to capture larger dinosaurs. Two of the vehicles served as a distraction, while one served as a chase vehicle, and sometimes a fourth was used as a lookout. *Sarcosuchus* was clearly a larger animal and was a classic example of when four vehicles were truly needed to capture with relative safety.

There were other vehicles on the island, notably a large semi and flatbed trailer. Glenn Hardcastle had often wondered if or when they'd even find a use for such a large vehicle, and now it seemed he had his answer. Although the semi would be present when the time arrived to catch the animal, it was nowhere near agile and quick enough to be used in a way like one of the jeeps. About the only help the semi would provide, aside from actually towing the monstrosity, would perhaps be as a lookout vehicle.

So now that Eric had ordered the use of two of the jeeps to go and find Dave, Hardcastle felt very uneasy and anxious. Losing another vehicle at this point would be catastrophic to the operation. This was a catch-22, Glenn knew, because venturing out into the harsh jungle in one vehicle could also result in catastrophic results—mainly, loss of life.

If it had been up to him, Glenn would've quickly briefed the new paleontologist of the situation, get whatever input she had to offer, and then an operation would be planned that would involve getting Dave and the super croc all in one swoop. This would of course probably mean a minimum of another day of planning, and he knew Eric would not settle for that. He wanted his precious Dave back as soon as possible, the best interests of everyone else be damned. At least this was all how Glenn Hardcastle saw it.

***

Charlotte Nelson arrived during the night by sea—by what seemed to her to be some sort of tugboat. She thought that was odd, but she didn't question it. She'd been waiting a long time for this opportunity, so it was no surprise to her when she finally arrived around one a.m. that morning that the very last thing she wanted to do was sleep. She couldn't see much, Eric had made it very clear after he saw her to her room that she needed to get a good night of sleep and to stay there until morning, but even if he hadn't made those demands, seeing anything was next to impossible in the pitch darkness of the night. So Charlie did the next best thing: she dragged a chair toward the door that led to the balcony. She then opened the balcony and listened to the hypnotic tones of the nearby surf gently rolling onto the beach. But it wasn't just the beach she heard. There were lots of unusual animal sounds. She realized how silly she probably would've looked to any of the employees that had worked for Eric Gill for a long period of time, but those people were used to the unusual sounds she was hearing. For someone like her, it was suddenly the only sounds she could hear anymore. The surf was gone and replaced by the wailing and moaning of the dinosaurs that had called the island home for undoubtedly millions of years.

Early the next morning, Charlie was awoken by a gentle knock at the door. When she answered it, Eric Gill was standing on the other side with a can of Diet Coke in hand. She glanced down at the beverage and then back up to Eric.

"This is your preferred soft drink?" Eric said...and it actually came out more like a statement than an actual question.

"Uh, yes, it is," Charlie replied, somewhat surprised. "How did you possibly know that?"

Eric smiled a mischievous grin. "There's a lot of things I know about you. I'm very careful about who I bring to this island, Ms. Nelson."

"I see," she replied, trying her best to not sound creeped out. "And please call me Charlie."

"Very well...Charlie," Eric said. "Please hurry and get dressed; we've got some scouting to do."

Charlie did as she was bade, and in less than half an hour, she stepped out of the pyramid-shaped building everyone on the island called home. Eric was waiting for her with a cigarette hanging out of his mouth.

"Do you mind?" he asked, gesturing toward the cigarette.

"No, of course not," she lied. Charlie had just managed to quit smoking and now the very thought of a cigarette was enough to make her nauseous.

Eric began walking toward a rather large building that appeared to be an aircraft hangar. Charlie observed numerous armored vehicles parked inside. Then she heard a rather curious sound coming from a trailer parked near the rear corner of the building. It sounded like a cross between an elephant and a mountain lion.

"What is that sound?" she asked.

"Why don't you go see for yourself?" Eric answered.

Charlie made her way toward the trailer and was nothing short of amazed when she found the source of the sound.

"Is this a—is this a...a...?"

"Dinosaur?" Glenn Hardcastle said, emerging from the shadows. "Why, yes, it is. A young tyrannosaur to be specific."

Charlie looked at him with wide-eyed amazement. "This isn't possible...I'm seeing it, but it's just not possible!"

"Honey, you're just getting started," Hardcastle said, offering a handshake. "My name is Glenn Hardcastle...I'm the dinosaur wrangler."

Charlie took his hand. His hands were large and rough compared to her small and dainty ones. "Charlotte Nelson," she replied. "But just call me Charlie."

"Okay, Charlie. Don't worry, the initial shock will wear off after a day or two and then you'll be able to work," he said.

"I'm afraid we don't have that much time to spare," Eric said, as he approached.

Charlie glanced over at him, breathing deeply, and still wide-eyed.

"I'm sorry about that, truly I am," he said. "But I'm afraid one of our men is out there hiding in a bunker waiting on us to retrieve him. And while we're out retrieving him, we're going to scout a location for a dinosaur we're pursuing. It's rather complex, and we need to work out the logistics of how we will get the animal to the sea."

Charlie nodded. "Alright," she said, feeling a bit overwhelmed. "I'll help you however I can."

"Good," Eric replied, rather pleased. "Well, we'd better get going then."

***

Glenn Hardcastle was immediately struck by Charlotte Nelson's appearance. She was very short, he estimated 5'5", and could not have weighed more than 120 pounds soaking wet. Her hair was short and so blonde it was nearly white. Her pink lips were so enticing; he'd almost forgot to check out the rest of her assets. There wasn't anything spectacular about the rest of her body, but she was exactly the sort of woman he'd be proud to bring home to his parents. He'd lobbied for her to ride along with him, but Eric had vetoed his request (like he always did) and she rode with him. Glenn got the pleasure of George's company instead.

They raced down the narrow dirt road that weaved its way through the outer edge of the jungle at a brisk pace. It was best to travel fast, and the sooner they retrieved Dave, the sooner they could scope out the super croc and then finally get back to base. That would be his moment to spend some quality time with Charlie and get to know her. That would be his moment to try and charm her. In the back of his mind, he knew Dave could potentially cause him problems once he got a moment to speak to Eric in private. Hardcastle decided he'd done enough worrying about that. If Dave was going to tattle to Eric, then so be it. He'd deal with the consequences when they came. The fact of the matter was that Eric Gill needed Glenn Hardcastle a lot more than he needed him.

CHAPTER 22

It seemed Jonathon hadn't gotten a good night's rest in many, many days. It all began when he received the terrible news about Lucy, and suddenly he remembered the reason why he'd returned to this island in the first place. It was because of Lucy, and although he'd ran into more than he'd bargained for since arriving on the island, her well-being was still the ultimate goal. Finding the fountain again before they left was just as important as stopping the dinosaur trafficking business he'd stumbled upon.

The previous night offered little sleep again, but this time it had just as much to do with the uncomfortable chair he'd tried to sleep in than anything else. Jonathon stood, stretched, and the popping sounds from his back were loud enough to wake Silas from his slumber on one of the cots. Henry had rested on the other cot, while Dave was tied down to the other chair.

"Sleep well?" Silas asked, and he yawned.

"No, not at all. You?"

"I've done worse," he replied.

Jonathon glanced up the staircase. "I've got to empty the bladder."

"Alright," Silas said as he was getting to his feet. "I'll follow you up and hold the door so you don't get locked out."

The two men left Dave and Henry to their slumber and made their way up the stairs and into the fresh air of the morning. Jonathon found a nearby tree, leaned against it, and relieved himself, while Silas stood in the doorway to the bunker. He occasionally glanced down the stairs, but there was no movement from either Dave or Henry.

Jonathon turned to walk back toward the bunker when suddenly something grabbed his attention. He stopped abruptly.

"What is it?" Silas asked.

"Quiet," Jonathon whispered. He turned his head sideways and then looked back over his shoulder, listening intently. "Do you hear a humming noise?"

Silas listened hard, and after a moment he heard it too. "That sounds like a vehicle headed this way."

"That's what I thought," Jonathon said. Panicked, he ran down the steps. "Okay, up and at 'em! We've got to go—now!"

Henry popped up and instantly grabbed his bag. He threw a few canned goods in it and began making his way up the stairs. Silas was already in the amphibious ATV and had it running by the time Henry got to it.

"Okay, Dave," Jonathon said as he untied his bindings. "Get in the ATV...quickly."

"Alright," he said in an agitated tone. "But you've got to know this is useless. They'll find me. You may as well let me go and take off alone. I won't tell them anything about you."

"Yeah, I don't think so," Jonathon said, clearly not believing him. "Get in the ATV—and be quick about it or I'll mess up your other leg."

Dave did as he was told and no sooner did Jonathon fasten down the protective cage, Silas had the vehicle rumbling along the road away from the approaching vehicle. Unfortunately, they were delayed just enough for Glenn to catch a glimpse of the fleeing ATV.

***

Hardcastle slowed just enough for Eric Gill to pull alongside him in the other jeep.

"There is no way they'll outrun us in that little ATV," he said, pointing toward the dust trail the fleeing vehicle was leaving behind.

"Well, we aren't taking any chances. We need to catch whoever that is and find out what they're doing on my island," Eric replied.

Glenn Hardcastle nodded and then accelerated after the small vehicle.

"Piece of cake," he muttered to himself. He glanced over at George Powell. "We'll try and do this peacefully, but if they don't obey, I'll be forced to run them off the road. This could get messy."

George nodded. "Do what you have to do," he replied, and then his expression hardened. "But just know we will not leave Dave behind again."

Hardcastle bit his lip and nodded.

***

"They saw us!" Jonathon shouted over the high-pitched wail coming from the ATV's engine. "Will this thing go any faster?"

"I'm afraid this is all she's got!" Silas replied.

"Pull over and let me reason with them," Dave said.

Jonathon glanced back at the first of two jeeps closing in on them rapidly. He immediately noticed the large turret machine gun mounted on the rear of the vehicle. "Somehow, I'm just not comfortable pulling over and reasoning with these guys," he said to Dave.

Jonathon could only watch as the jeep rapidly closed in on them until it finally was within shouting distance. An African-American man riding shotgun stood up and opened the protective cage on the top of the vehicle. He grabbed a roll bar to steady himself and then began shouting at them.

"Stop the vehicle and release Dave!" he said.

"How about you stop chasing us and we'll consider releasing Dave," Jonathon shouted back. "If it wasn't for us, Dave would be dead right now!"

The two men in the jeep glanced at each other, and Jonathon noticed the man driving shaking his head.

"I'm afraid we can't let you disappear with Dave," the man replied.

Suddenly, to Jonathon's dismay, Dave turned around and began shouting. "You can trust them, George! They will let me go further up the road, just stop chasing us before someone gets hurt."

Jonathon noticed the man driving look directly at Dave before shouting, "Can't do that, Dave! Eric wants you back, and we have no idea who these yahoos chauffeuring you around are." He then looked at Jonathon. "Sir, I'd strongly suggest you stop that vehicle immediately before I have to force you to stop it."

Silas glanced over his shoulder. "What do you want me to do, Jonathon? I can't outrun them."

"Don't stop!" Jonathon said. "Don't forget why we're here!"

The man driving the jeep grinned and shook his head, almost in disbelief. "Okay," he shouted. "Have it your way!"

Glenn Hardcastle mashed the accelerator and got a wheel alongside the ATV. He forcefully rubbed the jeep against the side of the amphibious vehicle in an attempt to run it off the road. The small vehicle drifted off the edge of the road and slid completely sideways. Hardcastle, thinking the vehicle was about to spin out, decelerated and waited.

Silas fought the steering wheel and miraculously regained control of the six-wheeled vehicle. Glenn Hardcastle could hardly believe it, and the act only angered him. The next hit would be much harder. He gunned the throttle and rammed into the back of the vehicle hard enough that the rear wheels came off the ground. Again, the little ATV fishtailed and slid all over the sandy road, but thanks to Silas's driving (and six wheels being better than four), somehow the vehicle stayed on the road.

Jonathon took a deep breath and then looked at his father. "Dad, whatever happens, you get that water to Lucy. It's why we're here…please don't forget that."

"What are you going to do, son?" Henry asked.

"I've got to ensure all of us are not caught," he answered, standing up. He then threw open the protective gate on the top of the cage.

Jonathon stood up just as Hardcastle began accelerating for another attack on the small ATV. Just as the jeep reached the rear of their vehicle, Jonathon leapt onto the hood. Glenn Hardcastle was stunned and began to slow down.

"Don't stop now!" Eric yelled at him as the jeep he was piloting raced ahead. "We can't let them get away!"

Jonathon noticed the familiar face in the other jeep, but it was obvious Eric didn't immediately recognize him.

Hardcastle gunned the throttle again and inertia forced Jonathon into the windshield.

"Get off my jeep!" Hardcastle yelled. He glanced over at George Powell. The man looked confused. "Get rid of him!"

George nodded and reached over the windshield to grab their unwanted passenger. Jonathon was ready and swiftly met George with an uppercut as he leaned over. George grabbed his mouth and fell backward, hitting his head on the rear cross bar which in turn knocked him out cold. Hardcastle rolled his eyes and became angrier. He reached into a holster mounted on the side of his seat and pulled out a small handgun.

"Last time I'm going to ask," he said, pointing the gun at Jonathon. "Get off my jeep!"

Jonathon glanced over his shoulder and noticed the other jeep closing in on Silas and his father.

***

Eric Gill aggressively piloted his jeep toward the ATV. He didn't know what Hardcastle had said to the men fleeing, but whatever it was, it had been unproductive and did nothing to end the confrontation peacefully. Now it was his turn.

"We're not going to hurt these people, are we?" Charlie asked from the passenger seat.

"No, we're not," Eric said. "But they've got one of my men. I've got to get him back, and I've got to find out what these men are doing on this island."

He raced the jeep alongside the ATV. He shouted toward the driver.

"Sir, stop the vehicle. We mean you no harm!"

"Yeah, I sort of don't believe that, Gill," the ATV driver said, glaring over at him.

Eric instantly recognized Silas Treadwell and his heart skipped a beat. "What are you doing here?"

"Funny, I was going to ask you the same thing!" Silas replied.

"Pull the vehicle over so we can talk about this!"

"I got a better idea," Silas said. "You pull over and I won't kill you...you can be on your way, and we'll be on ours."

Eric looked in his mirror just in time to see Hardcastle pointing a handgun at the man on the hood of his jeep. It was at that moment he recognized Jonathon. He feared this day may come, and he'd prepared himself for what needed to be done if it did happen.

"Shoot him," Eric shouted to Hardcastle. "Shoot him now!"

***

Hardcastle was somewhat shocked and stunned to hear Eric giving him the order to shoot the man on the hood of his vehicle. It must've meant Eric knew him and knew he was bad news. "No offense, pal, but it looks like you're a goner," he said as he pulled the trigger.

Jonathon instinctively rolled off the side of the vehicle and grabbed the side mirror. His legs were dragging dangerously close to the rear wheel, but miraculously, the side mirror held. He could hear bullets tearing through the windshield, piercing through the empty air where, a mere second earlier, he'd been lying.

"You slippery son of a gun," Hardcastle fumed. He pointed the weapon toward Jonathon, but because of the armored cage on the sides of the jeep, there was no clear view for a shot. He then redirected his attention out of the windshield and could see a dense patch of thorny, prehistoric brush lining the edge of the road. There was no way the man could hold on if he drove the side of the jeep into that.

Jonathon felt the jeep veer toward the shoulder of the road. He looked ahead and saw the nasty-looking foliage ahead. Remaining where he was suddenly was no longer an option. He held the side mirror tightly with his right arm and used his free left hand to remove the large knife from the holster on his belt. He suddenly flung the knife between the bars on the cage and landed it firmly into the thigh of the driver.

Hardcastle wailed and inadvertently dropped the handgun from his free hand. A hand reached out and yanked the knife from his thigh—it was George Monroe.

"Take the wheel," Hardcastle said through clenched teeth.

George was still groggy, but he quickly slipped into the seat just as Hardcastle had left it. Jonathon was climbing over the windshield just as Hardcastle had gotten to his feet. He lunged at him and began pummeling him as both men fell toward the empty space in the rear of the jeep just below the turret.

***

"Jump into the jeep!" Eric shouted at Dave. He drove the jeep gently against the back of the ATV.

Silas immediately reached up and pulled the open overhead door to their protective cage shut again. Dave reached for the handle, but Henry held it firmly in place.

"You're not going anywhere, son," he said.

Eric was now beyond angry; he was borderline furious.

"Dave, fasten your seat belt," he shouted as he intentionally decelerated the jeep. Now he was going to put enough distance between the two vehicles so that when he came charging back, the collision would be great enough to flip the ATV over if need be. Dave did as he was told and held on—he knew what was coming.

Henry leaned forward. "Silas, we've got to get off the road, it's our only chance!"

"We're on the same page, Henry," he replied, and he pointed at a clearing through the woods. Beyond the clearing, they could see the murky water of the small river than ran through the island.

"Alright," Henry said when he spotted what Silas was pointing at. "As long as you're sure she'll float!"

"She's never failed me before," Silas replied.

Eric began his charge toward the ATV for what he hoped would be the final time. Just as he was about to make contact, the little amphibious vehicle suddenly veered hard to the right and shot off the road through a narrow path that led to the river. Eric slammed on the brakes and the jeep slid to a stop.

***

Jonathon thought he'd gotten the upper hand when he fell forward and on top of Glenn Hardcastle. However, he quickly realized he severely underestimated the man's strength. Hardcastle managed to plant the foot on his uninjured leg into Jonathon's chest and pushed with enough force to throw him back and into the dashboard of the vehicle. Before Jonathon had a chance to lunge at him again, Hardcastle was already on his feet. Both men traded blows and it seemed both of them were on even ground.

George continued to motor ahead in an effort to catch back up to Eric. As he rounded a curve, he noticed the other jeep at a dead stop ahead of them. George grabbed the emergency brake in a desperate attempt to stop the vehicle. The jeep's wheels locked up and inertia caused Jonathon and Hardcastle to tumble over the windshield, onto the hood, and finally landing in the middle of the sandy road, the jeep stopping just mere feet away from hitting them.

The two men continued to roll around on the ground, throwing and landing punches whenever possible. Eric ran over to them and grabbed Hardcastle as George grabbed Jonathon.

"Stop it, both of you!" Eric yelled. He glared at Jonathon. "We've both got other problems right now!" he said, pointing toward the clearing that led to the river.

Jonathon immediately lost interest in Hardcastle and began running toward the murky water. He breathed a sigh of relief when he saw the amphibious vehicle floating, but it was short lived. A little further down the river, he noticed a large conglomeration of tree limbs, logs, and other shrubbery taking up half the width of the river. It looked similar to a beaver damn, but none of the tree debris showed signs of gnaw marks. It all looked as if it was simply collected and piled there. Jonathon could tell that the ATV was simply floating with the current. He could hear Silas desperately trying to re-fire the engine.

He looked over at Eric. "What is that?"

Hardcastle ran to the riverbank, holding his sore jaw. "*That* is bad news."

"Can you do something?" Eric asked in a very worried tone.

"No...I'm sorry, they're screwed," he replied.

Eric grabbed him by the shoulders and spun him around to face him. "You're the dino wrangler! Do something!"

Jonathon butted between them. "Someone tell me what that is!"

Charlie was standing beside George, behind the arguing men. "Oh my God," she whispered. "*Titanoboa*."

Jonathon looked toward the river again, and he could see the sickening sight of thousands of tiny brown scales moving at once as another horrific prehistoric beast uncoiled from somewhere behind the debris. It looked like an anaconda—only bigger. Much, much bigger.

Titanoboa was a prehistoric snake that grew up to nearly fifty feet long and easily weighed 2,500 pounds. The one Jonathon was looking at was every bit of that length and weight. It seemed that the enormous snake had somehow constructed the giant debris pile structure and used it much in the same way a spider uses a web. It collected living things that may have fallen into the river and quickly made a meal of them. Now, Henry, Silas, and Dave were headed toward it.

"Dad...Silas...you guys have got to get out of there!" Jonathon yelled.

"That vehicle they're in—is it strong enough to protect them?" Eric asked.

"Not a chance," Charlie said somberly.

"No," Jonathon agreed. "And even if somehow it could withstand the thousands of pounds of pressure that snake could put on it, they'd still be trapped when the snake drags it under water."

"Dave! Get out of there!" Eric yelled frantically.

CHAPTER 23

"Okay, fellas, this ride is over," Silas said, as he began unstrapping belts.

"Get this thing open," Dave said, panicked.

Henry was already trying to open the door, but it wasn't budging.

"You've got to be kidding me," Silas said in disbelief.

He put his large hand on it and jerked the lever hard. It still didn't move.

"It must've gotten jammed when we crashed into the water."

"Okay, we've got to go now!" Dave screamed, his eyes were wide and focused on something on the bank ahead.

Henry whipped his head around just in time to see the gigantic snake dive into the river, leaving a trail of swirling water in its wake. It was headed straight toward them.

Silas reached back toward the dash and opened a glove box. He retrieved a handgun.

"Shouldn't we be grabbing the rifles?" Dave asked.

"No time to try to shoot that thing with a rifle," Silas replied. "And this isn't for the snake anyway. Get back!" He pointed the gun toward the latch and fired the weapon. The thunderous blast instantly made all of the passenger's ears ring, but it did the job. The latch broke free and Dave immediately threw open the door.

Before Silas and Henry were even aware of what was happening, Dave jumped into the murky water and began frantically swimming toward the bank.

"What are you doing? You fool, you'll be the first one to go!" Silas yelled after him.

Henry watched in horror as the water began swirling just behind Dave. "Give me that gun!" he snapped with desperation, snatching the weapon from Silas. Henry began firing the weapon into the water where the swirling was occurring behind Dave. When he had fired the last shot, he and Silas watched the water intensely for any sign of movement. Silas glanced back up to check on Dave's progress.

"Well, what do you know?" he said. "The kid made it out of the water."

At that moment, the large head of the mammoth snake shot up from the murky water less than ten feet away from Silas and Henry.

"My God!" Henry shouted as he fell back in his seat.

The snake lunged for Henry, but Silas jerked the protective cage down just in time. The snake seemed to improvise. It glanced off the top of the vehicle, dove back into the water, and suddenly what they were all fearing began to become reality. The snake was wrapping itself around the ATV.

***

"Get Dave!" Eric shouted. George Monroe took off running back to the road where he would be able to cross the bridge and get to the other side where Dave was.

"We've got to do something," Jonathon said. "Do we have any weapons?"

"Sure, we've got lots of weapons, but nothing that won't risk tearing through those men at the same time. Open your eyes; the snake is completely wrapped around them now," Eric said. "We can't even see them anymore. They're completely entombed."

"Dad! Silas! Can you hear me?"

"I hear you, son." Henry's reply was muffled. "Get out of here. Save yourself! Finish what you came here for!"

"I'm not leaving, Dad," Jonathon answered.

They could all see the muscles in the giant snake's body tighten and the metal cage began to creak and bend in protest. Slowly, the vehicle began to submerge.

"Dad!" Jonathon screamed.

No reply.

Charlie Nelson began to sob. "Oh my God," was all she muttered over and over.

"Silas!"

No reply.

Eric grabbed Jonathon's shoulder and the vehicle sank further. "They're gone; there is nothing you can do."

Jonathon jerked free and began making his way toward the water. "I won't give up; I'm going after them."

"Are you nuts?" Eric said.

Jonathon just ignored him and began to wade into the water. Eric glanced over at Hardcastle. "Stop him!"

Hardcastle picked up a large stick and ran after him. Jonathon was concentrating so hard on getting to Silas and his father, he never knew what was coming behind him. Hardcastle swung the stick hard and made contact with the back of Jonathon's head. He fell like a sack of potatoes, and both Hardcastle and Eric had to pull him from the river.

"Why did you do that?" Charlie screamed.

"I saved him from himself, Ms. Nelson," Eric said coldly. "Now if you don't mind, please return to the vehicle. We've got to return to base."

"What about the croc?" Hardcastle asked, still rubbing his sore jaw.

"The croc will have to wait."

"Do you know this guy?" Hardcastle asked.

Eric nodded. "Yes, and his arriving on this island can't mean anything good for us. We've got to take him back and question him."

"Well, what makes you think he'll talk to us?"

"He may not talk to us, but I think I may know someone he will talk to," Eric replied. He looked back toward the river just in time to see the rest of the ATV disappear into the river. Moments later, both jeeps were rumbling back toward the base camp.

CHAPTER 24

"Jonathon is here? On the island?"

Annie was a combination of elation and concern all at once. She had not seen Jonathon since they'd both been on the island seven years ago. Last she'd heard, he and Lucy had gotten married and had seemingly moved on from their adventurous past. Try as she might, Annie could not think of a single good reason for Jonathon to return. After all, it was he that made them all vow to keep the place a secret. A vow that she'd only half-heartedly taken.

"Why on earth is he on this island?" she asked Eric emphatically.

"That's exactly what I'd like for you to find out," he replied.

They were in Eric's living room; the picturesque view from his open balcony lit the room up brightly.

"What do you mean—I mean, why me? Just ask him yourself!"

Eric shook his head, reached in his pocket, and retrieved a cigarette. "No," he replied, lighting it up. "He's never liked me, and he almost certainly disapproves of me being here running this operation. But you— he likes you—he knows you. He would be a lot more willing to talk to you than he would me."

Annie sighed and pushed her dangling red locks away from her face. "What is it you want me to ask him?"

"I want to find out why he is here and what he knows about my operation."

"He may be here for the fountain," Annie added.

The statement made Eric chuckle. "Ah yes, the fountain of youth," he said. "The fountain that neither you nor I have ever seen."

"The fountain is what drove my uncle here," Annie said. "Jonathon and the others found it...they told me about it."

"And yet I've been here for years and have never found it," he rebutted, blowing smoke out his nose.

"That doesn't mean it doesn't exist—I mean, how else do you explain all of these dinosaurs that have managed to avoid extinction?"

Eric paused and seemed to be in deep thought.

"I can't see Jonathon coming here for the fountain," Annie said after a few silent minutes.

Eric fell back into the soft cushions on the couch, looking defeated. "Well, we're never going to get any answers sitting here trying desperately to understand the psyche of Jonathon Williams," he said. "I need you to speak to him and get any information you can."

Annie stood up. She didn't want to admit it, but she was very curious and wanted answers too. "Okay, so where do I find him?"

***

Jonathon awoke groggy and plagued with a pounding headache. He was lying on a couch in what appeared to be some sort of break room. After a few minutes, he reluctantly propped himself up on the couch, and soon after, forced himself to get up. He rubbed his temples in a futile attempt to relieve some of the pain he was feeling. Then he surveyed the room.

On the counter, the first thing he noticed was a bottle of Tylenol. He made a beeline for the medication and wasted no time throwing a few pills in his mouth. Next, he rummaged through the cabinets for something to eat in hopes of ridding his body of the terrible hunger he was now experiencing. He found a box of cookies, half-full, and made quick work of the contents. He then eyed a Coke machine in the corner of the room. After fishing a couple of quarters from his pocket, he purchased the classic beverage and drank the entire can at once.

Suddenly feeling much better, Jonathon then made his way to the door and, as he suspected, it was locked. He thought of his father and of Silas. As tears began to well up in his eyes, he rubbed the moisture away and fought off the incredible urge to weep. There would be plenty of time for that later. For now, he had to focus on getting out of his current predicament. He pounded on the door and began yelling for someone to open it. There was no response, but Jonathon suddenly heard footsteps approaching. He began yelling again, demanding for whoever was on the other side to open the door and release him. There was no response, but the footsteps seemed to stop directly in front of the door. It was then that he noticed a folded piece of paper slide under the door. The footsteps then hurried away.

Jonathon plucked the sheet off the floor, unfolded it, and read the neatly printed words.

Stay Calm
You Have A Friend Here
Will Get You Out ASAP!

He crumpled the paper up immediately after reading it and stuffed it in his pants pocket. The author was a complete mystery to him, but it did

119

somewhat ease his mind. *Was it Dave?* There were a million questions running through his head like a freight train on the way to nowhere. It was undoubtedly contributing to his headache. He was anxious for the Tylenol to kick in.

Jonathon again looked around the room for any avenue of escape. There were no windows, and the door was very solid wood encased in a metal frame. It seemed that breaking out on his own would be impossible. Sooner or later, he knew someone was going to come and check on him. If he could find a suitable weapon, he could make his escape then. But then, where would he go? He knew nothing about the facility where he was being held. He assumed he was being held in one of the buildings where Dave had told him Eric's operation was. But for all he knew, he may not even be on the island anymore. Thoughts of Silas and his father once again tried to creep back in the forefront of his mind, and once again, Jonathon willed them away. Suddenly, he heard footsteps approaching again.

Quickly, he scanned the environment for something to use as a weapon. The footsteps drew closer and something in his gut told him that his opportunity was about to present itself. Instinctively, he grabbed a nearby chair. It was made of metal and plastic, but if the blow was landed right, it would do the job. He briskly moved to the space where he'd briefly become hidden by the opened door. Jonathon watched the knob begin to twist and readied the chair. The door swung open and as he prepared to unleash his fury, he saw something unexpected. A single open-toed shoe stepped into the room just enough for Jonathon to see it. The foot was feminine with toenails painted bright red. The woman on the other side of the opened door stood there for a moment before finally speaking.

"Jonathon?" she said meekly.

Jonathon recognized the voice and he couldn't believe it. He dropped the chair and reached around the door in a single motion. He abruptly pulled Annie toward him and pushed the door shut quickly behind her.

"What are you doing here?" he asked gruffly.

"I was going to ask you the same thing," she said with an innocent smile.

"Did you slide the note under the door?"

Annie squinted and her mouth opened slightly. "Note? What note?" she asked.

Jonathon shook his head, disappointed. "Never mind," he said. "Annie, tell me what you're doing here."

"You'll be mad," she replied.

"Sweetheart, I'm already mad," he said, trying not to sound annoyed.

"Well, first, I want you to know I just returned a couple of days ago for the first time since we were here all those years ago," she explained.

"Great, so you're here, Eric is here, Silas is here...it seems we've got a reunion of sorts going on."

Annie looked surprised. "Silas is here?"

Jonathon could see she genuinely didn't know. He decided to keep quiet about what had happened to Silas for the moment. "Maybe it's best if you start explaining to me what the heck is going on and why you are here," he said.

Annie nodded and took a deep breath. She thought a moment as she pondered what to say. "Okay, like I said, you're going to be mad...but, I've been seeing Eric Gill for a few years now."

Jonathon rolled his eyes. "You've got to be kidding me. That guy is a sleaze ball, Annie."

She held up a dismissive hand and shot him a look of anger. "Don't," she snapped. "Just don't even. I've not heard a peep out of you since everything went down here all those years ago. My uncle died in case you forgot. And yes, he was made from the scum of the earth, but I was the one that everyone in the family looked to for answers. Uncle Angus was always a black sheep in our family, and due to my shady association with him around the time of his untimely death, I too became an outcast. It certainly didn't help matters when the family discovered he'd left everything to those two goons, Travis and Frank. But since they were dead also, he'd put Eric next in line."

"That makes no sense; why would he leave his fortune in the hands of a pilot he'd only recently gotten to know?" Jonathon asked.

"Because of this island," she replied. "This island full of dinosaurs and the fountain of youth. He wanted someone who knew of its existence; someone that would have unlimited resources to look for him if he turned up missing."

"And the hierarchy eventually fell to Eric," Jonathon said, shaking his head. "And I suppose he came looking for him?"

Annie nodded. "Very shortly after we returned and told him what happened, he made his way here, but discovered quickly what we already knew: Angus was most likely already dead."

"Has Eric located the fountain?" Jonathon asked.

Annie shook her head. "No, he's looked for it and can't find it." She paused. "He's not all bad, Jonathon. When I was treated as an outcast, he saw that I was taken care of. He has been very caring toward me."

Jonathon yawned, and although he knew Annie would take it as boredom, he was genuinely tired. "Yeah, well he hasn't been telling people to shoot you, so forgive my reluctance to believe he's just a big old pussycat."

"Who tried to shoot you?" Annie asked.

"That thug that wears the hat with all the raptor claws around the band," he replied. "He tried to shoot me after your boyfriend ordered him to."

She lowered her head. "He wouldn't do that. After all, you're here and alive now."

"Yeah, so how about telling me why I'm still alive?"

She looked at him, puzzled.

"Don't play dumb with me," Jonathon snapped at her. "Why did he send you in here?"

Annie sighed, then gave another slight smile. Jonathon wanted to be angry with her, but she was just too darn beautiful.

"He wanted me to find out what you knew about his operation," she said, sounding defeated.

"You mean his black market dinosaur operation?"

She nodded. "He also wants me to find out what brought you here to begin with."

"Ah, now we're getting to the truth," he said. "So he's holding me here until I tell why I'm here."

She nodded again.

"And then what will he do with me after I spill it?"

Annie shrugged. "He'll let you go, I suppose."

Jonathon turned to her and grabbed her by the shoulders. "Surely you don't really believe that?"

She looked him in the eyes and seemed to ignore the question. "You mentioned Silas is here too?"

He held his eyes on her, doing his best to keep his composure. "Silas came here with me and my father to find the fountain one more time."

Annie pulled away from him. "What? Why? You're the one that was preaching to us about staying away from here!"

Jonathon nodded and held up his hands apologetically. "Yes, I did," he said. "But that was before Lucy was diagnosed with cancer."

Annie's jaw fell open. "Oh no," she muttered softly. "I'm so sorry."

He read her expression and answered the question he knew was running through her mind.

"Yes, it's bad," he said. "It's so bad that I became desperate enough to show up here so that I could retrieve the only way I knew to save her."

There was long awkward silence. Finally, she repeated her earlier question.

"So where is Silas?" There was a slight crack in her voice.

Jonathon shook his head. "He didn't make it." He paused. "And neither did my dad."

Annie's lip quivered and he saw a tear roll down her cheek. She reached up and pulled him toward her. It was at that moment he was unable to hold back his emotions any longer. He cried, and after several minutes, he felt somewhat better.

"I hate this island," Annie said after the long silence.

"Yeah, me too," Jonathon said. He looked her in the eyes again. "I've got to get out of here, and you've got to get out of here."

Annie nodded. "I can't leave—at least not yet. But, I can get you out of here."

Jonathon remembered the note that had been slid under the door. He retrieved it and showed it to Annie. "Do you have any idea who may have left this for me?"

She looked carefully at the writing. "No, I have no idea," she said. "Eric has all of these people in his back pocket; I can't imagine who would be bold enough to do something like this behind his back."

"Okay, here is what we're going to do," Jonathon said. "You're going to go tell Eric that Silas was determined to come here and get a tyrannosaur trophy and I came along in an attempt to stop him from doing it. Do not mention anything about the fountain. Agreed?"

She nodded in agreement.

"And you're not going to let me out—not yet anyway."

Annie was suddenly confused. "What? Why not? I can tell him you escaped. He'll be furious with me, but I'll smooth things out."

Jonathon took a breath and shook his head. "Annie, do you really think he hasn't thought about the possibility of me overpowering you and escaping? I'm sure he's got someone watching all of the exits. He trusts you, but he's not stupid. Letting me out right this moment would be a mistake, and besides, I need to figure out who left me this note."

CHAPTER 25

"If we're going to do this, we do it quickly and we do it early tomorrow morning," Charlie Nelson declared.

"I like the way you're thinking," Eric replied with glee. He glanced over at Hardcastle. "This one is full of spunk."

Glenn Hardcastle nodded. "That she is," he mumbled. "I'd like to see more of it."

Charlie ignored the comment. Truthfully, she'd been scared out of her mind since she'd watched two men be taken under the water by a *Titanoboa*. She already wanted to leave, but she had a job to do—an important job to do. This was not a time for her to show weakness. She'd had her moment to cry privately and then forced herself to regroup pretty quickly. She took a deep breath and continued.

"The truth of the matter is that if these prehistoric crocs are anything like the crocodiles of today, and there is nothing to suggest they're not, then these animals are mostly active during the early morning hours. What are we baiting it with?"

"Me and Dr. Cruz watched one of them chow down on an anatotitan a few days ago," Hardcastle said. "They seem to be pretty plentiful on that end of the island, and it's always been my experience you bait with whatever the animal typically feeds on."

Charlie smiled. "I agree," she replied. "But truthfully, a crocodile will pretty much eat anything you put in front of it. I just want to make sure you guys have something in mind."

"Okay, we bait it, we get it to come out of the water to feed, and once we get a clear shot, we tranq it in the fleshy part of the belly," Eric said.

"Sounds like a wonderful plan," Charlie said. "I'm just wondering why you haven't gotten it done already."

"Well, there's the matter of dragging the beast to the shoreline and then getting it on a barge," Eric explained.

Charlie crossed her arms. "I'm assuming that's why you have the large semi-truck I saw out there," she said with a raised eyebrow.

"Yes, but in case you didn't notice, we've sort of had a few setbacks during the last couple of days that has slowed progress," he said, glancing across the table to Dave.

Dave hadn't said much since he'd been brought back to camp. Eric had decided to give him some space while they finalized the plan to capture *Sarcosuchus*.

Charlie peered over a Dave and then back to Eric. "Well, you seem to have it all under control now." She quickly changed the subject back to the prehistoric croc. "Okay, so if the barge is in the water, and you drag the animal to the beach with the semi, how are you supposed to get it on the barge?"

Eric glanced over at Hardcastle for an explanation.

"We've got an industrial-strength wench mounted to one end of the barge," he explained. "We'll just pull her on board with that."

"Are you sure that the cable will be strong enough for that?" Charlie asked, clearly skeptical.

"We're using very high-grade steel cable," he replied. "I assure you we've got plenty of tensile strength to handle it."

"Alright," she said, convinced. "Okay, so you get it on the barge and...?"

"We've got a large ship with a crane," Eric said, as he rose from his chair to retrieve a cup of coffee from the corner of the conference room.

"Wait, you want to put this animal on the ship?" Charlie asked.

"Yeah, something like that," Hardcastle answered.

Charlie dropped her head back and laughed. She then leaned forward and dropped her face into her palms as if she were trying to hide her amusement.

"You can't put this animal on the ship," she finally said, deadly serious.

"And why not?" Eric asked, steaming cup of coffee in hand.

Charlie opened her mouth to speak, but Eric's coffee mug caught her attention. "Is that a *The Land Before Time* coffee cup?"

Eric smiled and took a sip. "I love that movie," he said. "I feel like I'm living it every day."

Charlie gave a slow nod and stared up at the ceiling. She was beginning to wonder how these idiots had gotten away with their illegal operation for so long.

"Okay, Littlefoot...you can't put an animal that large on the ship and risk the thing waking up. It would tear the ship apart. People would die."

"We will tranquilize it with enough juice to keep it under for the entire trip," Hardcastle said.

"Oh really?" she quipped. "And just how do you know how much to give it?"

Eric and Hardcastle looked at each other, neither saying a word.

"Just as I thought," she said. "You're guessing."

"It's an intelligent guess," Eric rebutted.

"It's still guessing," she replied. "And it's a dangerous matter to be guessing about."

Eric bit his lip as he considered what she'd said. Charlie could see the wheels in his head turning.

"Look," she said finally. "Is there some sort of reason why you're afraid to just pull the animal on the barge?"

"Yeah," Eric said. "We felt if we kept the animal close, we could monitor it, keep it sedated. If it wakes up on the barge, it's going to get loose and disappear into the ocean."

"And if it gets loose inside the ship, it'll also get free and disappear into the ocean," Charlie said. "And it'll kill everyone on its way out the door."

Eric nodded and looked over at Hardcastle. "She has a point."

"What if someone sees it?" Hardcastle asked.

"Cover it with a tarpaulin," Charlie replied. "How far are you going with it?"

Eric breathed deeply through his nose. "I can't tell you that."

"Are you taking it to the Great Valley?" She smirked at him, but he remained silent. "Come on...really?"

"Really," he replied. "Sorry, but some things you're better off not knowing."

"So who is the buyer?"

He shook his head. "Can't tell you."

There was an awkward silence. Charlie ran her fingers through her short, blonde hair. "Fine," she said finally. "But if it's going to be a long trip, you better make sure someone can get to that barge and monitor the animal's breathing every half hour."

"We can do that," he said.

"And you're not sedating the juvenile tyrannosaur, correct?"

He shook his head. "Don't see any reason to," Eric said. "We'll keep it caged."

"Very well," Charlie said. "It seems everything is settled. In the morning, let's get this done." She stood up from the table and briskly exited the room.

Eric, Dave, and Hardcastle remained, and they all looked at each other.

"I think I'm in love," Hardcastle said finally.

Dave rolled his eyes but kept his thoughts to himself.

"You're in love with every woman that comes to this island, Glenn," Eric said, annoyed. "You leave her alone; I think she's a keeper. She knows her stuff and seems to have more backbone than Cruz did."

"More backbone?" Hardcastle asked. "Didn't you see that gal crying when those two guys bought the farm in the river yesterday?"

"Give her a break," Eric replied. "I don't think she was banking on seeing people die her first day on the job. I think she rebounded nicely."

Hardcastle nodded. "Yeah, kinda like Littlefoot did after his mom died."

CHAPTER 26

Jonathon wasn't totally sure if he could trust Annie or not. Although he desperately wanted to, he knew the smart thing for him to do was wait and see who the mysterious person was that slid the note under the door. So he did the only thing he could do at the present time: He waited.

He wasn't sure how much time had passed because he'd spent at least some of the time sleeping. He wasn't sure how to feel about the fact that not one living soul had made any attempt to check on him since Annie had left. This could've been bad news. For all he knew, someone could've been listening in on their conversation and now Annie was paying for it. Or on the other hand, Annie could've done her part and told them what they wanted to hear which made him less than a threat now.

The concept of time was not totally lost on him. He knew he'd been in the room less than two days. He wasn't sure how he knew it, but it was just something in his gut—maybe his internal clock. Since there were not any windows in the room, he didn't have anything else to guide him. Perhaps his hunger, or lack of it, was another way that he knew. Since he'd eaten a bag of chips from the snack machine, he hadn't felt the ache in his stomach for more food since. With little else to keep him busy, Jonathon's thoughts again drifted to his father, Henry, and his friend, Silas. He lay on the couch in the corner of the room, he shut his eyes, and he wept quietly.

***

"So you're telling me they came all the way back over here just so Silas Treadwell could shoot a tyrannosaur he could mount on his wall?"

Annie had sat down on the couch and removed her shoes. She began massaging her feet; they ached fiercely. "Yes," she replied. "That's exactly what he said. I didn't believe it either, but he was very convincing." She leaned back on the couch and her body sank into the soft cushions. She glanced over at Eric who was seated in a chair near the coffee table, his legs crossed. The expression on his face was not a comforting one. She wasn't sure if he was buying the story or not.

"It doesn't make any sense," he said finally, rising from his seat. He strolled over toward the outside balcony and gripped the metal railing as he peered at the golden sun. It wasn't easy to see through the mist that always surrounded the island, but he could just make out a golden orb descending behind the horizon of the sea. He turned to face her. "I just remember how holier than thou he acted about this island and how we should respect it and stay away from it," he said bitterly. "For him to change his mind and return here for a reason like that..." He paused and took a breath. "...I just don't know."

Annie stood from her comfortable position and joined him on the balcony. She placed an arm around his waist. She wanted to say something, but frankly, she wasn't sure what to say.

"So do you believe him?" Eric asked suddenly.

Annie looked over at him, doing her best to look surprised that he'd even ask the question. "Of course I do," she replied quickly. "If I didn't believe him, trust me, you'd know it."

He gazed at her for a long moment, and she could tell he was really taking his time pondering what she'd told him. He finally leaned forward and kissed her on the head. "I believe you," he said. "I'm just not sure if I'm as quick to believe *him* as you are."

Annie breathed in the damp, cool breeze that rolled off the dusk sky and curved her bright red lips into her trademark beautiful smile. "Listen, when you've been chased by dinosaurs with someone, you get to know them for who they really are. If Jonathon tells me that's why they are here, then I have no reason to doubt him. I've seen him at his weakest moments and at his strongest."

Eric took a moment to enjoy the same air Annie had just breathed in. He considered lighting up a cigarette, but decided his lungs were currently enjoying the clean air too much. "Okay," he said. "But enough about him. I want you to know what's coming up tomorrow."

Annie's interest suddenly spiked. She turned to face him, her back against the railing. Eric took a moment to enjoy the view with her in the forefront. Her long, red hair blew wildly around her face. He couldn't help himself; he leaned forward to kiss her on the lips.

"What happens tomorrow?" Annie asked, trying to keep him on track.

He smiled at her. "Tomorrow, I finish up scoring the biggest pay day we've ever had. I want you to know that it'll be dangerous. Probably the most dangerous catch we've ever done."

Annie's smile straightened, and her expression turned to one of concern. "What are you going after that would be that dangerous?"

"*Sarcosuchus*," he replied.

She stared at him.

"It's a large prehistoric crocodile," he explained.

"Ah," she replied. "You know those long funny names have never made any sense to me." She wrapped her arms around his waist again and rested her head against his chest as the last few rays of daylight began to disappear. "If this dinosaur is as dangerous as you say, who in their right mind would want one?"

Eric thought about the mysterious buyer that only went by the name 'Mr. O.' "You know, I'm not sure about the guy's real name, and quite frankly, I don't care. If he wants to get a giant croc that could potentially swallow him whole, then more power to him. I'm just going to make sure I've got my money before I hand the beast over."

"So I take it you'll be out and about early in the morning?"

He nodded. "Probably before you get up for sure."

She made a mental note of it and looked up at him. "Just promise me you'll be careful."

He kissed her forehead and held her tightly. "I'm always careful," he assured her. "But it's going to be a long day. Don't wait up for me," he added.

***

Glenn Hardcastle and George Monroe looked over their vehicles and had been discussing the plan for the following day's activities. He took great care to check all points where the protective cages attached to all the vehicle frames. George took up his time checking and restocking the vehicles with ammunition for the powerful machine gun turrets mounted on the top of the jeeps. The semi was fitted with the equipment needed to drag the prehistoric croc to the beach, and crews would work to get the barge in position while they were busy catching the beast.

In order to get everything done as efficiently as possible, they were going to have to transport the juvenile tyrannosaur the next morning when they made the trek to the northern corner of the island. The trailer would be dropped near the beach, and they could take the animal to the ship once they had secured *Sarcosuchus*. They'd spent a great deal of time planning it all out, and now that Charlie Nelson had given her blessing, it was all finally going to be over. Hardcastle thought about it and could not remember a single time that a hunt and catch had ever exhausted him this much before. He'd be so relieved when it was all done and they collected the big payday. His thoughts were suddenly interrupted by echoing footsteps approaching across the hangar floor. He turned to see where George was and noticed him loading ammunition into the cab of the semi-truck.

"Hi, Glenn," a familiar male voice called about behind him.

He turned to face the man he knew he'd inevitably have to confront eventually. "Hiya, Dave," he said with a half-smile.

Dave crossed his arms and looked around to see if anyone was paying attention to them. When he was comfortable they were not, he looked back at Glenn who was now leaning against one of the armored jeeps. He noticed that he had a fairly large wrench in his hand.

"I think we need to clear the air about something," Dave said.

Hardcastle stared at him but said nothing.

"About what happened when we were hunting the young tyrannosaur the other day," Dave continued.

Hardcastle huffed. "What about it?" he asked.

Dave hardened his expression. "I think you know," he replied. "You were careless and almost got me killed." He then glanced down toward the leg he'd injured for extra emphasis.

"Dave, if I was trying to kill you, I'd have succeeded," Hardcastle said in a low voice.

Dave shook his head and smiled. "I never said you tried to kill me," he snapped. "I said you could've killed me."

Hardcastle bit his lip and looked away.

Dave continued. "I don't believe you went out there with intentions of getting me killed," he explained. "But I don't think you put much effort into keeping me safe either."

Hardcastle returned his gaze to Dave. "I led the charge to go and find you, Dave," he said. "Believe what you want to believe, but as I said, if I wanted you dead, you'd be dead."

Dave nodded. "Alright, well the point of this conversation is this: I'm keeping my mouth shut to Eric about everything."

"Well, thank God," Hardcastle said sarcastically. "I can't tell you how worried I've been that you'd tattle on me, Dave."

"And," Dave continued, "I'm going along tomorrow, and just know that if things go bad, I won't make any effort to save you."

Hardcastle laughed and turned way. "Duly noted," he said. "What makes you think I'd need your help anyway?"

"You're the dinosaur wrangler," Dave replied. "You'll be in harm's way when I will not. This animal is unlike any other we've tried to trap before. I'd be at least a little concerned if I were you."

"Well, thank God you're not me," Hardcastle quipped. "Will there be anything else you'd like to add?"

Dave stood still and thought a minute. "No, I think that's it," he said finally.

"Good," Hardcastle replied. "Then get out of my hangar," he growled, pointing toward the exit with the wrench.

Dave spun on his heel and exited the building without another word.

CHAPTER 27

Jonathon had been in another deep sleep when he felt someone aggressively shaking him.

"Wake up…wake up…" a female voice called out to him over and over again.

He'd been sleeping on the small couch in the corner of the break room. He rolled over and looked up through tired eyes to see the small blonde woman he'd seen at the river when Silas and his father were taken.

"Do I know you?" he asked groggily.

The woman looked around as if she was making sure no one was listening. She seemed very anxious. "No, but be glad you do now," she said, now tugging on his arm to get him up. "We've got to hurry before I'm spotted."

"Did you slide the note under the door?" Jonathon asked.

"Yes," she said quickly. "I'm getting you out of here." She again took a moment to look toward the door as if she was expecting someone to burst through it at any moment.

"Who are you?" he asked. He didn't know how much time they had, but he wanted a few answers before he darted out the door with a complete stranger.

She glanced at him, sensing his skepticism. "Look, we don't have time for this," she explained. "But I'll try to do this as quickly as I can."

"I'd appreciate that," Jonathon replied.

"My name is Charlotte Nelson. I'm a paleontologist, and I was just hired as a consultant for Eric Gill's little operation here on the island," she said. "I've been giving him advice on how to catch a large *Sarcosuchus* on the other end of the island. He collects these animals and sells them for a fee," she explained.

Jonathon held up a hand. "I know all about Eric's little operation," he said. "What I'd like to know is why you're helping me. If you're working for him, then how can you be on my side?"

She seemed to ignore the question. "Well, do you know who Mr. Gill is selling all of these animals to?"

Jonathon rubbed the back of his neck and stood from the couch. "Kind of," he replied. "I suspect he's selling them to a lot of wealthy and shady characters all over the globe."

Charlie nodded. "Yeah, and did you know his current customer is an international terrorist?"

Jonathon's mouth dropped open and his eyes widened. "A terrorist?" He let the words sink in a moment and slowly it began to make a lot of sense. He was fully aware of what sort of terror *Sarcosuchus* was capable of...much less a full-grown tyrannosaur. "Oh my God," he said softly. "The buyer wants to use these animals as weapons?"

Charlie nodded. "I know factually that the buyer is going to take the *Sarcosuchus* and release it in the Lake of Banyoles near Barcelona, Spain. The lake is over a mile long and about a half-mile wide. Large enough for the animal to thrive there. What's worse than that is that the lake borders the small town of Porueres. I don't think I have to explain to you why that is a terrifying thought."

Jonathon pulled his hat off his head and fanned himself with it. "Why would he do such a thing? And isn't that location somewhat random?"

Charlie licked her lips and looked around again, still visibly worried about someone discovering them. "It's not random at all," she said. "Where are the summer Olympics being held this year?"

Jonathon thought about it. "Spain," he said, thinking. "Oh my God...Barcelona, Spain!"

She nodded. "That's right, and guess where the rowing competitions will be held?"

"Oh my God," Jonathon said again in disbelief. "He'd have a spotlight in front of the entire nation. It would create massive panic."

"Yes, and that mass panic and hysteria would have a domino effect. Believe me, this would only be the beginning. Don't forget about the juvenile tyrannosaur. There is no telling what sort of plans he has in store for it too."

Jonathon stared at her in a trance for a few moments. He could feel that perspiration had formed on his forehead. He even felt a little dizzy. This had to almost be the worst-case scenario of all of the possibilities he thought were plausible. Then another thought suddenly occurred to him.

"How do you possibly know all of this?" he asked.

She sighed and again looked around. "Because the Central Intelligence Agency recruited me for this mission," she said very matter-of-factly.

Jonathon did a double take. "Wait…did you just say you're in the C.I.A.?"

She shook her head and chuckled. "No, I said the C.I.A. recruited me. I'm a paleontologist that just happened to get an unexpected visit from Eric Gill some time back. I thought the guy was nuts. A month later, a well-dressed man showed up at my office. He was handsome, and I thought maybe my luck was changing with men, but naturally, all he wanted to talk about was Eric. He wanted to know everything about what his visit was about."

"And you told him?" Jonathon asked in awe.

She looked at him like he'd grown another head. "Well, yeah," she replied. "When the C.I.A. shows up at your door, it's a little intimidating."

"So you spilled the beans and now here you are," he said, clearly still letting it all process.

"Well, actually, they told me to contact them if I ever heard from him again," she explained. "And well, I heard from him again…and next thing I know, I'm getting a good talking to about how this is my duty as an American. I'm hearing all sorts of horror stories about a specific Middle Eastern terrorist group that was interested in any sort of weapon they could get their hands on. Including dinosaurs."

Jonathon returned his hat to his head and took a deep breath. He truly felt lightheaded and the last thing he wanted to do was pass out. He walked briskly over to the sink, leaned forward, and put his mouth under the faucet. Charlie watched him drink a lot more water than she would've initially imagined. When he finally felt better, Jonathon turned around to face her again and wiped the moisture away from his mouth with his shirt sleeve.

"Well, how did they act when you told them all about the dinosaurs?" he asked.

"Oh that was the strangest thing of all," she said. "They barely acknowledged it. It was almost like they already knew about it. They seemed to be more concerned with the potential consequences of the animals reaching the mainland."

Jonathon pondered her statement; he clearly had more questions. Charlie decided her time was up.

"Okay, that's all I can tell you now," she said. "We've got to go immediately."

"Go where?"

"I've got to go with them to catch the *Sarcosuchus*. What I need—excuse me, what I'd like for you to do is to go down to the beach while everyone is gone and call for help," she said.

"I don't understand; why can't you just call for help right here?"

She held up her wrist and showed him what appeared to be a normal wristwatch. She pushed a small button on the side, and the face of the watch flipped up to reveal what looked like a tiny phone or radio of some sort. He grabbed her arm and looked at the watch up close.

"You're just a regular James Bond," he said in amazement.

"I know, right?" She pulled her arm back and closed the face. "I'd love to be able to call them right here, but it's not going to work. This mist screws up the signal. They told me this was a possibility and if it happened to get to the clearest area I could find and walk around until I found a signal. I've got to find somewhere with few trees and as much open space as possible. The only area I can think of that would be remotely safe would be the beach."

She began to unstrap the watch and hand it to him. "Here, take this and call them. You don't have to say anything. You need only to press the orange button three times. That part is important...don't screw it up!"

"Three times?" he said, wondering about the odd number to himself.

"I don't make the rules, but if you screw it up and punch the orange button anything other than three times, you're going to really make things difficult for us. So please be careful with that part." She handed the watch out to him.

Jonathon held up a hand and refused it. "I can't," he said. "There is something else I've got to take care of first."

She looked at him, confused. "What are you talking about? I watched your friends die. I don't think there is anything good planned for you here. You need to leave."

He shook his head. "I'm sorry, it's important."

She cocked her head slightly to the side and squinted at him. She was clearly bewildered by his decision. "You're telling me you're just going to sit back and let them take a tyrannosaur and prehistoric super croc to the mainland? You've got an opportunity here to stop something catastrophic from happening and you're not going to take it?"

Jonathon crossed his arms and shook his head. He smiled. "I never said I was going to sit back and do nothing," he said. "I'm telling you I've got something else I need to do. But before I do it, I'm going to stop this from happening."

"So call the C.I.A.," she pleaded.

"I can't call the C.I.A. until I've completed what I need to do," he said. "I've got one chance at it and I'm not going to blow it."

"Well, what is it exactly that you just have to do?" she asked.

Jonathon stared into her blue eyes for a long moment. He wanted to tell her because she'd already shared so much with him. But truthfully, he didn't think she was ready to hear about the fountain of youth. The only reason she'd accepted the dinosaurs so easily was probably because the C.I.A. had her doing a mission for them. She was laser focused on her objective, he could certainly see that.

"I promise I'll tell you what I had to do once it's done, but until then, I need you to hold off calling the C.I.A."

Charlie opened her mouth to argue further but quickly decided it was a futile effort. She refastened the wristwatch and turned to head out the door. Jonathon quickly followed.

As they snuck down the hallway, Jonathon could see from a doorway at the end of the hallway that it was still dark outside.

"What time is it exactly?" he asked.

"You mean after I repeatedly waved my watch around in your face, you never took a moment to check the time?" she asked, and she looked at the timepiece, herself obviously unsure of the time. "It's a quarter till five," she whispered. "I've got to be in the hangar at 7:00 a.m. to ride out with these lunatics."

They eventually slipped out of the doorway at the end of the corridor and into the outdoors. Jonathon motioned for her to stay within the darkness as much as possible. Although he was completely unsure of where she was going, he followed her. She suddenly stopped and crouched down. He copied her movement and crouched down near her side. It was only then that he saw the reason for her abrupt halt. He could see the silhouette of someone walking in their direction and away from the pyramid-shaped structure near the back of the compound. The two of them held their breaths and hoped that they had not been spotted. Jonathon squinted and strained his eyes in a desperate attempt to make out who the person was, but the darkness was too much.

"Do they see us?" Charlie whispered.

Jonathon continued to stare at the mystery person and his heart stopped when he realized that the individual had stopped walking and appeared to be looking at them!

"Crap," he muttered. "Yeah, they see us."

Charlie cursed under her breath. "Well, what do we do now?" she asked.

"Nothing, hold tight," he replied still keeping his undivided attention on the person that seemed to be staring right back at him.

It was then that the strange silhouette began moving straight toward them with cautious steps. Jonathon kept waiting for whoever the person was to call out to them, but it didn't happen. He was just about to suggest that they take off running when the person finally stepped into the light.

"I know her," he said, standing up.

Charlie, still unsure about the situation, remained where she was.

"Annie?" Jonathon called out cautiously.

"Jonathon?" she replied. "What are you doing there? Who is that with you?" she asked as she briskly moved to where they were.

"Is anyone coming behind you?" he asked, ignoring her questions.

"No," she said assuringly. "It's just me. Do you still not trust me?"

"I'm getting there," he answered. He then reached down and helped Charlie to her feet. "It's okay, we don't have to worry about her."

When Annie realized it was a pretty blonde woman crouched down in the shadows with him, she flashed a mischievous grin.

"My, my, Jonathon," she said, almost purring. "I was never able to get you down in the dark with me," she said.

He thought back to a brief moment many years before when Annie had drunkenly come on to him while they were on Angus Wedgeworth's ship on their way to the island. He'd rejected her then, and she'd apparently never forgotten it.

"It wasn't like that," Charlie snapped, obviously completely oblivious to their past history.

"Sweetie, I'm kidding," Annie replied. She held out her hand and introduced herself.

"I'm Charlotte Nelson," she replied. "But call me Charlie."

Jonathon looked at her. "Why can't I call you Charlie?"

She smiled at him. "Sorry, it's been all business with you since we met."

Annie chimed in. "I've heard your name. You're the new paleontologist."

Charlie nodded. "That's right, what do you do here?"

Annie looked at Jonathon, unsure if she should say. Jonathon shrugged.

"You might as well tell her," he said. "She's going to find out one way or the other."

"I'm kind of Eric's girlfriend," Annie said sheepishly.

Charlie instantly shot Jonathon a distasteful look. "Are you kidding me? Why are you involving her?"

Jonathon grabbed her by the shoulders. "Relax," he said calmly. "We've got history."

"Yeah, she was just referring to your uh…history," Charlie replied, looking past him and to her. "That's not helping."

Jonathon looked at Annie and then back to Charlie. "No, there was no romantic relationship between us…ever," he explained.

Annie nodded. "It's true. He rejected me."

Jonathon rolled his eyes. "Look, she found us. So now she is involved whether you want her to be or not."

"And just how do we know she won't run and tell her boyfriend that you and I are sneaking around out here?" Charlie asked.

"Because," Annie interrupted, "any relationship I have with Eric right now is nothing more than a smoke screen to get more information. Jonathon told me a few things yesterday that have opened my eyes up about Eric. I don't think he's all bad, but he certainly hasn't been honest with me. When I get off this island, he and I are through. That is a promise."

Maybe it was female intuition. Or maybe it was something else. Whatever 'it' was made no difference to Jonathon. He could see that Charlie still didn't trust Annie, but she seemed to be biting her tongue and ready to press on.

"So where were you two sneaking off to in the early morning hours?" Annie asked.

Charlie pushed some wild strands of hair out of her face. "I was taking him to the hangar. I was hoping I could find somewhere to hide him so we can sabotage your boyfriend's efforts to catch a *Sarcosuchus* here in a few hours."

Jonathon looked at her, surprised. "And just when were you going to let me in on this plan?" he asked.

She glared at him, and for the first time, he saw a flash of annoyance. "About the time you completely screwed up my original plan," she said, holding up her wrist so he could get a good look at her C.I.A. watch. "You're the one that is adamant that you've got other business to attend to and you'll handle the situation with the *Sarcosuchus* and juvenile tyrannosaur. You've forced me to come up with a plan on the fly, so cut me some slack."

Jonathon smiled at her. He would've laughed, but he was afraid her annoyance would evolve into full-blown rage.

"This spy stuff is a tough gig, isn't it?" he asked.

Annie looked at both of them, confused. "Did I miss something?"

Jonathon shook his head. "No time…I'll explain later. Let's get to the hangar. We have very little time to come up with a plan."

CHAPTER 28

The trio snuck into the hangar, and Jonathon got his first moment to really survey the surroundings. The ceiling was illuminated with fluorescent lighting and the concrete floor was almost spotless. Jonathon hated to admit it, but he was actually somewhat impressed with everything Eric Gill had managed to put together over the last seven years. He noticed there were four armored jeeps in the building, one of which had a significant amount of damage.

"I don't even know if I want to know what happened to that one," Annie said, pointing toward the mangled vehicle.

"*Tyrannosaurus rex* got a hold of it," Jonathon muttered, still staring at the damage.

"How do you know that?" Charlie asked. She strolled over to the jeep.

"Because I saw it happen," he replied.

Annie wanted to ask more questions but decided she really didn't want to know.

Charlie also remained silent and unwilling to press him for more information.

Jonathon looked around the room again and noticed an unattached trailer parked near the corner of the room. He walked over to it and peered at the sleeping animal inside.

"This is why the tyrannosaur mangled that jeep," he muttered softly. "These morons stole their baby."

"It's not going to matter much longer," Charlie said, pulling his arm to guide him away from the trailer. "We'll set it free tomorrow. Our top priority right now should be figuring out how to keep them from capturing a *Sarcosuchus*."

Jonathon nodded. He briefly removed the hat from his head and wiped the sweat from his brow. It was a smothering hot and humid night. "Right," he said, returning the hat to his head. "We could sabotage the vehicles," he added, looking around at the fleet again.

Charlie shrugged, showing her displeasure. "You know as well as I do all that would do is prolong the inevitable. They'll get these vehicles going again as soon as possible and continue on with their plans."

"Okay," Jonathon said. He paused, waiting for her to elaborate.

She sensed it and continued. "I think the best thing to do here is let them think they've completed their mission and then sabotage it."

Jonathon crossed his arms, intrigued. "I'm listening," he said.

"Their plan is to tranquilize the animal and then tow it on a barge," Charlie explained. "I think you need to be on that barge."

Jonathon shook his head. "I told you I've got something here I need to do first," he said.

Charlie sighed and it was clear she was annoyed. "Jonathon, there is no time. This all goes down tomorrow. You help me with this, and I promise I'll help you with whatever it is that you've got to do."

Jonathon breathed deeply through his nose. He was tired of having this conversation.

"No," he argued. "You're not risking your life for me."

Charlie opened her mouth to speak, but Jonathon snapped at her before she could.

"No," he spat. "We're not discussing this further. I'll help you tomorrow with this, but if I'm going after the croc, I'm going to need some help with the juvenile tyrannosaur."

"I'm already ahead of you," she replied, glancing back toward the caged trailer. "Leave the tyrannosaur to me."

Annie stepped forward. They'd almost forgotten she was there. "And what about me?" she asked.

Jonathon stared at her, confused. "What about you?"

"Well, what do I do?"

Jonathon smirked at her. "You go back to your boyfriend and act like nothing is wrong."

Annie crossed her arms, obviously not happy with his response. "That's it?" she asked.

"Actually," Charlie interrupted. "There is one thing you can do."

Annie perked up. "What?"

"You can lock Jonathon back up in the breakroom," she replied.

"Excuse me?" Jonathon muttered.

"I don't understand," Annie said. "Why would we want to do that?"

Charlie yawned and rubbed her eyes. "Because right now, he has nowhere else to hide," she said tiredly. "We lock him back up until everyone leaves…then you come down and let him out."

Jonathon considered it for a long moment. "I don't know," he grumbled.

Charlie looked at him and stepped forward. "You're the one that said we can trust her," she said, gesturing toward Annie. "If we're going to let them think they've succeeded before we sabotage their mission, then they can't be worried about any kind of threat. If they discover that you're gone in the morning, you can rest assured they'll be constantly looking over their shoulders for you."

"I can do it," Annie added. "She's right, Jonathon. I let you out after they're gone, and then you chase them down with whatever vehicle is left here."

Jonathon took a deep breath and released it slowly. He knew both women were right. Unfortunately, he couldn't shake the sensation that he was losing control of the situation. It was a feeling he didn't like.

"Alright," he agreed finally. "If this is the plan, let's get going. There isn't much time left."

Charlie reached into her pocket and retrieved the key she'd acquired and had subsequently used to release him. She glanced at Annie and rather reluctantly handed it over to her.

"We can trust you to release Jonathon after me and the others are gone...right?" she asked. Her words came out more as a plea than a question.

Annie sighed as if she were growing tired of trying to convince Charlie of her trustworthiness. "Yes," she replied sternly. She took the key and shoved it into her own pocket. "You can trust me with this."

Suddenly, the trio heard loud footsteps approaching the entrance.

"Someone is coming," Jonathon whispered, doing his best to not sound panicked.

"Who would that be?" Charlie asked, directing the question to Annie.

Annie scowled at her, disgusted with the suggestion that she had something to do with it. "I have no idea...and I'm getting a little tired of feeling like an outsider here."

"Ladies, we don't have time for this!" Jonathon snapped as the footsteps drew closer. "Does anyone know of another way out of here?"

Both women shook their heads and turned toward the back of the hangar.

"There has to be a back door or something," Charlie said, and she began to sprint away.

Jonathon and Annie followed her just as the door opened behind them. The three of them hid behind the mangled jeep in the rear corner of the building. Fluorescent lights began to come alive above their heads, and now Jonathon could feel his pulse quicken. He got down low, almost on his belly, and peered underneath the jeep to see if he could get a look at who the visitor was. The boots looked familiar; he thought it was George. Just then, he felt a tug on his shirt sleeve. It was Annie. She was pointing toward Charlie, and Jonathon noticed she had indeed found a back door. The only problem was that the door was in the center of the back wall and there was nothing hiding it.

Jonathon looked for George again and found him shuffling around through some boxes near the front door of the hangar. If they were quick, it was possible they could make it; but he felt that the risk was just too great.

Charlie motioned at him, trying desperately to get his attention. She glanced to the door and her demeanor seemed to suggest to him that she was going to make a run for it. He quickly shook his head to make it clear to her that she should wait. In response, she just smiled at him and began removing her shoes, another clear indicator she was going to try it despite him. Annie just glanced at her and then back to him, visibly confused on what to do. He could see the terror in her eyes and he wondered how Eric would react if he found out she'd been conspiring with them. He knew he had to think fast, otherwise Charlie was about to make a huge mistake that could potentially foil their entire mission. It was at that moment that an idea came to him.

Charlie was beginning to crawl toward the rear of the mangled jeep when Jonathon grabbed her by the ankle and dragged her back. She scowled at him, and for a moment, he wondered if she would spit venom. He waved her off and pointed toward the trailer attached to the other jeep near them. She glanced at the trailer and then back to him. He could tell she immediately picked up on his idea, and after mulling it over for a short moment, she nodded in agreement.

Jonathon scanned the environment again for George's whereabouts. He was now filling a large can with fuel, still completely oblivious to their presence. Jonathon belly crawled to the trailer and peered up at the large black eyes looking back at him. He wasn't real sure how aggressive a juvenile tyrannosaur would be, but judging by the animal's size, and more importantly, the size of its teeth, he didn't feel that anyone's life would be in any significant danger. He carefully and quietly removed the pin that held the door shut. He then slowly opened the door widely so it would be very obvious to the animal that freedom was in front of it. The baby tyrannosaur cocked its head to the side and took a cautious step forward. It looked at the opened door, and then it peered at Jonathon, Annie, and Charlie. Jonathon resisted the urge to call the animal much in the same way he'd always called his dog Rex when he wanted him. All they could do was wait for the animal to make its way out of the cage and prey that it got far away from them before George noticed. After what seemed like an eternity, the dinosaur finally crept timidly out of the cage and onto the smooth concrete floor. It sniffed at Jonathon, and for a brief moment, he thought the animal was going to bite off his nose.

However, somehow, he remained as still as a statue, and before long, the animal had calmly strolled out into the middle of the hangar. It sniffed and pawed at everything in its immediate vicinity, investigating everything and leaving nothing to chance.

Jonathon motioned for Annie and Charlie to get ready. The two of them crawled to the rear of the mangled vehicle and crouched down, ready to sprint toward the door the moment George's attention was captured.

George had just finished pouring fuel into the first jeep when he heard the strange pitter-patter sound the juvenile tyrannosaur's feet made as it searched for a way out. He calmly put the can down and walked around the front of the large semi-truck that was parked in the center of the hangar. It was then that he caught a glimpse of the young tyrannosaur's tail as it disappeared behind a large crate on the opposite side of the hangar from Jonathon.

"Hey, stop!" he cried out instinctively. He chased after the animal and, with his back completely to them, Jonathon motioned for the women to go. They did so, and in what appeared to be one choreographed motion, the three of them opened and slipped through the back door all at once. Jonathon carefully shut the door behind them.

Once outside, they all breathed a sigh of relief. Charlie smiled widely. She'd enjoyed it, and it made Annie want to smack her.

"Okay, no more talk," Jonathon said. "We all know what to do, now let's execute the plan!"

Charlie nodded and said, "See you tomorrow." With that, she vanished in the shadows.

Jonathon motioned for Annie to follow him, and the two of them began the short trek back toward his makeshift prison. He moved quickly and Annie was on his heels. She kept up and kept quiet for the duration of the short walk back. When they finally arrived, Jonathon began to pull the door shut. Just before he closed it completely, he glanced up and met Annie's eyes.

She shook her head. "Not you too," she whispered.

Jonathon smiled. "I trust you," he said. "See you in a couple of hours."

He shut the door the rest of the way and heard Annie promptly lock it. Once he came to the total realization that he was completely alone yet again, he decided to lie on the couch and get a power nap. After all, he was pretty certain he'd need it. Once he'd settled down for the nap, he closed his eyes and, to his surprise, falling asleep suddenly became easy again.

CHAPTER 29

Charlie arrived in the hangar at seven o'clock, right on time. She was not surprised at all to discover she was the second person there. George was there, still readying the vehicles and equipment. She glanced toward the cage near the back of the hangar and could see that he'd managed to catch the juvenile tyrannosaur and return it to the trailer.

"Good morning, sir," she muttered, trying to be polite.

George looked at her and grumbled some sort of incoherent response, but he at least seemed friendly.

"How many vehicles will we be taking?" Charlie asked.

George had an arm full of ammunition, and he was neatly stacking it beneath the large gun on the back of one of the jeeps. He paused a minute and wiped a bit of sweat from his brow with a bandanna he retrieved from his back pocket. She knew he'd been busy for a couple of hours now.

"We will be taking every vehicle available, except for the wrecked jeep over there," he said, pointing.

It was at this point that she noticed one of the jeeps was missing. She wanted to ask where the other vehicle was but knew if she did, it may give her away.

"Will you be driving one of them?" she asked, trying to warm up to him. He nodded in response.

"Well, would you mind if I travel along with you?" she asked.

This time, George shook his head. "No," he muttered. "I'll be driving the semi. I'll have to pull the croc to the beach. It's too dangerous."

Charlie nodded. "I see," she said. "Well, which vehicle do you think will be the safest?"

George checked the sight on the large mounted machine gun and then gave Charlie a look. "Probably the jeep pulling that baby dinosaur," he said, pointing toward the juvenile tyrannosaur. "Job number one for whoever is pulling it is to get it to the beach and in the hands of our shipping team."

Charlie nodded and did her best not to smile. "Well, I think maybe that's the ride I'll shoot for then."

A rumbling sound approached from somewhere outside the hangar, and moments later, the missing jeep rolled in. There was a trailer attached to the back with another cage and a large dinosaur was inside. Charlie got closer for a better look. The dinosaur appeared to be a not yet fully-grown *Corythosaurus*. *Corythosaurus* was a duck-billed dinosaur with a helmet-shaped crest that adorned the top of its skull like the brush on top of an ancient Roman soldier's helmet. The animal was a forest green color, with dark speckles of black splattered across its back. A fully-grown *Corythosaurus* could reach a length of thirty feet, which would be far too large to fit into the cage. This one would have had to be pretty young. The dinosaur was clearly distressed, making a pitiful sound that sounded eerily like a trombone. The sound originated from the crest atop its skull.

"I'm assuming you know what this is, Doc?" Glenn Hardcastle said as he exited the vehicle and stared at the panicked animal with indifference.

"Yes," she replied, turning her attention to him. "It's a *Corythosaurus*. It appears to be quite young."

Hardcastle shook his head. "Nope," he replied. "That there is bait!" He laughed, seemingly very amused at his own joke.

Charlie did not laugh; she only stared at him.

"Why would you use this particular animal to bait *Sarcosuchus*?" she asked.

"Because this particular animal is semi-aquatic," he began, then paused to see how she would react. She stared at the animal and took a deep breath as she considered what he'd said. "I bet you didn't know they spent a lot of time in water, did you?" he asked.

Charlie shrugged. "Well, there has been some speculation about that, but I personally never believed that they did. That is quite interesting though." She paused and forced a smile. "It's why I signed up for this job."

Hardcastle nodded. "Well, since the super-croc spends so much time in the water, we hope that maybe this one will take off into the drink when we release it. Obviously, it won't take long for the croc to show itself if that happens."

"And then you spring into action?" she asked, trying to sound like an ignorant woman (she could tell Hardcastle loved that).

"That's right," he added, and he then reached in the jeep and pulled out a very large rifle. "I figure two darts from this baby will put that croc to sleep pretty quickly."

"I bet," she replied. "Just be careful that it doesn't drown."

Another man approached from behind her and said, "Trust me; we won't go to this much trouble to let the animal drown." It was Eric Gill. He approached the trailer and gazed upon the *Corythosaurus*. "Nice job, Glenn," he added. "This one should serve the purpose nicely. Don't you agree, Doctor Nelson?"

Charlie nodded. "I think it will do just fine," she agreed.

"Very well, I think we're just about ready then?" he said, peering back toward George in the hangar. George gave him a thumbs up, and a few other men that Charlie had never seen before headed toward the vehicles and took their places on the guns. George made his way to the semi and Eric sat down behind the wheel of one of the jeeps.

Charlie watched all of the men scrambling to their positions and, although she knew where she wanted to go, she figured she'd ask Eric.

"Why don't you take a seat with Dave and help with the handoff of the tyrannosaur?" he said to her. "He could probably use your expertise in case the animal does something unexpected."

Charlie nodded and did her best to refrain from smiling. "Sounds good…I just want to help," she said modestly.

"Besides," Eric added as he started the engine of his jeep, "you'll be much safer handling that part of the mission. If we need you, I'll come for you."

With that, he gunned the throttle and began the convoy toward the other end of the island.

***

Jonathon spent every minute of time since he had parted ways with Annie pacing back and forth across the break room floor. His heart leapt when he heard the key hit the lock and he was tugging on the door the second Annie had it unlocked. This surprised her and Jonathon quickly grabbed her and pulled her into the room.

"Quickly," he said, "Tell me what is going on."

"I don't know anything," she replied. "All I know is that Eric left about 20 minutes ago headed for the hangar."

"Alright, that means it's all about to start. Annie, I need you to go back to Eric's room and wait for all of this to be over. It really shouldn't take long, but in case things go sour, you need to be within the safety of this compound."

Annie gave no argument. "Jonathon, be careful. Eric is a determined guy, but I know deep down he's a good guy. Please don't hurt him," she said.

He gave her an odd look and a slow nod before heading out the door without another word.

***

Jonathon reached the hangar just in time to see the semi pulling away with George at the wheel. The jeeps were kicking up dust in front of him, and he could clearly see one of them was still towing the juvenile tyrannosaur.

I guess George managed to catch it, he thought to himself.

He peered in all directions and carefully made his way into the deserted hangar. He immediately made his way to the battered jeep and prayed that it would start. The key was already in the ignition, and as luck would have it, the first turn of it was enough to bring the vehicle to life. Black smoke billowed from the tailpipe and the engine sounded awfully sick, but all he needed was for it to get him close to where the action would be taking place.

Jonathon put the vehicle in drive and took off in pursuit. He stayed far enough back to remain unnoticed, and the fresh cloud of dust in the air gave him an idea of how far behind he was. He continued following the convoy until he met a fork in the road. This concerned him because he could see dust settling down both roads. He knew that he needed to follow whichever vehicle was headed to the beach.

Quickly, he hopped out of the jeep and looked around in both directions to make sure no one had spotted him. Satisfied his presence had not been detected, he examined the tire tracks leading away in both directions. After a moment, he decided that the deeper and wider depressions that veered off down the road to the right must have belonged to the large semi-truck. The semi would not be heading toward the shoreline yet; it was going after the super croc.

Jonathon jumped back in the battered vehicle that was currently barely sputtering enough to idle. He reached over to the glove box and opened it. Too his surprise and delight, there was a 9mm handgun inside. He snatched the weapon out, released the magazine, and was further surprised to find that it was loaded. After laying the weapon down on the passenger seat, he again took off to continue the pursuit.

The steering wheel pulled badly to the left and shook to the point that Jonathon felt his teeth would rattle loose. He wanted to ponder exactly what he was going to do when he caught up with the jeep towing the juvenile tyrannosaur, but the relentless shaking was making his head hurt. He believed thinking and planning was just going to make it worse.

After what he estimated to be another three miles of driving, Jonathon rounded a sharp curve and spotted the sandy beach of the ocean. The gray mist that surrounded the island was still prominent, and for a split second, it surprised him. With everything that had been going on, it was easy to forget about the supernatural aspects of the island.

As Jonathon peered out over the ocean, in the distance, he could see the end of a large rectangular object sticking through gray mist. It was dark in color, and after straining his eyes, he decided it must've been a dark shade of red. Suddenly, it occurred to him that the object was a large barge floating in the deeper waters off of the beach.

That's the ride for the Sarcosuchus, he thought.

He then noticed a large spool of cable mounted on the end of the barge.

Probably a wench of some sort to reel the large beast onto the barge...

When Jonathon returned his attention to the road, he could see the jeep and trailer pulling off the road and onto the beach straight in the direction of the barge. It was then that he noticed a smaller boat onto the beach and three men standing in front of it. So far, he knew he was outnumbered at least five to one. He suddenly jammed on the brakes and brought the jeep to a sliding stop in the dirt.

This is going to be tough, he thought.

If he didn't do something quick, the men were going to load the cage holding the juvenile tyrannosaur onto the boat. Jonathon suspected there was a much larger vessel beyond the mist that was going to tow the barge and also transport the tyrannosaur. If the tyrannosaur made it to the large vessel, he knew stopping the entire ordeal would become significantly harder. As far as he could tell, under the circumstances he had but one option. He slid the lever into drive but held his foot on the brake for a few more moments.

He thought of Lucy and his mother. Lucy was the entire reason he even came to the island. He'd come to find a solution—the only miracle he knew of in the entire world that would save her life. Jonathon wondered if he'd have even come to the island if he'd known how deep he would've gotten into this crusade he now found himself in. A crusade to keep the dinosaurs exactly where they belonged: on the wretched island that they'd lived for thousands of years. If he got himself killed all in the name of this crusade, everything he came to the island for in the first place would be lost. Would that mean his death would be in vain? It was hard to see it that way if it kept the rest of the world safe from rampaging super crocodiles and terrifying tyrannosaurs. But still, hope of his wife beating her illness would become slim to none. And worse yet, would she even find out what happened to him? Who would tell her? She'd just lie in bed waiting...waiting for a husband that promised her he'd return. And what about his mother? She'd never learn of what happened to her husband. Jonathon felt responsible for his father tagging along and the weight of his death was heavy on his heart. It would be a very cruel and unfair twist for his mother to never know the truth of the terrible fate of her husband, and obviously, it would be even worse if she lost a son too.

Jonathon chewed his lip another minute while he pondered the situation. There was still a chance—although a slim one—that he'd manage to stop the atrocities occurring on the island *and* manage to escape back to his home with his wife's miracle water in his possession.

What the hell, he thought. He'd cheated death on more than one occasion. He thought back to his last visit to the island. He remembered the large tyrannosaur that literally chased him over the edge of a cliff. Then he thought of the monstrous pterosaurs that he'd narrowly escaped from off of Angus Wedgeworth's ship. Was that luck? Or did that mean there was still purpose in his life?

Of course that's what it meant, he finally convinced himself. *I've cheated death before, and it could've been for this very moment. This is the moment that could save lives on the mainland.*

With that final thought in mind, Jonathon released the brake and accelerated toward the boat on the shoreline.

CHAPTER 30

So far, Eric Gill was very satisfied with how things were going. All of the vehicles had managed to form a sort of half-moon shape around the shoreline of the swamp. The jeep with the trailer containing the *Corythosaurus* had backed up in the center with Hardcastle perched on top of the cage, awaiting the signal to pull the gate upward.

Once the young *Corythosaurus* was released, Eric's hope was that the strategic positions of all the park vehicles would be enough to force the animal into the water. Even if the *Sarcosuchus* was unable to catch the bait, it would at least lure one of the beasts to the surface and close enough for Hardcastle to get a clear shot at it.

"I'm waiting," Glenn Hardcastle said impatiently. He directed the statement to George who was holding binoculars to his face, scanning the waters for movement.

"See anything?" Eric asked as he stepped beside George.

He pulled the binoculars down from his face and shook his head. "Nothing," he said with a tinge of his own impatience rolling off the words.

Eric looked back and up to Hardcastle. "How hard was it for you to catch that thing?" he asked, glancing toward the *Corythosaurus*.

Hardcastle glared down at him taking his meaning. "It took some time," he replied sharply. "If we let this thing go and there are no crocs around to hear it, it's gonna take me a little time to hunt down another one."

Eric gritted his teeth a moment and then spat on the ground. He reached into his shirt pocket and retrieved the pack of Jupiter cigarettes. He lit one, took a puff, then said, "So really all we need is something in the water splashing and making noise?"

Hardcastle's eyes narrowed. "Yeah, pretty much," he replied.

"So I've been wondering what we're going to do with Jonathon," Eric said, staring at the water.

George abruptly looked up at Hardcastle, unable to hide his shock. Glenn shrugged in response and said, "If you throw a man in there, he'll probably make more noise than this *Corythosaurus*."

"What if we tied a rope to him? Do you think we'd be able to snatch him out of there before the croc could get his jaws on him?" Eric asked, still staring into the murky water.

Hardcastle thought a moment. "Maybe," he said finally. "But I'm sort of thinking it won't break your heart too much if we can't get him out."

Eric gave a slight nod in reply, and George thought he noticed the faintest hint of a smile as well. "Release the dinosaur," Eric said. "We'll take our chances."

Without hesitation, Hardcastle pulled the rope attached to the gate upward. The *Corythosaurus* slowly moved toward what it perceived to be its freedom, but there was obvious skepticism in the animal's movements. It seemed to sense something was off.

"Come on, you idiot! Let's go," Hardcastle grunted, and he began to stomp the top of the cage with his heavy boots.

The loud noises above its head frightened the animal, and suddenly it darted out of the cage. Just as Eric had hoped, the animal leapt into the water and frantically tried to distance itself from its strange captors. The men watched as the *Corythosaurus* swam further and further into the swamp. Finally, it approached a large crop of cypress, and soon after, they lost it behind the trunks of the trees.

"Well, that's that," Hardcastle said, sounding defeated. He jumped from the top of the cage, the rifle loaded with tranquilizers in his hands. "I think it might be time for Plan B, boss."

George dropped his head, clearly concerned and not fully on board with Plan B, but he said nothing. Eric noticed his demeanor but did not acknowledge it.

"Looks like we don't have a choice," he said, and it sounded as if he were trying to justify it for George.

"No sense in all of us going after him," Hardcastle said as he approached the jeep with the cage attached. "I'll go get him and be back here in a jiffy."

"Okay, but if you bring him back here unconscious, it's not going to do us any—"

Suddenly, there was a loud shriek of terror from somewhere beyond the crop of cypress trees. Hardcastle ran back to the edge of the swampy water and readied the rifle.

"What was that?" Eric asked.

"There—look!" George shouted, and he pointed toward the *Corythosaurus* swimming frantically back in their direction. The animal was wailing and sounded strangely like a baby crying. The sound was unsettling and gave all of the men goose flesh.

Roughly ten to twenty yards behind the *Corythosaurus's* wake, what appeared to be a massive stone with two very large eyes protruding from it quickly closed the gap behind the animal. Of course all of the men knew it wasn't a stone; it was the large head of the beast that they'd come for.

"What are you waiting for?" Eric asked, his voice shaking a bit. "Take the shot!"

Hardcastle had the stock of the rifle against his shoulder, but he wasn't firing the weapon. "I can't take the shot just yet," he said calmly, just above a whisper. "All I can see is the thing's head; I need to see the rest of the body."

Eric looked back to the prehistoric crocodile and then back to his employee holding the rifle. "You can't see the body because it's under the water," he snapped back. "The only way you're going to see the body is if the animal gets out of the water!"

"That's right," Hardcastle whispered, and he began to slowly walk backward.

Suddenly, a horrifying realization overcame Eric. The *Corythosaurus* was headed straight toward them, and it looked as if the *Sarcosuchus* would be unable to catch it before it reached land.

"George," Eric said as he began to back way. "Get to the semi and ready the wench. We're not in a safe spot right here." He turned to see if George had heard him and was surprised to see that his other employee had disappeared. "George? George, where are you?" Eric shouted. With George nowhere to be found, he began to run. He ran to the nearest jeep and closed the cage over him. He didn't have a lot of confidence in the strength of the roll cage against the power of the monster he saw swimming in their direction. It was then that he remembered the handgun in the glovebox. Deep down, he knew a weapon like that was useless, but something about holding it in his hands comforted him slightly. It was at that moment that he heard the scream. The next thing he knew, he felt the jeep being tossed into the air with him still inside it.

***

Jonathon had a tight grip on the steering wheel and he sawed it back in forth, desperately trying to keep the fishtailing vehicle under control. The damaged jeep no longer had the luxury of four-wheel drive, so the loose sand on the beach made it very difficult to keep the vehicle pointed in the right direction.

The right direction just happened to be the large wooden boat that was undoubtedly a transport vehicle for the juvenile tyrannosaur. Jonathon's current mission was quite simple: destroy the boat at all costs. The men did not immediately seem concerned when they noticed the approaching vehicle. After all, he was piloting a Gill Enterprises jeep, and there would be no reason to assume that anyone besides a Gill Enterprises employee would be driving it.

It wasn't until Jonathon saw Dave step out of the driver side of the parked jeep that the chaos began. He assumed that Dave recognized him and immediately alerted the other men. Before Jonathon even had an opportunity to react, one of the men, a tall and slender man with what appeared to be a cowboy hat, pulled a handgun from his waist and began to open fire. Jonathon figured he had at least another thirty yards to go before he reached the boat. All he could do was lean over for cover and keep his foot planted firmly on the accelerator.

It wasn't easy for him to keep the vehicle straight in his current position, but moments later, Jonathon knew he'd reached his target as he felt a sudden jolt and noticed an explosion of splintered wood sailing over the top of him. Unfortunately, there wasn't a good way to destroy the boat without also driving the jeep into the water. *If* the four-wheel drive had been operational, there *may* have been an opportunity to get the vehicle back to dry land. The water came into the floor of the vehicle quickly, and Jonathon's boots were covered before he'd even realized what was happening. He attempted to steer the vehicle back to the shore, but quickly realized it was a futile action.

"Jonathon, get out of the jeep!" a man yelled. It was Dave.

Jonathon stayed slumped over onto the passenger seat as the vehicle came to a final halt. He hadn't forgotten about the man that had shot at him. "You know, I'm not so sure I want to get out with a guy shooting at me!" he shouted back.

There was a long pause.

"No one is going to shoot at you," Dave replied in a calmer voice.

Jonathon kept still. He didn't trust him.

"Come on out, you've got my word," Dave said.

Jonathon held his ground and frantically searched his mind for some sort of solution to his predicament. He noticed the gun he'd placed on the passenger seat lying on the floor, submerged in water. He grabbed it and began to consider his chances with the weapon.

Was it really a good idea to roll out of the jeep, gun blazing? He didn't think so. After all, he'd just made a very rash decision that had put him in the current jam he now found himself in. Still, what choice did he currently have? Jonathon didn't feel like he had a choice when he made the decision to crash into the boat, and now he had that same feeling again.

"Jonathon, it's okay, come out. He's telling the truth." It was a different voice this time. A female's voice. Charlie.

With the gun still tightly in his grasp, Jonathon slowly crept out of the driver's side of the jeep. Fortunately, the vehicle came to rest with that particular side facing away from the shore. There were waves rolling in that quickly had him soaking wet up to his stomach. Jonathon kept low and made his way to the front of the jeep in an attempt to get a look at Dave and the other men before he came out fully into the open. It didn't take long for him to discover he had nothing to fear.

The first thing he noticed was the man that had shot at him. He was no longer wearing the cowboy hat and there was no gun in his hand either. He was lying on the beach, and Jonathon could only guess he'd been struck by the jeep. The other two men were on the ground tending to him—he seemed to be unconscious. Dave stood in front of them with his arms raised. Charlie was standing behind the turret machine gun mounted on the rear portion of the jeep. She had the weapon pointed toward Dave, but kept her eyes focused on the other men tending to their injured counterpart.

Jonathon stepped out from behind the vehicle and trudged through the weight of the water. Once he reached the sand, he asked, "Is he alright?"

One of the men tending to the unconscious man shot up from his kneeling position, an evil scowl on his face. "Does he bloody look alright to you, mate?"

The man's accent was thick and Jonathon guessed he was British. He seemed to be in his early thirties with a crewcut and goatee. He looked as if he spent a great deal of time in the weight room, and Jonathon could just make out the lower half of a tattoo on the man's right arm that peaked out from under the cuff of his tight sleeve. It appeared to be the lower half of a heart, bright red in color.

"Well, is he breathing?" Jonathon asked, genuine concern in his voice.

"Yeah, he's breathing," the man barked back angrily, and he pointed at Jonathon's gun. "Good thing you got that gun or I'd make bloody sure *you* stop breathing!"

"Load him into the jeep, we'll get him back to the compound and get him medical attention," Jonathon replied, ignoring the threat.

The British man looked down at Dave. He nodded, and the men immediately began moving the injured man toward the jeep. Jonathon noticed Charlie giving him a worried look.

"When they load him up, get him back," Jonathon told her. "He needs help. I'll finish what I've started here."

Charlie shook her head. "No," she said. "You can't do it alone, and I sure can't leave these guys here with you."

"You're not going to leave them with me," he replied. "We're going to let the tyrannosaur go, and then we are going to lock them into that cage."

The men suddenly stopped in their tracks and then the British man spoke up. "Like hell you are!" he shouted furiously. "That dino is worth a lot of money, and it's not leaving this trailer!" As if on cue, the young tyrannosaur began to wail and march nervously back and forth in the cage.

Jonathon chuckled and shook his head. He felt a mosquito buzzing around his head and tried to wave it away with the gun. "Oh yes," he said. "I guess we should've explained what this is all about."

"They're here to stop us from taking any of the animals off the island," Dave explained. He closed his eyes and appeared to be deep in thought. Jonathon wondered if he was already rehearsing how he'd explain what all had happened to Eric.

"Bingo," Jonathon replied. He pointed at the pacing tyrannosaur with his free hand. "That dinosaur is not leaving this island." The animal wailed again. It was an unsettling sound.

The British man turned another shade of red, and Jonathon could've sworn he saw a puff of steam leave his ears. The man began unleashing a barrage of expletives at him, but he never heard him. Instead, his attention had turned toward the nearby jungle. A massive flock of birds burst upward from the green canopy like a volcanic eruption. The birds disappeared in the gray, misty sky above, and Jonathon could've sworn he felt the slightest vibration under his feet moments before the birds took flight.

Out of the corner of his eye, he spotted the angry man approaching him, but he kept his attention on the jungle. Again, he felt a slight vibration under his feet. He looked to the juvenile tyrannosaur and noticed the animal was still wailing and pacing even more frantically than before. Suddenly, he realized what was happening and it terrified him.

"Charlie, get out of there and release that dinosaur...NOW!" he shouted, panicked.

"Are you bloody deaf, mate?" the Brit screamed at him. "I said that dinosaur is not going anywhere!"

Jonathon finally returned his attention to the man, but before he could explain, the gun was slapped out of his hand. Both of them dove for the weapon, but much to Jonathon's dismay, the Brit grabbed it first. He wasted no time pointing the barrel of the gun at him.

Jonathon looked back to the jeep, desperately hoping Charlie was still on the turret, but she'd already exited the vehicle and was attempting to open the cage.

"Don't you dare, missy!" the man yelled, and he pointed the gun at her. He then looked to one of the other men that was still tending to the unconscious man. "Jimmy, get her away from that bloody cage!"

The man took one step and immediately stopped dead in his tracks. A frightening and deafening roar boomed from somewhere in the nearby jungle.

"That's why we've got to release that tyrannosaur," Jonathon said, doing his best to sound calm. "That sound you just heard is daddy…he's come to collect his baby."

The British man lowered his gun and his jaw dropped. Oddly, the first thing he asked was, "How do you know it's the daddy?"

"Because I watched some of the fools on this island kill the mother a couple of days ago when they captured the juvenile," Jonathon explained. "Now we don't have any time. We've got to release that dinosaur now or things are going to get really bad."

"Do as he says," Dave said, panicked. "We've got to release the animal right now!" He suddenly looked as if he was going to be sick.

Charlie didn't wait another moment. She began to quickly release the Master lock and release the dinosaur. The animal cocked its head to the side and looked at her curiously, as if it was trying to figure out if the gesture was some sort of trap.

"Come on, let's go!" she shouted at the young dinosaur, which unfortunately only made the animal more timid.

At that moment, there was another roar, this time much closer. Now, all of them could feel the rhythmic vibrations of the very large beast that was moving quickly toward them. The juvenile tyrannosaur suddenly leapt from the cage and onto the sand. Clearly, it had heard the adult animal's call drawing closer as well.

"Okay, it's out, let's get out of here," the Brit said, and he sprinted into the driver's seat of the jeep. Dave leapt into the back seat, and the other men began to fumble with the rear gate so they could load the injured man.

"Hurry up!" Dave shouted.

Jonathon and Charlie walked toward the vehicle to leave with them, but the Brit quickly pointed the gun at Jonathon's head when he was within arm's length.

"Don't think so, mate," he said coldly. "You got your wish—the dino is free. You're not going with us."

Jonathon felt his jaw literally drop. "Come on, you can't be serious!" he shouted. "You're going to leave us here to die?"

"We have room, Scott," Dave said. "We can't leave them here."

"Sure we can," Scott replied with no emotion. "We leave them here and that bloody dinosaur will chase after them instead of us!" He looked over his shoulder at his counterparts, still struggling with the rear gate. "For Pete's sake, bring him up here," he growled.

Dave reached over and grabbed the British man's arm. "Scott, we cannot leave them here," he said very sternly.

Scott took a deep breath and released it through his nose. His jaw was set tight as he briefly contemplated what to do. Finally, he looked over at Jonathon. "Tell you what, mate," he began. "We'll take you along."

Jonathon felt a huge rush of relief, and he heard Charlie whispering a big thank you to God.

"But..." Scott continued. "You're riding back there," he said, and he jerked a thumb back toward the cage.

Jonathon wanted to argue, but another deafening roar that seemed less than fifty yards away reminded him there was no time. "We'll take it," he said quickly, and he grabbed Charlie's arm and all but dragged her to the cage. The two of them hopped inside and pulled the door shut.

"The door won't stay shut!" Charlie said, panicked.

"Do you still have the lock and key?" Jonathon asked.

She immediately reached into her pocket and retrieved the lock with the key still inserted. Jonathon snatched it from her and quickly locked the door. He then dropped the key into his pants pocket and watched as the other two men loaded their injured friend into the rear of the jeep.

The moment Scott mashed the accelerator, the adult tyrannosaur came crashing through the palm trees and other tropical plants that bordered the road. It immediately noticed the young tyrannosaur scurrying toward it and briefly paused to sniff at its young. However, the moment was short-lived. Jonathon and Charlie watched as the monster then raised its head and released another thunderous roar in their direction.

"I think you're gonna want to step on it!" Jonathon yelled toward the jeep. He was unaware if Scott or Dave actually heard him, but he could feel the vehicle picking up speed. Unfortunately, the tyrannosaur was too.

"We're not going to outrun it in this sand," Charlie said, her voice quaking.

Jonathon opened his mouth to speak, but thought better of it. He wanted to say something—anything—that would give her hope that she was wrong. But he knew she was right, and there was nothing in him that would be able to convince her otherwise. All he and she could do was move to the front of the trailer and hunker down.

It seemed to be only a mere few seconds before the lumbering tyrannosaur caught up to them. As it ran along the right side of the jeep, Jonathon closed his eyes. He knew what was coming next. Suddenly, without any warning at all, the dinosaur thrust itself into the side of the jeep, and the vehicle rose from the ground and fell onto its side.

Jonathon fell hard against the iron bars on the side of the cage, and Charlie came crashing into him. He felt for a moment as if he would lose consciousness, but another hard jolt seemed to stir him back awake. A moment later, he heard a blood-curdling scream from one of the men in the jeep.

He glanced toward the front of the jeep and watched the tyrannosaur rise from the wreckage, the legs of a man dangling from its jaws. Jonathon noticed Charlie watching, wide eyes full of terror, and he quickly tugged at her, as he knew what was coming next. He wanted to pull her away, to shield her from the gore that he, unfortunately, knew all too well. As he heard the sickening sound of bones being crushed, he knew he was too late. A shower of bright red poured from the tyrannosaur's terrifying maw.

Jonathon heard another scream, but this time it was female. It was Charlie. The dinosaur quickly gobbled up its first victim and then snapped its large head around in the direction of the screaming woman.

"Charlie, stop," Jonathon whispered in her ear. He grabbed her and held her toward the ground, his hand over her mouth.

He could see the terror in her eyes, and he knew that she probably now had lost any control she previously had over her screaming. Jonathon could clearly see the look in her eyes that seemed to suggest she truly believed she was living the last moments of her life.

The tyrannosaur lunged toward them and the cage clanged loudly when the beast's head rammed into the bars. The jolt threw Jonathon into the side of the cage again, and he lost his grip on Charlie. It was at that moment that he noticed one of Charlie's legs sticking out of the front of the cage between two bars. The enraged dinosaur seemed to see it too and the animal dove for the unprotected limb. Jonathon knew there would be no time to pull her back in, and he was already playing out the scenario in his head. She'd either be screaming even louder, or she'd pass out from shock when she realized her leg had been bitten off. Then he'd have to quickly apply a tourniquet while still trying to figure out a way of the mess.

Just as the blood-thirsty animal was about to snap off Charlie's leg below the knee, Jonathon heard shots ring out from the jeep. He whipped his head around to see Dave, standing on the side of the vehicle, the 9mm gun in his hand. He was firing off shot after shot. Jonathon pulled Charlie toward him and he was just about to yell at Dave to stop and take cover, but he was too late. The tyrannosaur dipped its head downward, and when it arose, there was another sound of crushing bones and a sight of raining gore. Dave never even had a moment to scream. He was literally there one second, gone the next.

"Okay, come on," Jonathon said, pulling Charlie to her feet. "We've got to get out of here."

No sooner had he gotten her up, Charlie slumped back down—she'd passed out.

Great, he thought. Then he heard more screaming—this time, it sounded like the British man, Scott. Jonathon quickly reached for his pocket to retrieve the key, but before he even got his hand in his pocket, the entire cage began to roll toward the surf.

Jonathon held on and rode the chaos out the best he could, and he could only wince and grit his teeth as he watched Charlie's limp body tumble round and round in the metal cage. She reminded him of a shoe in a clothes dryer, and the sickening sound of her body slamming into the cage did too.

He tried time and time again to get a hand in his pocket to retrieve the key so that they could escape, but the violent rolling of the cage prevented him from getting it. Before he knew it, the cage was in the water and becoming more and more submerged with every roll. Just as he began to think he was going to have a fate just like his father and Silas, the rolling stopped. He had just enough room to get his neck and head out of the water. Much to his surprise, he could see the jeep was still attached to the trailer.

He quickly reached down, grabbed Charlie by her shirt collar, and pulled her head above water as well. He was unsure if she was breathing, or if she was even alive, but he could only assume that she was. Jonathon moved toward the rear of the cage, dragging Charlie along with him. When he reached the door, he wedged her against it with his knee to keep her head above water. He then thrust a hand down into his pocket again to retrieve the key.

There was another scream of utter terror from the jeep, and Jonathon then noticed the water around him turn red. He quickly reached between the bars, and fumbled at the lock. His hands were shaking so badly he could barely insert the key. Just as he was about to turn it, the cage again violently rolled forward. This time, they were fully submerged.

Jonathon felt his body fall away from the door, and Charlie fell from his grasp as well. Holding his breath, he swam back toward the lock and again tried to reach for it, but again the cage shook violently. He then thought he heard a crack of thunder and suddenly a dark shadow fell over him. The cage was pushed hard into the sandy bottom and he then realized that the tyrannosaur was lying on top of the cage. Again, the water began to turn red.

Jonathon again reached between the bars and tried desperately to feel for the lock and key. Due to the stirred-up sand and bloody water, he could see nothing. He could no longer ignore the burning desire inside of him to take a breath of air. It was no longer a choice any longer. In mere seconds, his mouth would involuntarily open, and his lungs would fill with water. Oddly, he thought, *At least I won't be eaten alive.* Just as he was about to embrace death, the death that had been chasing him repeatedly on the cursed island, he felt the cage door swing open and a strong hand pull him upward.

Jonathon burst through the surface and gulped a sweet breath of air. His first thought was Charlie, and just as he was about to reach into the cage for her, he was pulled away. Someone was dragging him toward the beach, and when they reached the sand, an older man fell down beside him. He was dressed in a khaki shirt and shorts to match. He had a graying beard that still had hints of the blond color it once was.

"Just lie still a minute," the man barked at him.

"But you're—you're…" Jonathon mumbled.

"Dead?" the older man asked, and he laughed. "Don't you know me better than that?"

Jonathon stared at him and then saw someone drag Charlie ashore next to him. It was another older man, and he looked up at his partner, concern etched in his already wrinkled face.

"Silas, she's not breathing!" Henry said, panicked. "How is Jonathon? Is he alright?"

"He's fine," Silas said, dropping to his knees. "He looks like he's seen a ghost though."

For a long moment, Jonathon could not speak. He could only watch in amazement as his father and Silas Treadwell worked together to perform CPR on Charlie.

CHAPTER 31

Eric had no idea how long he'd been unconscious. All he knew was that when he awoke, he had a splitting headache and some sort of makeshift bandage wrapped around his head.

"What happened?" he asked, still groggy.

Glenn Hardcastle leaned over to where he was lying and pushed his hat back, exposing more of his forehead. "That happened," he said with a smirk and he gestured toward the semi-truck idling on the road behind them.

Eric slowly turned his head and looked at the truck. The trailer was obviously enduring a great deal of weight. The *Sarcosuchus's* tail was so long that it hung limply off the rear of the flatbed. The prehistoric crocodile had multiple straps and chains draped over the body, but it was clearly unconscious.

Eric allowed a half smile and then returned his attention to Hardcastle. "How difficult was it? I hate that I missed it..."

"Yeah, be thankful you slept through all of it because that old girl is nasty," he said, his tone turning serious. "We had to put about four darts in her before she finally began to calm down. And I'm real glad you spared no expense on the wench or the cable. Truth be told, the tensile strength is probably still a little low...but somehow it held."

Eric took a deep breath and nodded. "Okay, help me up," he said, raising his hand.

Hardcastle pulled him to his feet and Eric walked toward the trailer. His first few steps were wobbly, but his balance got better with every step. He felt the urge to reach for a cigarette, but he was afraid if he did, he may just throw up. Right now, he didn't have time for throwing up.

He slowly placed a hand on the side of the large animal's belly. Although he was fully aware that it was unconscious, part of him was still terrified to touch it.

"How long was I out?" he asked.

Hardcastle glanced at his watch. "Ah...well, it took us about twenty minutes to get the croc out and loaded on the trailer. When I came back to check on you, you were already lying here with your eyes open. I'd guess ten or fifteen minutes."

"So you're telling me the animal has been asleep at least twenty minutes?"

Hardcastle nodded. "Give or take a few."

"And remind me how long the tranquilizer will last."

Hardcastle gave him a puzzled look for a moment. "Well, it's hard to say."

Eric's eyebrows tightened. "What do you mean 'it's hard to say'?"

"Well, it's just that none of us anticipated it taking four darts to put the thing to sleep. We'd anticipated two darts doing the trick and keeping it out cold for at least an hour before another dose would have to be applied. My guess is we'll get at least an hour with four darts, but someone has gotta keep a close eye on this beast in case she begins to stir sooner."

Eric pondered that a moment and bit his lip. "Alright," he said finally. "If that's the case, let's get a move on. The doc should be at the beach waiting. Maybe she'll have a theory."

Hardcastle looked toward the cab of the truck and made a circle motion with his arm and finger in the air. George took the signal's meaning and immediately began to move forward with the semi.

"Come on, boss," Hardcastle said, gesturing for Eric to follow. "You're gonna have to catch a ride with me I'm afraid."

Eric rubbed his aching head and began following him. "So where is the other jeep?" he asked as they walked.

Hardcastle said, "Your ride is over there," and he pointed toward the tree line on the other side of the road.

It took Eric a moment to find it, but eventually, he saw it. Beyond the colorful flowers and vegetation that bordered that particular part of the road, he could see what appeared to be the bent and mangled wreckage of the jeep he'd been driving when he'd lost consciousness. The vehicle was standing on its rear bumper, the roll cage resting against the trunk of a large tree. The distance from the road to the tree gave him a chill.

"That thing threw me *that* far?"

"Well, at least you got a nap in while me and the other guys were doing all the dirty work," Hardcastle said, still walking with his back to Eric.

***

The tyrannosaur was sprawled lifeless across the top of the cage that still rested underwater and several yards away from the beach. Silas and Henry arrived just in time, and Silas finally got the opportunity to bring down the tyrannosaur he'd dreamed about killing since he'd left the island the first time.

"Dad," Jonathon said, still in awe. "How? How are you guys alive?"

The two men were seated on the sandy beach. Henry looked over to Silas as he tended to Charlie a few feet away. "How is she?" he asked.

Silas glanced over at him and gave a thumbs up. "Way better than one would expect," he said. "She's banged up, and her left arm may be fractured, but all things considered, she's in pretty good shape."

Henry breathed a sigh of relief, and Jonathon could see that the weight of some burden seemed to be lifted from his father's shoulders.

"Thank goodness," he said gratefully. Then he gave a bit of a stern look to Jonathon. "You both are very lucky. How on earth did you get yourself into that mess?"

Jonathon shook his head and chuckled. "Excuse me?" he said in disbelief. "How about you tell me how you and Silas aren't trapped on the bottom of the river and then I'll fill you in on what I was doing."

Henry took his straw hat from his head and fanned himself. Jonathon couldn't tell if the older man was hot, or just trying to swat insects away. "Well," he began, "I thought I was a goner, son, I really did," he said. He paused and scratched his head before returning the hat to its rightful place. "All I knew to do as that monstrous snake pulled us beneath the water was to take in the biggest, deepest breath of my life and hope for a miracle. And well, I got one."

Jonathon crossed his arms. "Go on," he said, leaning back slightly.

"Well, I suppose it was all thanks to a couple of miracles," he replied, pointing to Silas. "That man must've been a boy scout because he is the most prepared individual I've ever met."

Silas had gotten up and strolled over to them. Charlie seemed to be unconscious.

"I was one hell of a boy scout," he said as he took a seat next to them. "But none of that would have mattered if our old friend didn't show up just in the nick of time."

Jonathon rolled his eyes and stood up. He dusted the sand off his pants. "Okay, alright," he said, patting his legs down. "You guys have obviously begun a lifelong friendship, and that's all fine and dandy, but will one of you please tell me what exactly happened?"

"Alright, alright," Silas said, clearly enjoying the moment. "Remember the *Spinosaurus*?" he asked. "Did you know those things are aquatic?"

"There has been some debate about that," Jonathon said. "There are a lot of paleontologists that believe the *Spinosaurus* was a good swimmer and spent a lot of time hunting in water."

Henry smiled. "Well, son, I'm here to tell you that they *are* indeed spectacular swimmers. That same *Spinosaurus* that we saw when we first arrived on the island showed up and attacked that giant snake. Fortunately, Silas had some Spare Air to keep us alive until it was safe to surface."

"Spare Air?" Jonathon asked, confused.

"It's a tiny submersible air tank," Silas explained. "It has a mouthpiece on it and it gives you an additional ten to fifteen breaths in case there is an emergency. Since the vehicle I brought is amphibious, I knew we'd probably find ourselves in some water at some time or another. I also knew that since I'd built the protective cage that there would be an added danger if something happened and the vehicle began to sink."

Jonathon's mouth opened slightly, and he tilted his head as he began to play it all out in his mind. "So you're telling me when the vehicle was going down, you were going for the tanks?"

"Actually, Silas already had his hands on the tanks before we were all the way underwater," Henry added, and Silas nodded in agreement.

"So you're telling me the *Spinosaurus* killed the *Titanoboa*, and you guys used the Spare Air to stay alive until it was all over?"

Henry nodded. "That's exactly what happened. If that big dinosaur hadn't shown up, I'm not sure we'd have made it."

"Once the snake was removed, I wrestled the cage open and we swam to the river bank. By the time we were out of the water, the *Spinosaurus* was feasting on its kill. Of course, you and the goons that were chasing us were long gone," Silas said.

Jonathon crossed his arms and chewed his lip. "So what have you gentlemen been doing these past two days?"

Silas and Henry looked at each other, both of them smiling simultaneously. Jonathon blinked at them and raised an eyebrow. Silas began walking toward him and as he did, he reached into one of the large cargo pockets on his khaki shorts.

"We knew you were detained," he said, still walking. "So your father and I thought it was best to go and take care of the very thing we came here for."

Jonathon watched as Silas retrieved an object wrapped in a handkerchief. The older man unwrapped it and proudly held a small glass vial out to him.

Jonathon's eyes widened and now he felt a smile of his own spread across his face.

"Is that what I think it is?" he asked, taking the vial. He held it up to the bright light originating from the sky and could see the propitious liquid sloshing gently around the interior.

Silas didn't speak; he only nodded and then reached over and embraced Jonathon. Henry joined them and said, "Son, we've got what we came for. Now let's get off this island before things get worse."

Jonathon hugged his father for a long moment and clutched the vial tightly in his right hand. He then pulled away from his father and clutched his shoulder with his free hand.

"Dad, I can't do that," he replied with a sad reluctance. "As much as I know you're right, I can't leave here knowing that Eric Gill is about to take a very dangerous animal off this island. People could die, and if that happens, I won't be able to forgive myself."

Henry closed his eyes and slowly dropped his head. After a moment, he looked over his shoulder to where Charlie was lying on the beach.

"What about her, son?" he asked, looking back to Jonathon. "She needs some medical attention, and we aren't doing her any favors by sticking around here."

Jonathon stared at Charlie and felt a pang of guilt. "You're right," he said. "Take this vial of water and take Charlie back to Silas's ship. It's probably best if you both head back without me."

Silas looked to Henry and then over to Jonathon. He began to laugh, a slight chuckle at first, and eventually swelling into a full-blown hearty cackle. "Jonathon, I can always count on you for a good laugh, you know that?"

"We're not leaving you here, son," Henry said very sternly. "You may as well get that idea out of your head. We didn't just become reunited only to separate once again."

Jonathon clenched his jaw and considered his options. Time was running out.

"Okay, how about this," he began. "Dad, you take Charlie back to the ship and me and Silas will stop Eric. Give us two hours, and if we're not back, then you head back without us."

Henry shook his head, seemingly just as defiant as he was after the first suggestion. "Absolutely not."

Jonathon opened his mouth to argue, but before he could speak, Silas trudged past him and leaned over to whisper something to Henry. He watched as his father looked into his new friend's eyes and then slowly nodded his head.

"Alright then," Henry said, looking toward his son. "I'll give you both two hours."

Jonathon's eyes narrowed and he looked to Silas for some sort of explanation regarding what had just happened. Silas only shrugged in response as he knelt down to pick up Charlie.

"How are we going to get them safely to the ship?" Jonathon asked, peering out to sea.

"The same way we got here," Silas answered. "The ATV is parked just beyond the beach over there," he added, pointing.

Jonathon was puzzled. "I figured it was resting at the bottom of the river."

"Nah," Silas replied, carrying Charlie across the sand with ease. "We managed to use the winch to get it out. She's not running great, but she's running good enough to get to the ship."

Once Henry and Charlie were safely in the water and headed toward the *Wild Lady*, Jonathon and Silas found a hiding spot behind a collection of large jagged rocks that bordered the surf.

"So, what's the plan?" Silas asked, checking the chamber of his rifle.

Jonathon removed his hat and wiped the sweat from his brow with his sleeve. "Well, I'm thinking when they arrive and see the carnage of all their dead guys and the large *T-rex* lying in the water, they'll be pretty surprised and confused."

Silas nodded. "Yeah, that's a safe bet."

Jonathon looked at him. "I think we better take advantage of that confusion. We've got to attack them quick. If they get that dinosaur onto the barge and into the water, our job is going to get significantly more difficult."

"Okay," Silas replied. "How many guys do you think we will have to contend with?"

Jonathon leaned back against one of the tall rocks and pondered the question. "Well, of course there is Eric," he said. "And I think George is behind the wheel of that semi."

"That it?" Silas asked, sounding hopeful.

Jonathon shook his head. "Nope, there is at least one more guy…goes by the name of Hardcastle, and he is the one that we've really got to worry about."

Jonathon retrieved the 9mm handgun he'd stuffed into the back of his pants and checked the magazine. There were only six bullets left, and he knew he'd have to make each one count. He looked over to Silas and was glad the big man was by his side once again.

"So what did you say?" he asked.

Silas looked over at him, confused. "What are you talking about?" he asked.

"To my father," Jonathon explained. "You whispered something to him and suddenly he was on board with my idea. What did you say?"

Silas nodded and smirked. "Oh, I just reminded him that he didn't know how to pilot that ship—that he may be able to figure it out, but it would take him a little while to do it."

Jonathon huffed and shook his head. "So you two are conspiring against me now?"

Silas glared at him. "Well, when you come back from the dead with someone, you form a special bond. We wouldn't expect you to understand."

CHAPTER 32

The moment that Glenn Hardcastle brought the jeep to a stop, Eric Gill hopped out and drew his gun.

"What in the hell happened here?" he asked, his jaw dropped wide.

The first thing he noticed was the fully-grown—and recently deceased—tyrannosaurus rex resting on top of one of his jeeps about fifteen yards out into the water. The next thing he noticed was the vast amount of bright red blood splashed and splattered all over the brilliant white sandy beach. In addition to the blood, he noticed a severed human leg and what appeared to be a portion of a man's hand several feet away from that.

"Oh my God," Hardcastle said, stepping out of the jeep. He was seldom emotional, but the scene before him was unlike anything he'd ever seen before. "Dr. Nelson...Dave...Scott—Oh my God, they're all gone!"

Eric gritted his teeth and felt his pulse begin to race as the full weight of what had just occurred began to hit him. He scanned his environment once more, and as if the blood and gore of his deceased employees were not enough of a kick in the gut, he also suddenly realized that the trailer behind the jeep—the same trailer that had contained the juvenile tyrannosaur—was now empty, the metal door to the cage opened and closed lazily with the incoming surf.

George Powell, seemingly unfazed and still focused on the job at hand, had swung the semi-truck into a wide semi-circle and then began to back the flatbed trailer containing the mammoth crocodile onto the sandy beach as close as he could get it to the water.

Hardcastle glanced over at George and then over to Eric. "Well, what do we do now?" he asked.

Eric spat on the ground, clearly disgusted. He swallowed hard, doing his best to contain his rollercoaster of emotions, and then turned his attention to Hardcastle.

"We move forward with what we have?" he said with renewed determination. "Mr. O will have to understand the setback. We'll meet with the croc as planned and deliver the juvenile *T-rex* to him later."

Glenn nodded and then began jogging toward the water.

***

"Where is he going?" Silas whispered, his eyes focused on Hardcastle.

Jonathon gazed out into the sea and raised his chin toward the large barge roughly a hundred yards off shore. "Probably to go and retrieve the cable off that barge. Then I'm guessing they'll tie onto the croc and use the winch to pull it out there. Once on the barge, they'll be ready for their package to be picked up."

Hardcastle waded into the water until it was waist deep and then he dove forward, seemingly prepared to swim the rest of the way.

"Well, are we gonna stop him?" Silas asked, readying his rifle.

Jonathon reached over and pressed the barrel of the gun downward with the palm of his hand. "There is no reason to," he whispered. "Let him get a little further out and then we can take down Eric and George."

When he was convinced that Hardcastle was a safe enough distance away, Jonathon crept out from behind the large rock and rushed toward Eric with the handgun pointed toward the back of his head. Eric was standing beside the trailer, preparing to loosen the straps holding the *Sarcosuchus* down. He never knew he was being approached.

"Stop right there!" Jonathon yelled, still pointing the gun toward Eric.

Eric immediately pulled his hands away from the trailer and raised them over his head.

"Jonathon?" he asked, his back still turned. "Is that you?" He didn't sound surprised.

"The one and only," Jonathon replied, and he began peering in all directions in search of George Powell.

"Did you have anything to do with all this?" Eric asked, clearly referencing the death and carnage that occurred at the jaws of the dead tyrannosaur.

"Maybe," he replied, still looking around. "George?" he cried out. "Where are you at?"

"Don't answer him, George," Eric commanded. "I'll be fine. Stay put."

Jonathon pressed the gun against the back of Eric's skull. "On your knees," he hissed through clenched teeth.

As Eric complied, Jonathon thought he saw a shadow move under the trailer. George was apparently just on the other side of where they were.

"George," Jonathon called out. "I've got no problem with you. Just walk away and let me do what needs to be done. I'm not interested in hurting Eric; I just need to stop him."

Silas Treadwell stayed hidden behind the rock and kept his rifle pointed toward the end of the trailer. From the distance he was at, and the unique perspective, he could clearly see George's legs moving beneath the gap under the trailer. George was moving slowly toward the back of the trailer and appeared to be planning a surprise attack.

Silas waited patiently, and as George slowly moved into position at the back of the trailer, he took a deep breath, held it, and fired a shot toward the metal bumper just in front of where George was standing.

The shot thundered loudly, and there was a loud *clang* as the bullet glanced off the trailers metal bumper. Silas was surprised to see George immediately fall to the ground and begin screaming.

"I've been shot!" he screamed over and over.

Silas darted out from behind the rock and jogged toward the fallen man that seemed to be writhing in pain on the sand.

"Did you shoot him?" Jonathon asked, wide-eyed and surprised.

"Absolutely not," Silas snapped. "I hit exactly where I was aiming!"

George continued to yell, and as he drew within twenty yards, Silas could clearly see blood on the sand. He could also see a handgun still in George's grasp.

"Can't you see the man has been hit?" Eric asked furiously.

"Toss that gun away!" Silas roared, ignoring Eric's question. "Do it now, or I'm going to really give you something to scream about!"

George immediately complied, throwing the gun wildly toward the surf. As Silas and Jonathon turned their attention to the flying gun, they suddenly realized what was happening, but it was too late.

Glenn Hardcastle had just stepped back onto the beach and made a diving catch for the gun. Silas immediately pointed his rifle in Hardcastle's direction and fired. The sand exploded at Hardcastle's feet as he rolled across the ground, and in one solid motion, he regained his footing. He then immediately crouched to one knee and fired the gun toward Silas.

Silas howled as the bullet tore through his right thigh and he immediately collapsed to the sand. He instinctively let go of the rifle and grabbed his wound with both hands.

"No!" Jonathon screamed. He kept the gun pressed hard against the back of Eric's head, and leaned toward him. "Tell your man to drop that gun, or I'm going to blow your head off!"

"You do it, and I'll finish the old man off!" Hardcastle yelled in reply.

Silas rolled onto his side and peered over at Jonathon. He clenched his teeth and shook his head hard. Jonathon took the act as Silas's blessing to forget about him. He then looked away from his injured friend and directed his attention to George Powell, still injured and lying on the ground.

"Okay!" Jonathon shouted. "I won't shoot if you won't!"

"Deal!" Hardcastle replied, and then he too directed his attention to George. "You okay buddy?"

"Yeah, I think so," George answered breathlessly. "Bullet ricocheted off the trailer and got me!"

"Ah," Hardcastle replied, and he glared over at Silas. "I guess you meant to do that old man?"

Silas shook his head as he pressed hard on his profusely bleeding wound. "Nah...if I'd meant to do it, I'd have made it count," he said through clenched teeth.

Hardcastle eyed the blood that seemingly poured from Silas's leg. The splotch of red on the white sand underneath him was growing wider every second. He then redirected his attention to Jonathon.

"Okay, pal, here is the deal," he said. "Your old friend here is bleeding to death and George is not. Now you can you stay right where you're at and hold that gun to the back of Eric's head if that makes you feel safe, but while you're doing that, your friend is going to die."

Jonathon felt his heart sink as he came to the realization that Hardcastle was right—and Silas saw it hit him too.

"Don't you even think about it," he muttered, sounding half-groggy and half-angry. "This is just a flesh wound. I'm holding pressure on it. I'll be fine."

Jonathon took a deep breath. He could see the color leaving Silas's face...there was really no choice to be made. Slowly and reluctantly, he pulled the gun away from Eric's head.

"Good choice," Hardcastle said with a smirk. He kept his gun pointed at Silas and commanded Jonathon to drop his weapon on the ground. Jonathon did as he was bidden and immediately jogged over to where Silas rested on the ground.

"Hang on and remain calm," he said, quickly pulling his belt off.

Silas looked up at him and there was a glazed over look in his eyes. "I'm cool as a cucumber," he replied softly.

As Jonathon applied a tourniquet to Silas's leg, Eric approached him from behind. He'd picked up Jonathon's gun and now held it tightly in his right hand.

"I should kill you both right now," he said peering down at the both of them with a coldness in his eyes.

"So why don't you?" Hardcastle asked. He made his way toward the rear of the trailer, the winch cable in his left hand. "You alright, George?" he asked.

"I'm okay," George replied, finally getting to his feet.

Eric watched as Hardcastle climbed onto the back of the trailer and attached the cable to the loop on the large harness wrapped around the *Sarcosuchus*. He glanced at his watch.

"Our client is scheduled to arrive in about fifteen minutes," he said. "You and George see to getting the croc loaded up and ready to go. I'll join you after I deal with these two."

Jonathon wanted to protest and he wanted to come up with some sort of plan to stop them. But truthfully, none of that seemed to matter to him anymore. George remained behind and began limping around and loosening the straps holding the *Sarcosuchus* down while Hardcastle swam back toward the barge. Jonathon could only watch helplessly as the life seemed to slowly leave Silas.

"He needs a doctor," Jonathon said, still holding the tourniquet tightly.

Eric knelt down beside them and reached over for Silas's rifle.

"Forgive me if I sound cruel, but quite frankly, I don't really care," Eric said as he stood back up. "Look around you," he added suddenly. "There were several good men that were supposed to meet me here, and now all that is left is blood and body parts."

"I had nothing to do with that," Jonathon replied trying his best to sound calm. "You took the juvenile tyrannosaur and the father followed its scent." He paused a moment and looked up at Eric. "If there is anyone to blame for their deaths, it is you."

Eric sighed deeply and tightened his jaw. A rage built up within him that he hadn't felt in years. He had been on the fence about what to do with Jonathon, but now he knew.

"You know, I really didn't want it to end like this," he said, pointing the barrel of the gun toward the back of Jonathon's head. "How dare you blame me for their deaths."

Jonathon did not turn to look back at him. "I just call 'em like I see them."

Eric chuckled. He was amused with Jonathon's arrogance; he couldn't help it. "Well, if it's like you say and their deaths are my fault, there is no reason for me stop with them," he said as he thumbed the hammer back on the gun.

Jonathon closed his eyes and quickly thought of Lucy. His heart began to ache as he came to the realization that not only would he never see her again, but he would also never get to see his child.

"You don't have to do this," he whispered, a final last ditch effort to save not only his life, but Silas's.

"Oh, but I do," Eric replied, smiling.

A thunderous boom rang out, and once again, the sand turned red.

CHAPTER 33

Jonathon fell backward onto the sand, but for some reason, he felt no pain.

Was I hit? he wondered. *I heard the gunshot…am I already dead?*

Slowly, he opened his eyes and began feeling around his head for blood. When he found none, he began to survey his environment, and it was then that he spotted Eric, seated in front of him with what appeared to be a gunshot wound to his chest.

He was breathing very deeply and his teeth were clenched tightly. There was no mistaking the grimacing expressions etched on his face were driven by blinding pain.

"Why?" he rasped. But he wasn't talking to Jonathon. He was looking toward the front of the semi-truck.

Jonathon blinked as he began to make sense of what was going on. Standing near the driver side door of the truck and holding a revolver, the barrel still smoking, was Annie. She was shaking, and there were tears streaming down her face. The gun she was holding was now pointed at George, who was now standing across from her with his hands raised.

"Because you were about to kill him!" she screamed. "You were about to murder him!"

Jonathon returned his attention to Eric. He wondered where the gun he'd been holding was at. He quickly noticed in lying in the sand next to him, but Eric seemed to have absolutely no interest in picking it up, and even if he did, he didn't appear to be in a condition to use it. He then looked back down to Silas and the old man blinked and gave a weak smile.

"Annie, bring me the gun," Jonathon said as he clambered to his feet. He looked past her and could see one of the Gill Enterprises pick-up trucks parked up the road. "Why did you come out here? I told you to stay put."

Annie handed him the gun, which he immediately pointed at George. She said nothing and the tears continued to flow down her face. Jonathon embraced her and kissed her on the forehead. "It doesn't matter," he said with a smile. "You saved my hide."

Annie looked over at the gigantic prehistoric crocodile, and Jonathon watched as her eyes widened. The enormous animal breathed in and out deeply, and there was a rumbling sound with each breath. Suddenly, the *Sarcosuchus* lurched forward. Jonathon jumped back, startled.

"It's waking up!" Annie screamed.

For the briefest moment, Jonathon thought she was right, but then he noticed the cable that was stretched out toward the ocean. It was suddenly tight with no slack at all. The prehistoric croc began to slide forward, and when Jonathon looked out toward the barge, he could see Glenn Hardcastle standing over the winch, waving at him.

Jonathon knew he had to act fast. He grabbed Annie by the shoulders and looked her in the eyes.

"Annie, Silas is hurt and he needs medical attention," he said. "Is there anyone back at the compound that can give him that?"

Annie looked down at the older man she hadn't seen in years. "Oh my God," she whispered. "Is he dead?"

Jonathon looked over at him, and truthfully, he wasn't sure. Silas certainly looked like he may be dead, but he wasn't about to assume that.

"No," he said quickly. "He's not dead yet, but he will be if we don't get him medical attention!"

Annie stared at Silas and remembered how he'd saved her life when they'd been on the island seven years ago. She looked back to Jonathon, suddenly focused and determined. "Yes, there is a nurse on the staff— she can help."

"Okay good," he replied. "Go bring that pickup truck over here so we can load him up."

Annie began sprinting toward the truck without saying another word. Jonathon noticed the *Sarcosuchus* was almost completely off the trailer and would soon be in the water. He looked back to Eric and noticed that he was now slumped over on the ground and appeared to be unconscious—or dead. George was still standing nearby with his hands in the air, his face ashen. Jonathon quickly grabbed the frightened man by the shirt collar and mashed the barrel of the revolver under his chin.

"George, I don't have a lot of time," he growled. "At this point, you're either with me or against me. If you're against me, I've got no use for you anymore." Jonathon pulled the hammer back on the gun. He never intended to use it, but he couldn't allow George to realize that.

George swallowed hard and was now sweating profusely. "What do you want me to do?" he asked, stammering.

Annie brought the pickup truck to a sliding stop in the sand next to an unconscious Silas. Jonathon then grabbed George by the arm and all but dragged him to the truck.

"Help me get him in the truck," he commanded, gesturing toward Silas.

Due to the injury to his leg, George wasn't a lot of help, but somehow he and Jonathon managed to drag the big man into the bed of the truck.

"Now, get in and go back to the compound with them. Keep Silas's legs elevated," Jonathon told him, pointing to the back of the truck. "You need medical attention too."

He then handed the gun to Annie. "You get back to the compound—don't stop for anything." He paused and eyed George a moment before looking back to Annie. "If he tries anything, kill him."

Annie nodded slowly and climbed back into the truck. She craned her head around in an attempt to get another look at Eric. Jonathon went out of his way to block her view. Annie looked up at him and asked, "What are you going to do?"

Jonathon looked over to the *Sarcosuchus*. It was now being dragged through the sand and almost into the water. "I've got to stop them from taking that animal off this island," he grumbled. "If I'm not back in another hour, my father and Charlie are in a ship just off the shoreline a little south of here," he said, pointing. "You get to that ship—my dad will know what to do."

Annie told him to be careful and then sped away in the truck. Jonathon ran toward the *Sarcosuchus* and quickly climbed onto the large animals back. It was now halfway into the water, and he knew that once it was entirely in the water, Hardcastle would be able to reel it in faster. He made his way to where the cable was fastened onto the harness. It was his hope that he'd be able to simply unhook the cable, but he was dismayed to find that it was padlocked.

With no other options and little time to ponder them if he did, Jonathon quickly made his way toward the head of the animal so he could dive into the water and shimmy along the line until he made it to the barge. As he crawled over the *Sarcosuchus's* large skull, he was suddenly overcome with an uneasy feeling. He prayed the animal wouldn't suddenly awaken and gobble him up whole.

Fortunately, his worst fears didn't happen. Jonathon dove into the water and began pulling himself along the cable ahead of the giant croc. He could see Hardcastle still standing over the winch and smiling like a madman as he realized what Jonathon was about to attempt. The man was younger than him, more athletic, and undoubtedly crazier than him to boot. Hardcastle had taken his shirt off but was still wearing cargo pants and his hat—he was quite an intimidating sight. As he considered the challenge before him, Jonathon silently cursed himself for not picking up the other handgun that was lying on the beach.

When he reached the barge, he was very much aware of the fact that the water was way over his head. If he didn't get onto the barge quickly, Hardcastle would probably pummel him into submission and then there would be a real danger of drowning. To his utter surprise, instead of immediately attacking him, Hardcastle all but pulled him up onto the barge.

"Came here to assist me?" he asked, still smirking.

Jonathon shook his head and clenched his jaw. "I came here to stop you," he replied sternly.

Hardcastle stood up straight and cracked his knuckles. "Are you sure? I *really* hoped you were coming to assist me." The winch was still reeling in the croc and it whined stubbornly in protest.

Jonathon smiled and took a deep breath, fully aware of what was next. "Yep, I'm sure. Stop this madness before someone gets killed!"

Hardcastle shook his head. "You know, somehow I kinda thought you were gonna say something like that."

At that moment, Hardcastle took a wild swing at Jonathon's head, but he managed to duck in time. Jonathon threw a counter shot at Hardcastle's ribcage and connected with a tremendous punch that stunned the younger man and sent his hat flying off his head. Hardcastle grabbed his side and yelped in pain, but instead of slowing him down, it only seemed to make matters worse. He quickly spun around so that he was behind Jonathon. Hardcastle then wrapped both arms around his waist and threw him around wildly through the air like a rag doll.

Jonathon estimated that he'd traveled roughly six feet through the air when he finally fell hard onto the metal surface with a loud bone-rattling *thud*. He winced at the pain caused by the impact but was cognizant of the fact that he had no time to lick his wounds. Out of the corner of his eye, he saw Hardcastle charging at him, and he managed to roll out of the way just as a heavy boot came stomping down right where Jonathon's head had just been.

As he rolled over he managed to get onto his feet and throw a quick right hook that connected with Hardcastle's jaw. The younger man rubbed at his lip and then angrily spat out blood. He then smiled at Jonathon, his teeth smeared red.

"Ah, now you've really done it," he said with a sinister look in his eye. "Now I'm *really* pissed!"

Hardcastle then lunged at him, and as he did so, he punched Jonathon hard in the mouth. The blow to his face dropped him immediately to his knees, and for a moment, he felt as if Hardcastle was going to finish him off. However, it suddenly became apparent to him that the *Sarcosuchus* has regained the other man's attention. The large animal was now sliding onto the ramp at the end of the barge. Upon realizing this, Glenn Hardcastle ran back to the winch controls.

There was a throbbing sensation in his mouth, and Jonathon could feel a couple of his teeth wiggling around when he mashed his tongue against them. Every ounce of his being was telling him to count his losses and head back for the beach, but the sight of the terrifying dinosaur that was being hauled onto the barge would not allow him to do it. He began his approach toward Hardcastle yet again.

"Who is Eric selling the croc to?" he asked as he continued walking.

Hardcastle turned to look at him, keeping one hand on the winch controls and using his free hand to wipe blood away from his mouth.

"I don't know his name, nor do I know his game," he said staring him down. "Eric refers to him as Mr. O."

Jonathon shook his head and laughed. "Come on now," he said. "You can't really be this stupid. The man is a terrorist and he plans to use this animal as a weapon."

Hardcastle took a deep breath and narrowed his eyes. He was not in the mood for insults, and he certainly didn't believe a word of what Jonathon was saying.

Jonathon could see his anger building and held up his hands in an apologetic fashion. "Don't take what I'm saying the wrong way—it's just...well, look at this thing," he explained, gesturing toward the *Sarcosuchus*. It was now fully on the barge. "Are you really comfortable selling an animal as dangerous as this one to someone that you know absolutely nothing about?"

Hardcastle released the winch control and marched straight toward Jonathon. He stopped directly in front of him and drew his face close to Jonathon's, almost to the point their noses were touching.

"I'm not the one selling this thing," he grumbled. "Eric is. And just how do you know what he's going to use it for?"

"First of all, you're helping Eric," Jonathon countered. "And if this thing gets a hold of someone back in the civilized world, you've got just as much blood on your hands as he does. How I know what he's going to do with it doesn't matter, just know that it isn't speculation—I genuinely know what he's planning with this animal, and it's pretty terrifying."

Hardcastle pulled back and crossed his arms. "I'll keep that in mind," he said completely unconcerned. "Now you can either leave or help me. If you refuse to do either, I'm going to be forced to kill you."

"Eric's dead," Jonathon blurted out, hoping it would make him reconsider.

Hardcastle's mouth dropped open slightly, and he looked past Jonathon back toward the beach. "What? You killed him?" he asked, sounding genuinely surprised.

Jonathon shook his head. "No, Annie did," he explained. "She showed up just as he was about to shoot me in the head."

Hardcastle's face hardened, and he remained silent for a long moment. Finally, he began to laugh.

Jonathon wasn't sure what to make of the laughter. "So now you're not working for him anymore—you need to stop this," he added, almost pleading.

When Hardcastle finally stopped laughing, he opened his mouth to speak, but before he could say a single word, the sound of an approaching vessel caught his attention. He looked toward the mist, scooped his hat off the metal platform, and whispered, "He's here."

CHAPTER 34

The ship that approached was not at all like what Jonathon expected. In his mind's eye, he pictured Eric Gill's wealthy client to show up in some sort of sleek, modern ship with a fresh coat of paint that would shine brilliantly even in the mist-darkened skies of the island. Instead, what emerged near the edge of the veil was a rusty old vessel that barely appeared to be seaworthy.

"*This* is your rich client?" Jonathon asked.

"It would seem so," Hardcastle replied replacing his hat, and there was a hint of worry in his tone.

As the ship drew nearer, Jonathon could see two men of Middle-Eastern descent on the deck, and they appeared to be carrying automatic weapons.

"I've got a bad feeling about this," he muttered softly.

Hardcastle ignored him and raised his hand to wave. The men on deck did not wave back; they just peered at him with icy stares. A moment later, another man that was taller than the other two stepped out from the cabin. He was dressed in a black business suit and there was a turban upon his head that shared the same color. His face was dark and etched with wrinkles; the bottom half covered completely with a long salt-and-pepper beard that dropped low enough to hide his neck.

"Mr. O, I presume?" Hardcastle called out.

The man's demeanor appeared to be softer than the other two, and he allowed the slightest hint of a smile.

"My, what an impressive animal," Mr. O said, gazing past Jonathon and Hardcastle to the prehistoric crocodile. His English was good, but accented thick with Arabic. He stared at the *Sarcosuchus* for a solid minute before speaking again. "What about the other animal?" he asked. "Do you have it?"

Hardcastle sighed deeply and made an annoying clicking sound with his mouth. "Well…no, I'm afraid not," he said.

Suddenly, Mr. O's eyes widened, and his once relatively friendly features began to turn dark.

Hardcastle noticed and spoke quickly. "Look, we had one—but it escaped just this morning," he explained. "I can get you another one!"

Mr. O stared at him but did not speak. Instead, he leaned over and said something to one of the men standing beside him. There was a brief exchange in Arabic when finally Mr. O returned his attention to Hardcastle.

"Where is Eric Gill?" he asked calmly. "I need to speak with him about this."

Hardcastle frowned, and Jonathon wasn't sure if it was because he was going to have to tell Mr. O what happened to Eric, or if it was because he took the question as a slight to him and his position in the company.

He pondered the request for a few seconds, then cocked his head and said, "Mr. O, I'm afraid Mr. Gill isn't available right now. He asked me to handle his affairs and—"

Mr. O held up his hand in interruption—a dismissive gesture. "Sir, I have traveled a long way for these animals. If *both* of the animals are unavailable, I'm afraid that this deal is off." Without saying another word, the man turned away and headed back to the cabin.

"Wait," Hardcastle called out, somewhat panicked. "Give me an opportunity to make good on the deal."

Mr. O stopped momentarily and half-turned back toward the railing of the ship.

"No, the deal is off!" he repeated loudly. "We will take the animal as compensation for this waste of time."

Jonathon had been watching the awkward exchange between the two men with a lot of interest, but remained silent. The expression of anger that now began to creep across Hardcastle's face began to worry him, and he wondered if he should speak up. It was very clear that he was not interested in giving the animal away as Mr. O had suggested.

"Sir, I'm afraid that isn't how we do business at Gill Enterprises," he replied. "This animal isn't going with you unless you are prepared to pay for it." When he finished speaking, he crossed his arms and produced a big toothy grin. When Jonathon saw Mr. O's reaction, he *really* wished he hadn't done that.

Mr. O suddenly charged toward the railing and grabbed the rusty metal with both hands. He jerked backwards on it furiously and began to scream something in Arabic.

"You shouldn't have done that," Jonathon whispered, finally unable to remain silent any longer.

"Don't worry," Hardcastle replied very calmly. "I know what I'm doing."

Jonathon glared at him and then returned his attention to the screaming man on the ship.

"Really?" he asked. "Because it looks to me like you're about to get us killed."

Hardcastle shook his head. "He's not gonna shoot us if that's what you're worried about."

Jonathon looked on as Mr. O turned toward the other two men and because shouting at them. He didn't understand Arabic, but the body language seemed to suggest he was ordering the men to kill them.

"It sure looks like he's about to have his men shoot us," Jonathon said, and he contemplated jumping off the barge.

"No, he's not," Hardcastle replied, still unshaken. "If he starts shooting at us, he will risk hitting the croc. He's not going to risk that."

One of the men wielding an assault rifle stepped away momentarily and then returned with the end of a heavy cable.

"Attach the cable to the barge if you want to live," Mr. O called out to Hardcastle. "We will take the animal and leave. If you refuse, we will be forced to kill you and your friend. Then we will take the animal anyway."

Hardcastle stared at Mr. O for a long minute, and Jonathon could tell he was trying to come up with a way out of his current predicament that didn't involve allowing the *Sarcosuchus* to be taken by force.

"Don't be an idiot," Jonathon said. "Let him go; we'll alert the authorities. He won't get far."

Hardcastle took a deep breath—he sounded almost defeated. "Get off this barge," he said, still staring upward at Mr. O.

"Sure, but you're coming with me," Jonathon replied.

Hardcastle shook his head. "No, I'm not," he said calmly.

Jonathon looked up toward Mr. O and the henchmen that flanked him. They had raised their weapons, and he was beginning to think that Hardcastle was completely wrong when he dismissed the notion that they would not fire on them for fear of hitting the *Sarcosuchus*.

"What are you going to do?" Jonathon asked quickly, and he began to raise his hands in surrender—it was instinctual.

"Is Eric really dead?" he asked softly.

Jonathon looked back toward the beach and could just make out what appeared to be the lifeless body of Eric Gill slumped over motionless in the exact same spot that he'd left him.

"I think he is," he responded. "I'm sorry."

Hardcastle nodded slightly and said, "Well, if that's true, there is no reason for me to stay here. I think I'm going to bargain with them. They're my ticket out of here."

Mr. O seemed to be getting restless as he apparently noticed the soft conversation occurring between Hardcastle and Jonathon. He leaned over and whispered something into the ear of the man on his right. The man nodded and immediately pointed his gun toward the barge and opened fire.

At least ten shots rang out and ricocheted loudly across the metal platform mere feet away from Hardcastle and Jonathon.

"Whoa! Hold on!" Hardcastle shouted, throwing his hands in the air. "Okay, okay, the animal is yours."

Mr. O's features immediately softened again. "I was beginning to think that you were a typical American fool," he said with a laugh. "Attach the cable and I will let you live—but hurry before I reconsider." He then crossed his arms and waited to see if his demands were met.

Hardcastle nodded. "No problem," he replied quickly. "But, sir, I must insist that you take me with you." It was more of a demand than a request.

Mr. O stroked his beard and narrowed his eyes. "And why exactly would I want to take you with me?" he asked, sounding a little intrigued.

Hardcastle calmly walked from behind the winch controls and looked over his shoulder at the gigantic creature slumbering behind him.

"You know nothing about this thing," he said, gesturing toward the *Sarcosuchus*. "And in case Eric didn't tell you—and I'm assuming he didn't—this thing is not going to stay asleep until you get to wherever it is that you're going."

Mr. O took a deep breath and moved his hand from his beard to the back of his neck. "Do you have more tranquilizers for us to give the animal?" he asked.

Hardcastle reached down and retrieved a large black duffel bag that Jonathon had not noticed. The bag had been sitting behind the winch controls completely out of view. He held it up high so that Mr. O could get a good look at it.

"This bag has enough tranquilizers to keep this animal out for a few days if need be," he said. "But you really need someone that knows what they're doing when it comes to administering the correct dosage. You need to not only know where to apply it, but you also need to know how much to give. Give too much, and you kill the animal. Give too little, and you or your men will end up dead."

There was a long silence as Mr. O seemed to mull over everything that Hardcastle had said.

"Are you nuts?" Jonathon whispered. "We can't let this animal leave this island!"

"Yeah, you keep saying that," Hardcastle whispered back with his back turned. "Look, I don't really like you, but we've got one thing in common. We're both American—if you think I'm going to let them use this dinosaur for terrorism, then I assure you, *you* are the one that is nuts."

Jonathon was surprised and bewildered all at the same time. He opened his mouth to reply, but Hardcastle began calling out to Mr. O again before he could.

"And to sweeten the pot a little, how about this?" he offered with a big smile. "How about you take me out of here…let me work for you…and I'll help you get as many of these animals that you want," he said very matter-of-factly.

For the first time, Jonathon could see that Mr. O was finally seriously considering Hardcastle's offer. He quickly weighed his options but realized there were few left.

"And what of your friend?" Mr. O asked, now looking beyond Hardcastle to Jonathon.

Hardcastle glanced at him over his shoulder and then looked back to Mr. O.

"He's not affiliated with me," Hardcastle said. "He stays behind."

Mr. O clenched his jaw and then asked, "And what about Eric Gill?"

Hardcastle laughed. "What about him? He has nothing to do with this. This is between you and me. You take me on your boat, and we sail away. You let me take it from there—just trust me, I can get more dinosaurs if that's what you want." He crossed his arms and quickly became still and silent. He reminded Jonathon of a used car salesman that had just made his pitch.

For what Jonathon counted as the third time, Mr. O leaned over and whispered something to one of the men holding a machine gun that flanked him. While he did this, Hardcastle slowly turned to face him and whispered, "This is your chance. If I were you, I'd dive into the drink and get back to the beach."

"You can't possibly think that you'll be able to stop them all by yourself," Jonathon said.

"Not your problem," he replied. "I'm not going to tell you again to get off this barge. Whatever happens next is on you."

Jonathon looked back toward the beach and thought of the men on the ship holding the assault rifles. There was absolutely no reason for them to let him go because he was absolutely no use to them. A chill ran up his spine as his imagination began to run wild. The bottom line was that he wasn't going to do Lucy any good at all if he was dead.

"Good luck," Jonathon whispered, and he suddenly turned and dove into the water.

As he swam he could hear Mr. O shouting in Arabic and he even heard Hardcastle shouting back at him, though he could not make out anything that was said. He figured that the man—for whatever reason— had decided to help him escape. Maybe Hardcastle wasn't as bad of a guy as he thought. Perhaps the good fight he'd given him had earned his respect. For what it was worth, Jonathon decided that Glenn Hardcastle had certainly earned a little of his.

CHAPTER 35

When Jonathon finally made it back to the beach, the first thing he did was check on Eric Gill. As he'd suspected, the man had bled to death right where he'd left him on the sand. Jonathon sighed and rubbed the back of his neck. He noticed his hat lying on the ground next to the large trailer that the *Sarcosuchus* had been on a short time earlier and scooped it up. The realization that his hat had been missing made him chuckle and it was a testament to just how busy he'd been. He had no idea that he'd even lost it.

Jonathon knelt beside Eric and stared into the deceased man's lifeless eyes for a solid minute. Although he'd created a nightmarish situation—and sure seemed as if he was about to commit murder—Jonathon could not help but pity the man. It was a tragic end for him, and Jonathon was pretty certain that the last person Eric thought would kill him would have been Annie.

"Were you really gonna kill me, Eric?" Jonathon asked the dead man. He genuinely wanted to know. It was then that he began to notice a dozen or so *Parksosaurus* dinosaurs approaching from the jungle. They were seemingly aware of the freshly dead mammal on the beach.

"I ought to leave you here for the dinosaurs to eat," he grumbled, but then immediately felt guilty for saying it. As bad as he was, Jonathon didn't feel that the man deserved an ending such as that. *Angus Wedgeworth? Maybe...but Eric? No—not at all.*

Instead, Jonathon stood up, dusted the sand off his pants, and retrieved the very same jeep Eric and Hardcastle arrived in. He then carefully loaded the dead man into the back of the jeep and caught glimpses of the tiny dinosaurs watching his every move. They didn't frighten him, but all of the eyes focused on him was somewhat unsettling. After slamming the tailgate and climbing back behind the wheel, Jonathon sped away toward the road that led back to the compound.

***

Annie ran out the front door of the medical ward as soon as she heard Jonathon piloting the jeep through the gate. This scared him as his first thought turned to Silas. *Was he dead too?*

"What's wrong?" he asked as soon as he brought the vehicle to a stop.

"Is Eric alive?" she asked, her voice quaking.

Jonathon gripped the steering wheel tightly and stared forward through the windshield for a few seconds as he contemplated how to approach the question.

"Annie," he said softly as he climbed out. "You did nothing wrong—like I said earlier, if you hadn't shown up, I'd be—"

"Oh my God," she said as her eyes widened and she covered her mouth with her hand. "I killed him, didn't I?" The tears began to flow.

Jonathon sighed and reached out to embrace her. "He killed himself," he said, desperately trying to console her. "Eric didn't give you much of a choice in the matter."

She continued crying and buried her face in his chest. In between sobs, she looked up at him and said, "I just couldn't sit here wondering what was going on. That's what I did the last time we were here—I just couldn't do it again. I decided I had to face my fears, and now I'm wondering if I made a bad decision."

Jonathon shook his head and smiled. "And as I said...I for one am very thankful that you showed up when you did. If you hadn't made that decision, you and I wouldn't be talking right now."

"This makes my head hurt," she complained, closing her eyes. A strong breeze blew across the open lot and her red locks partially covered her face. "I just want to go to sleep. Then I want to wake up and find out all this was just a bad dream."

"Me too," he replied softly. He then grabbed her by the shoulders and gently forced her to look at him. "How is Silas?" he asked unable to contain the worry in his tone.

Annie bit her lower lip and closed her eyes. "He's still alive," she replied, sounding both relieved and grateful. "But just barely. The nurse here did all she could, but he needs a hospital. He nearly bled to death."

Jonathon looked to the heavens and said a quick prayer of thanks. It was good to get some good news for a change. He looked around the compound—it looked deserted.

"How many people are still here?" he asked.

Annie scrunched up her face as she pondered the question. After a moment of thinking she said, "There is the nurse, George—Silas of course." She paused. "Probably another five employees total."

"Alright, I want you to round everyone up and tell them that Eric is gone—I wouldn't go into much more detail than that. Tell them that if they want to leave, they're welcome to come along with us back to the mainland, but we're leaving in fifteen minutes. I don't think it's safe to stay here," he said.

"And if they refuse to leave?" Annie asked.

"Then they're on their own," he replied with no emotion. "Tell me where Silas is."

Annie looked back toward the door she'd just came out of. "The medical ward is the first door on the left," she said.

"Okay, meet me back at the jeep in fifteen minutes," he replied, glancing at his watch.

Jonathon stormed through the entrance and immediately made his way into the clinic. The first thing he noticed was Silas lying on a gurney in the center of the room. His skin was pale and he suddenly looked very old and frail. His appearance was unsettling, and unfortunately, the relief he'd felt when Annie told him Silas was still alive was beginning to fade and turn into despair.

"How is he?" Jonathon asked.

He'd never seen the woman seated at the small desk in the corner of the room before. She was middle-aged, Hispanic, slightly overweight, and appeared to be exhausted. She had been leaning back in her chair, massaging her temples when Jonathon had entered the room. It did not appear that she even realized he was in the room until he spoke.

When she heard his voice, the woman became so startled she nearly jumped out of her chair. She placed a hand on her chest and took a deep breath, trying to calm herself.

"He's not good," she finally said, her words heavy with somber. "I'm just not equipped to deal with someone that has lost as much blood as he has."

Jonathon nodded and stared at his unconscious friend. "Do you think he can survive a boat ride back to the states?" he asked.

The woman got up from behind her desk and walked to the opposite side of the gurney from Jonathon. "It's possible," she replied. "But his odds are decreasing with every minute."

"I figured so. That's why I'm taking him out of here right now," he said, determined.

The woman looked at him, puzzled. "I'm sorry, sir, but who are you?" she asked.

Jonathon looked up at her and smiled. "I'm Jonathon Williams." He held out his hand. She shook it and then he said, "Silas came over to the island with me, and I feel responsible. I've got to make sure he gets the best possible chance to pull through this."

"I'm Sandra Martinez," she replied. "And I'm sorry, but I have to ask…who shot him?"

"Glenn Hardcastle," Jonathon answered. As he said the name, the rush of conflicting emotions made him nauseous. Hardcastle had stuck his neck out for him and allowed him to escape, but he also came very close to taking Silas's life.

Sandra winced when she heard the name. "That's not surprising," she replied. "I've always been a little terrified of that man."

"Really?" Jonathon asked. "Why is that?"

Sandra raised an eyebrow. "Have you ever met the man?" she asked, placing a hand on her hip.

Jonathon chuckled. "Point taken," he replied. He then began unlocking the wheels on the gurney with his foot. "Sandra, I'm not going to force you to do anything," he said as he moved toward the end of the bed. "But I'm about to take Silas here off the island and back to the mainland. I'd *really* appreciate it if you'd join us."

Sandra looked at him, puzzled by the request. "This is my job. I can't just leave or Mr. Gill will—"

"Eric is dead," Jonathon interrupted. "He was shot also. I'm going to take his body back to the states."

Sandra's expression turned to obvious panic, and Jonathon could imagine how it all sounded to her.

"Look," he said softly. "I know we just met and you have absolutely no reason to trust me—but, I'm asking you right here and now to do just that...trust me."

"Did you or Glenn shoot him?" she asked, staring at him.

He shook his head. "No. Actually, Annie Wedgeworth did—and she did so to keep Eric from killing me. He's not exactly who you probably thought he was."

Sandra was taken aback. "But Annie is his girlfriend!"

Jonathon sighed and looked at his watch. He was running out of time—Silas was running out of time.

"Sandra, I realize this is all a lot to process and it must sound absolutely nuts, but I've got to get Silas some help. Now I'm prepared to go without out you, but there are a couple of things you should know," he said. "Firstly, Silas's best chance of making it is going to include having someone with medical training on board with us—and that is obviously you. Secondly, your former boss, Eric, was selling dinosaurs to a really bad man, and he's going to be back for more. I'm fairly certain that you don't want to be here when he returns."

Sandra stared into his eyes for a few seconds and then slowly dropped her gaze toward Silas. She took a deep breath, closed her eyes, and then nodded. "Okay," she whispered. "Give me a couple of minutes to gather some medical supplies that we may need and I'll meet you outside."

Jonathon immediately felt relief and he reached across the gurney and grabbed Sandra's hand. "Thank you," he said with as much sincerity as he could muster. "You're making the right decision—for both of us."

***

As it turned out, aside from Sandra Martinez, none of the other Gill Enterprises employees dared to desert their jobs, and even seeing the lifeless body of Eric Gill wasn't enough to persuade them. In a sense, Jonathon understood their position just as he had with Sandra when she was reluctant to go with him. He was a stranger to them, and if they were aware of his presence, he was certain that Eric Gill and Glenn Hardcastle had not painted a very pretty picture of him. As much as he hated to leave them on the island—because he truly believed it wouldn't end well for them—he was also aware that getting the other people that were close to him off the island was a priority.

It was a bittersweet moment for Henry when Jonathon and the others returned to the ship. He was more than happy and relieved to see his son arrive unharmed, but then his emotions flipped upside down when he discovered the condition of his new friend, Silas. Jonathon was met with a barrage of questions from his father, and his answers basically rehashed everything that had occurred after Henry and Charlie had left them on the beach.

With his father caught up on Silas's fragile state, it was Jonathon's turn to ask questions regarding Charlie's well-being. He discovered that her condition had improved significantly since he'd seen her last, and she was now conscious and speaking. Sandra looked her over and proclaimed that aside from a possible concussion, a fractured arm, and a possible broken rib, Charlie was going to be just fine.

"Are you regretting coming to the island yet?" Jonathon asked her, taking a seat beside the couch where she'd been resting.

"I'm past that phase," she said with a forced smile. She held up her wrist and showed him her watch. "I wanted to alert my C.I.A. contacts, but I couldn't—the watch was damaged."

Jonathon shrugged. "That figures," he said. "I was hoping to get them on Mr. O's trail as soon as possible. He got away with the *Sarcosuchus*."

Charlie frowned. "Well, you know as well as I do that he will never be able to control that animal. That thing is going to make a meal out of him."

"Yep, but that's not what I'm worried about," he replied. "I'm worried about what innocent person will be the *next* meal—and the meal after that."

She shifted onto her side and the pain made her wince. "I will contact the authorities as soon as we're back on the mainland," she said through gritted teeth. "He won't get far."

"Glenn Hardcastle is out there with him, and believe it or not, I think he wants to stop him," Jonathon added, almost as an afterthought.

Charlie was surprised. "I don't buy that," she said. "I spent a lot of time with that man, and he never gave me a reason to trust him."

Jonathon pondered what she'd said and wondered if he had indeed been duped.

"Well, all I know is that he bought me enough time to get away," he replied. "Whether he had my interests in mind, or his own, he still seemed to do his best to make sure I got back to the beach unharmed."

Charlie closed her eyes and repositioned the pillow she'd been resting her head on. "I guess we'll find out more when the C.I.A. catches up to them," she said, and she yawned.

"You sound pretty confident that they'll find them," Jonathon replied.

She opened one eye and peered at him. "Trust me…it's pretty much a certainty," she said.

Although it got off to a rocky start, the voyage back to the mainland was for the most part uneventful. Silas had regained consciousness and even managed to talk Henry through getting the ship going and in the right direction. As they drifted further away, Jonathon took a stroll onto the stern and took one last look at the mysterious island shrouded in mist. It was almost impossible to see it thanks to the camouflage the mist provided, but he knew what to look for. He watched it and didn't blink until the ghostly presence disappeared over the horizon. He wondered if he'd ever see it again—and secretly hoped he never would.

CHAPTER 36

Silas survived the trip back to the states and began receiving blood transfusions shortly after arriving at Mercy Hospital in Miami, Florida. The medical staff gave their assurances that his condition was improving and that they expected him to fully recover from his injuries, but it was going to take some time. There was a great deal of questioning from the staff as to why Silas had a gunshot wound, and they noticed that Charlie had significant injuries as well. Jonathon was unsure what to say, and since his face was now showing a great deal of bruising from his fight with Hardcastle, he wasn't sure if they'd believe anything he said even if he tried to come up with an excuse.

Fortunately, Charlie intervened and gave the staff a telephone number for one of her contacts with the C.I.A. A short time later, a short man in a black business suit showed up and spoke with the hospital staff. He later questioned Jonathon and all of the others that had escaped the island. Each of them cooperated and told him everything that they knew about Eric Gill's operation.

When the man was finished with his questioning, he made sure to get everyone's contact information and left a business card with his information it. Each of them was told—politely, yet firmly—that they had to make themselves available for further questioning when needed. After spending what Jonathon estimated to be a total of six and half hours at the hospital with them, the man finally left.

After receiving medical attention of her own, Charlie urged Jonathon and Henry to head home so that he could see after Lucy. At first, both of the men were adamant that they needed to stay longer for Silas, but after further urging from Annie, they finally headed home.

"I'll let you know if anything changes and of course when he is going to be released," Annie said as she walked them to the elevator.

Jonathon shook his head and reached out to embrace her. "Thanks again for saving my life," he said. "If it hasn't occurred to you yet, by saving my life, you also saved Silas's."

She pulled back from him, surprised. "I hadn't thought of it that way," she said. "That's a far cry from what I did the last time we were on the island."

He smiled at her. "Exactly," Jonathon replied. "If you ever begin to feel guilt, you think about that."

Once he and Henry finished their goodbyes, they left the hospital and took a bus home to Jackson.

***

The long ride allowed Jonathon and Henry plenty of time to discuss how they would handle things when they arrived back home. They were both fully aware that Julianne would greet then with a flurry of questions regarding their whereabouts over the past few days. They decided the best course of action would be for Henry to take his wife aside and gently explain everything that had happened while Jonathon met with Lucy and gave her the water they'd all risked their lives to get.

As expected, as soon as they entered the house, Julianne became hysterical.

"Oh my God, what has happened to your face?" she asked, running to Jonathon. She gently grabbed his head between her soft and delicate palms.

Jonathon could see the utter worry in his mother's eyes and suddenly felt guilty for putting her through it. She still appeared to be as well put together as she'd ever been. Her hair and clothes were just right, and her trademark pearl necklace adorned her neck. Even her makeup was as perfect as ever. Yet, there was no mistaking the turmoil in her eyes. She'd been worrying for quite a while now—it was very obvious.

"I'm alright, Mother," he said, gently pulling her hands from his face. He smiled at her. "Everything is going to be alright now."

She gave him a confused looked, and then suddenly looked past him to where Henry was standing, his arms crossed.

"Where have you two been?" she asked. Her eyes began to well up at the sight of her husband.

Henry approached his wife and immediately wrapped his arms around her. "It's good to see you, Julie," he said softly, and Jonathon could clearly see his father's eyes beginning to well up too.

"Mom, how is Lucy?" Jonathon asked.

Julianne slowly pulled away from Henry and turned to face her son.

"Jonathon, the last twenty-four hours have been bad," she whispered, clearly trying to keep Lucy from hearing their conversation from the nearby master bedroom. "She's been really weak and refuses to eat or drink. I'm so glad you're back—she'll be glad to see you." She then paused and looked from Jonathon, back to Henry. "The two of you were gone a little longer than I expected…I'd really like an explanation."

Jonathon looked to his father for help.

"Julie, why don't we take a drive over to the Buddy Burger up the road? I haven't had a decent meal in a few days, and I could really use a good ole American hamburger," Henry said, draping an arm around her and steering her toward the door. "I'll explain everything while we're out."

Julianne looked over her shoulder to Jonathon. "Are you going to be alright, son?" she asked.

Jonathon reached into his pocket and wrapped his hand around the vial of water.

"Now I am," he said with a smile. "You two go on...we'll catch up some more when you get back."

Julianne's eyes narrowed and she slowly returned her gaze to Henry. "Alright then," she said as she reached to her neck and fumbled her fingers across her pearls. It was something she'd always done when she was nervous or anxious. She pointed a finger at him with her free hand. "We will talk when I return?"

Jonathon nodded. "I promise."

Julianne turned away and Henry led her out the door. He looked back to his son as he pulled the door shut and gave him a wink of encouragement. Jonathon smiled in reply.

When he entered the bedroom, it was dark and it took a couple of minutes for his eyes to adjust. He could hear Lucy's light, steady breathing and realized she must be asleep. He decided not to wake her, and instead, he slunk down into the rocking chair in the corner of the room. When he did so, the old wooden chair made a popping noise in protest—a sound that was much louder than it should've been in the almost complete silence of the moment. Much to his dismay, he heard Lucy stir, and it was suddenly apparent that she'd woken up.

"Julianne?" she called out, her voice raspy.

Jonathon rose from the chair and drew toward her, kneeling beside the bed. He reached out and took her small hand.

"It's me," he said softly.

He felt her brush a hand across his face. "Oh thank God," she replied weakly. "Where have you been?" The question was a combination of hurt and anger.

"I'm sorry I left the way that I did," he said, his best attempt to avoid the actual question. "But the important thing is that I'm back now—and I'm not leaving again. That's a promise."

"No," she replied, a tinge of defiance in her voice. "You're not getting off that easy. Where have you been?"

Jonathon sighed and then he couldn't help but smile. Although she was sick and frail, she was still the same determined woman at her core.

"Mom tells me that you haven't eaten or drank anything in quite a while," he said, again avoiding the question.

He heard her make a grumbling noise of annoyance before saying, "I'm just not hungry."

Jonathon nodded. "Okay," he said. "How about drinking a little water for me?"

Now that his eyes had fully adjusted, he could clearly see the silhouette of her head shaking back and forth. "No, not right now," she said.

"Tell you what," Jonathon said, as an idea popped into his head. "I'm going to fix you a small glass of water and if you drink every drop, I'll tell you where I've been."

Lucy sniffed and turned onto her side. "I'm not really thirsty, but if it'll get you to tell me what's been going on, then fine," she said, sounding a bit childish.

Jonathon stood back up and patted her shoulder. "That's a deal," he said. "I'll be right back."

He strolled into the kitchen and retrieved a glass from the cabinet. Just as he'd pulled the vial of water from his pocket and prepared to open it, the doorbell rang. Jonathon stood there for a moment staring at the vial of water and the empty glass. The bell rang again and he considered ignoring it. After the third ring, he reluctantly returned the vial to his pocket and decided to quickly run off whoever was on the other side of the door.

The bell rang yet again as he opened the door, and though it was a familiar face standing on the mat, it was by far one of the last people he expected to see.

"Mr. Williams," the man in the black suit and sunglasses said. It was the C.I.A. agent that had questioned him in the Miami hospital. "I told you we'd be in touch."

Jonathon was taken aback by the man's sudden visit. "We were in touch less than twelve hours ago," he said, looking down at his watch.

The man nodded. "May I come in?" the man suggested. "I've got news."

Jonathon took a deep breath. "Do you realize you've never even given me your name?"

The man removed his sunglasses to reveal his piercing blue eyes. "Sorry, in my line of work, I don't often give my name. Call me Mr. Cold," he said, offering a handshake.

Jonathon narrowed his eyes and took the man's hand. "You don't have a first name Mr. Cold?" he asked.

Mr. Cold smiled—it was the first time Jonathon had ever seen him do it—and cocked his head to the side. "It's Cornelius," he said flatly. "And if you share that with anyone, I *will* see that you regret it."

Jonathon smiled in response but stopped short of laughing.

"Now have I earned enough trust to come in?" Mr. Cold asked. "As I said, I have news."

Jonathon wasn't sure about the man in the black suit, but there wasn't anything about him that seemed threatening. And as bad as he hated to admit it, he was very curious about what exactly the news he wanted to share was all about. Calmly, he stepped to the side and motioned for Mr. Cold to come in.

After closing the door, he led him to the living room and offered him a seat on the sofa. Jonathon decided to take a seat in the nearby recliner.

"How is your wife?" Mr. Cold asked.

The question alarmed Jonathon. "How do you already know about my wife?" he asked, unable to hide the surprise in his tone.

Mr. Cold held up his hands. "Relax," he said. "I can find out pretty much anything I want to find out about anyone. I had my agency look into your background, and I discovered the news about your wife's unfortunate condition. I'm betting a man in your position would do absolutely anything in his power to save the life of not only the woman that he loves, but also the unborn child still in her womb."

Jonathon felt his pulse quicken. *Did Mr. Cold know about the fountain? Did he know about the vial of water in his pocket?* He didn't see how that was possible.

"You said you had news," he said, trying desperately to change the subject.

Mr. Cold smiled and took a deep breath through his nose. "That I did," he said, and he leaned forward. "The U.S. military caught up to those terrorists and the giant crocodile they were hauling."

"You're kidding," Jonathon replied. "That was fast."

Mr. Cold nodded. "Yes, it was a very serious situation, and there was little time for us to act. The man that Eric Gill was dealing with is a very dangerous terrorist, and he had some awful plans for that animal."

Jonathon nodded but said nothing; he wasn't sure what he should say. He looked down at the carpet and there was a long awkward silence.

"What is it like?" Mr. Cold asked suddenly.

Jonathon looked up at him. "What?"

Mr. Cold shifted his weight on the couch and leaned over the arm. "What is it like to see real living, breathing dinosaurs? Is it terrifying? Shocking? Magical?" He smiled.

Jonathon shifted in his chair and suddenly become quite uncomfortable. "So you know all about the island?" he asked.

Mr. Cold nodded in reply.

Jonathon crossed his arms and let the full weight of his body sink into the chair. He let his head roll back onto the headrest and he stared at the ceiling. "It's all of those things," he said softly. "But mostly terrifying to be quite honest."

"We've known about it for quite a while, but we've been unable to locate the island. It's our understanding that there is some sort of trick to finding it, but we haven't been able to figure it out yet," he replied.

Jonathon closed his eyes. He didn't know what to say.

"It's also my understanding that you know a little about how to find it," Mr. Cold continued.

Jonathon sat up suddenly. "Is that what this is about? You want me to show you where the island is?" he asked.

"Eventually," Mr. Cold replied. "But right now, I've got a more pressing matter that I was really hoping you'd be willing to assist the agency with."

Jonathon peered over at him and raised his eyebrows. "What exactly do you guys need *my* help with?" he asked.

Mr. Cold stared at him and suddenly seemed much more serious. "As I said, the U.S. military managed to take the terrorists into custody, but during the assault, the dinosaur managed to escape."

"Escape where?" Jonathon asked.

"Into the Atlantic Ocean of course," he replied. "We have no idea where that beast is going to pop up, but when it does—"

"That's not good at all," Jonathon interrupted. Suddenly, something else occurred to him. "You said your men took the terrorists into custody?"

Mr. Cold nodded.

"Was there a man named Glenn Hardcastle among them?" he asked.

"You know him?" Mr. Cold replied, nodding.

"Yes, I do," he answered. "And he is not one of the terrorists. I think he went along to try and stop the whole thing. He was not assisting them. If you have him in custody, he knows these animals even better than I do. He will be the man that you need to talk to about tracking the *Sarcosuchus* down."

Mr. Cold shook his head and began to laugh.

"What's so funny?" Jonathon asked, annoyed.

"I'm sorry," Mr. Cold said, sounding genuinely apologetic. "But I find what you're saying funny only because Mr. Hardcastle said the exact same thing about you. Why do you think I came to you in the first place?"

Jonathon sighed as it all began to make sense. "Hardcastle sent you to find me?"

Mr. Cold nodded in reply. "He has been cooperating fully and even explained that he was somewhat responsible for the animal escaping...something about he'd shorted the dosage that was supposed to keep the animal sedated. He wanted it to escape so that the terrorists would be unable to use it."

"That's right," Jonathon said. "And chances are high that the animal is going to swim right back to the island. That's where its home is at, and it would only make sense for it to return there."

"That's our sincere hope," Mr. Cold responded. "But we'd like your assistance in locating the animal, and later, we'd like your assistance in locating the island."

Jonathon stood from his chair and paced to the opposite side of the room. Mr. Cold eyed him suspiciously.

"I can't leave my wife right now," he said. "You know the obvious reasons why."

Mr. Cold nodded and rubbed both hands on his pant legs as if he were smoothing out the fabric. He then looked up at Jonathon and said, "If it's the cancer you're worried about, I've got wonderful news."

Jonathon cocked his head and stared at him. Mr. Cold slowly stood from the couch and walked over to him.

"If you agree to help us, the cancer is gone," he said very matter-of-factly.

"What are you talking about?" Jonathon asked, unable to contain his skepticism.

"I'm saying that I have a cure for your wife's cancer," Mr. Cold replied. "The cure has existed for quite a while, but the damn pharmaceutical companies pay a lot of big money to keep it under wraps."

Jonathon gave him a disgusted look.

Mr. Cold held up his hands defensively. "I know, I know," he said. "I agree—it's vile and it's terrible. But it's also the truth." He paused and considered his next words. "Look, we don't have time to get into all of the politics regarding the cure, but all you need to know right now is that it exists and my agency has access to it. You tell me that you will help us, and I'll see to it she begins receiving the cure no later than tomorrow morning."

Jonathon shook his head. "I don't believe you," he said. "That sounds way too easy."

Mr. Cold sighed and placed his hands in his pockets. "Jonathon, no one is going to force you to assist us—that much I can assure you. Your situation is sensitive, and I get that, but think about this...what other options do you have? Do you want to save your wife's life or not?"

Jonathon thought again about the vial inside his pants pocket. It didn't seem that Mr. Cold had any knowledge about the fountain of youth. He obviously was unaware of the fact that Jonathon did indeed have another option—but this option had the added consequence of not only immortality for Lucy, but for the baby as well. He'd felt nothing but guilt when he decided he had to trick her into drinking the water—but that was before he had another choice. And besides, he could always hang onto the water and use it if it became necessary.

"Okay," he whispered. "But I'm not moving on anything until my wife begins receiving this miracle drug you've got."

Mr. Cold smiled at him. "Very good," he said. "Your country thanks you. I'll see you in the morning." With that, he turned away and headed back toward the door.

"Mr. Cold," Jonathon called after him.

He stopped at the door and looked back at him. "Yes?"

"You're not really with the C.I.A., are you?"

The man laughed and returned the sunglasses to his face. "All you need to know is that I'm on your side," he said, and he quickly closed the door behind him.

EPILOGUE

One Month Later...

"What is it?" Lucy asked as she flashed a lovely smile.

Jonathon watched as she waddled across the kitchen floor to retrieve a container full of icing. He was seated at the counter where she'd been working on a cake.

"What is what?" he asked, smiling back at her.

"You're looking at me funny," she said as she refocused her attention to applying the icing on the cake.

"I'm just stunned at the amazing turn around you've made," he said. "I feel almost as if I'm dreaming."

She shot a quick glance his direction. "Well, you're not dreaming," she said. "I feel wonderful—I still can't believe the drug worked."

Jonathon shifted uneasily in his chair. "Yeah, me either. We got pretty lucky."

"You can say that again," she said as she carefully smoothed out the chocolate goodness all over the top of the cake. "For me to be offered a chance to take part in a clinical trial just when it seemed as if all hope was lost—and then it actually worked!"

"Yep, we're blessed," Jonathon replied, and he walked over to Lucy and put his arms around her large belly. "Talk about answered prayers…"

"And as usual, I've got you to thank," she replied, turning and giving him a quick kiss on the cheek. "You could've told me that was the reason you left for a few days," she added. "I would've understood."

"I didn't want to give you any false hope," he replied, and suddenly, he felt guilty for lying to her. He had decided one day he'd tell her the truth, but not until he was certain all of the cancer was gone and their new baby arrived.

"And now you've got a new job working for the government," Lucy said. She paused for a moment and stared at him. "I'm not so sure this new government job of yours isn't connected to my treatment," she added.

Jonathon suddenly felt a bit uncomfortable. "And what would an unknown paleontologist have to do with a trial drug for cancer?" he asked, hoping she was kidding. "I've already explained this. Now that the government has discovered the existence of the island, who better to help them keep it under wraps?"

Lucy smiled and returned her attention to the cake. "I know," she said. "I just wish it was still hidden away out there in the Atlantic. It needs to be left alone."

"They *are* leaving it alone," Jonathon lied. The truth was that some unknown department of the federal government had in fact taken control over Eric Gill's compound, but so far, they'd left the animals of the island alone. Jonathon was going to do everything in his power to keep it that way.

Suddenly, the phone rang.

"Who in the world would that be at this hour?" Lucy asked, glancing at the clock. It was almost nine p.m.

"Probably Mom," Jonathon replied, stepping toward the wall mounted phone. "She hasn't made her daily call to check up on you yet—you know how worried she gets."

Jonathon answered the phone and the voice on the line immediately brought him to alarm.

"Jonathon, you need to turn on the news right now," Mr. Cold said.

"Which channel?" Jonathon asked.

"It doesn't matter," he replied. "Start packing, and I'll call you in another twenty minutes with further instructions."

Before Jonathon could say another word, he heard a dial tone. He slowly returned the phone to the wall and turned to face Lucy. She had finished icing the cake and was licking the spatula.

"Who was that?" she asked.

Jonathon didn't answer; he just headed for the living room to turn on the television. Lucy followed him and asked him again who was on the phone. Again, he didn't answer. As the picture inside the tube television gradually illuminated, he could tell by the tone of the reporter's voice that something bad had happened.

"Details are still pouring in, but at last count, there have been six casualties and dozens injured in the attack," the reporter said. "Authorities are adamant that all residents in the city of New Orleans are to seek refuge indoors at once. No one should be on the streets right now until the animal is caught."

"Oh my God," Lucy said. "Jonathon, what animal is he talking about?"

Jonathon felt his jaw drop as the weight of what he was seeing was beginning to set in. "It can't be," he whispered. The pictures on the television revealed what appeared to be an attack on the marketplace in the French Quarter of New Orleans. The structure where all the shops had once been looked as if a tornado had ripped through it. There were flashing strobe lights originating from ambulances, police cars, and firetrucks painting the chaotic scene in hues of red and blue.

The reporter continued: "In case you're just joining us, it seems that there has been an attack in the French Quarter of New Orleans by what witnesses are describing as a giant crocodile. Authorities on the scene are telling ABC News that the animal seems to have emerged from the Gulf of Mexico and immediately began attacking unsuspecting patrons as soon as it climbed onto dry land. There are six confirmed casualties, two people are missing, and dozens more are injured. The animal is still at large and is extremely dangerous." The reporter paused and appeared to be listening to someone speaking into his earpiece. "And now we're getting word that the National Guard has been called and is being utilized to stop the giant crocodile before anyone else is harmed."

Jonathon had heard enough. He turned away from the television and raced into the bedroom to begin packing. Lucy chased after him.

"What are you going to do?" she asked.

"I've got to get down there," he answered as he threw clothes into a duffel bag. "The giant crocodile the news is referring to is a *Sarcosuchus*, and it came from the island. If they don't hurry up and stop it, a lot of other people are going to get killed."

"Oh my God," Lucy whispered. "If one of those things wants to get inside a building, it will."

"Exactly," he replied.

Suddenly, the phone began ringing.

Jonathon jogged over to it, picked up the receiver, and immediately said, "I'm on the way to New Orleans…I'll contact you when I get down there." After hanging up the phone, he reached over and threw the strap on the duffel bag over his shoulder.

"Promise me that you'll be careful," Lucy said as he drew near her to say goodbye.

He leaned over and kissed her. "You don't worry about me. Worry about those folks in New Orleans."

Lucy chased him to the door and watched as he jumped into his Jeep Wrangler. Their dog Rex stood beside her on the front porch, and they both watched as the taillights of his vehicle disappeared into the darkness.

THE END

CHECK OUT OTHER GREAT DINOSAUR THRILLERS

WRITTEN IN STONE
by David Rhodes

Charles Dawson is trapped 100 million years in the past. Trying to survive from day to day in a world of dinosaurs he devises a plan to change his fate. As he begins to write messages in the soft mud of a nearby stream, he can only hope they will be found by someone who can stop his time travel. Professor Ron Fontana and Professor Ray Taggit, scientists with opposing views, each discover the fossilized messages. While attempting to save Charles, Professor Fontana, his daughter Lauren and their friend Danny are forced to join Taggit and his group of mercenaries. Taggit does not intend to rescue Charles Dawson, but to force Dawson to travel back in time to gather samples for Taggit's fame and fortune. As the two groups jump through time they find they must work together to make it back alive as this fast-paced thriller climaxes at the very moment the age of dinosaurs is ending.

HARD TIME
by Alex Laybourne

Rookie officer Peter Malone and his heavily armed team are sent on a deadly mission to extract a dangerous criminal from a classified prison world. A Kruger Correctional facility where only the hardest, most vicious criminals are sent to fend for themselves, never to return.

But when the team come face to face with ancient beasts from a lost world, their mission is changed. The new objective: Survive.

SEVEREDPRESS

 facebook.com/severedpress
 twitter.com/severedpress

CHECK OUT OTHER GREAT DINOSAUR THRILLERS

SPINOSAURUS
by Hugo Navikov

Brett Russell is a hunter of the rarest game. His targets are cryptids, animals denied by science. But they are well known by those living on the edges of civilization, where monsters attack and devour their animals and children and lay ruin to their shantytowns.

When a shadowy organization sends Brett to the Congo in search of the legendary dinosaur cryptid Kasai Rex, he will face much more than a terrifying monster from the past.

Spinosaurus is a dinosaur thriller packed with intrigue, action and giant prehistoric predators.

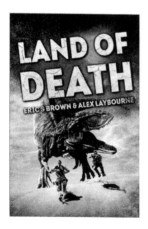

LAND OF DEATH
by Eric S Brown & Alex Laybourne

A group of American soldiers, fleeing an organized attack on their base camp in the Middle East, encounter a storm unlike anything they've seen before. When the storm subsides, they wake up to find themselves no longer in the desert and perhaps not even on Earth. The jungle they've been deposited in is a place ruled by prehistoric creatures long extinct. Each day is a struggle to survive as their ammo begins to run low and virtually everything they encounter, in this land they've been hurled into, is a deadly threat.

CHECK OUT OTHER GREAT DINOSAUR THRILLERS

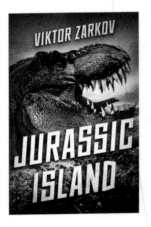

JURASSIC ISLAND
by Viktor Zarkov

Guided by satellite photos and modern technology a ragtag group of survivalists and scientists travel to an uncharted island in the remote South Indian Ocean. Things go to hell in a hurry once the team reaches the island and the massive megalodon that attacked their boats is only the beginning of their desperate fight for survival.

Nothing could have prepared billionaire explorer Joseph Thornton and washed up archaeologist Christopher "Colt" McKinnon for the terrifying prehistoric creatures that wait for them on JURASSIC ISLAND!

K-REX
by L.Z. Hunter

Deep within the Congo jungle, Circuitz Mining employs mercenaries as security for its Coltan mining site. Armed with assault rifles and decades of experience, nothing should go wrong. However, the dangers within the jungle stretch beyond venomous snakes and poisonous spiders. There is more to fear than guerrillas and vicious animals. Undetected, something lurks under the expansive treetop canopy . . .

Something ancient.

Something dangerous.

Kasai Rex!

Printed in Great Britain
by Amazon

61049487R00119